FOOL'S ERRAND

Works by Marc Norman

Oklahoma Crude
Bike Riding in Los Angeles

Fool's Errand

a novel by

MARC NORMAN

Holt, Rinehart and Winston
New York

Copyright © 1978 by Marc Norman
All rights reserved, including the right to reproduce
this book or portions thereof in any form.

Published simultaneously in Canada by
Holt, Rinehart and Winston of Canada, Limited.

Library of Congress Cataloging in Publication Data

Norman, Marc, 1941–
Fool's errand.

I. Title.
PZ4.N8475Fo   [PS3564.O62]   813'.5'4   77-13608
ISBN 0-03-019301-X

FIRST EDITION

Printed in the United States of America

1 3 5 7 9 10 8 6 4 2

For Alex and Zack, Skypals

Part one

1

SKY TO HAZE, haze to ocean. Fingertips drumming on the bakelite wheel.

Forney wears a business hat when he flies, wants so badly to look legitimate. He bought the hat in St. Paul ten years ago, the day he founded Forney Air Service and flew off to Alaska in a DH–4. The hat has stayed with him since, through the various rebirths of FAS. Clattering rocker-arms have sprayed it with engine oil. Slipstreams from run-ups have blown it pell-mell across frozen fields. Sweat has stiffened the liner. It fell out of a Jenny at one thousand feet over Bremerton, Washington, once—Forney searched for two days and finally found it on a store roof. That was lucky, but it is not a lucky hat, because Forney has never been lucky. Since his slow slide down the western slope of the continent carried him over the Mexican border, the hat's been used as a fuel filter, straining out the dirt, water drops, and other crap always present in Latin American gas.

Out the side window, the port engine streams oil. Forney glances at the instruments mounted on the engine strut. Oil temperature is rising, oil pressure has a cracked face and a milky fog behind it. The tachometer needle points to zero, always has. Forney doesn't need instruments, though not because he's so smart. The engine's leaking oil—naturally, pressure drops, temperature rises. The propeller is going around—need no dials for that. Forney looks ahead, at the cockpit panel. Some instruments are dead, some are missing altogether. Forney can tell when he's flying, when not. Level, the horizon looks so, engine sounds so, the wind whistles that note. Climbing, the horizon falls, the engines strain louder, wind more quiet. Gliding, all that reverses. If the starboard engine quits, the airplane tries to turn right. If the port engine quits, the airplane banks left. If the third engine, the noisiest, out on the nose, quits, Forney will see the propeller windmilling five feet in front of him. It's a large airplane, the Trimotor, but simple for an average man to understand. It's a Ford; Ford builds machinery for jerks, rubes—a Ford tractor is meant to be overhauled by hayseeds in barns. So with this airplane: three big engines, a riveted aluminum alloy frame; corrugated aluminum skin layered across the wings and down the fuselage like a shingle roof. It's as though Henry Ford assembled three engines in a metal shed, bolted the engines to the walls, and flew the shed away. Forney's seen pictures of Henry Ford; he imagines if he ever met him, Ford would resemble one of his own tractors—hard, cold, dirty.

BELOW IS GATUN LAKE; a freighter has just cleared the southern locks, now disappears beneath a wisp of cloud. The flat jungle throws off heat like a man sleeping. Forney pulls the port throttle, then the mixture—the engine shudders to a stop. Forney locks his right knee, opposite rudder to the yaw. He feels a leg cramp building; pain runs up his side into his belly.

He looks aft, into the cabin. Cargo this day is two lepers and two nuns for company. Every Tuesday, he runs up to David and back, to the Benedictine Leprosarium, for the lepers on sick call. This is his only permanent route; the Benedictines pay him fifty bucks a month. His bank payment for his three machines and the hangar lease is a hundred and twenty bucks alone; there's avgas at thirty cents a gallon, oil at twenty-seven cents a quart, two hundred and thirty gallons per machine, thirty quarts. Miscellaneous, such as food. The nuns look out at the dead engine, fingering their crosses. Their lips are moving in catechism—one leper prays along. The other seems to be having a great time; he looks ahead at Forney, gives him the high sign, as if he knows him. Forney won't wave back. The leper's face is runny, like the cherry center of a chocolate candy. The leper flashes his teeth, opens his eyes as wide as he can. Hi pal, thinks Forney.

WHERE THE SUN SPLITS the water is Cristobal, seven minutes away. Forney will land okay on two engines, could land on one, could land on none, given a fair-sized field. He's done it, so many times. In a backwater pond off the lake shore, an Indian chops out a dugout. Things on the ground grow larger. All routine—even engine failure is routine. The wreck of a beached barge—six minutes now. Forney could trim for a glide this minute and bring it in strictly by juggling throttles, hands off the wheel, except what's the point?

He's not feeling well at all: tight heart, eye ache, hard, impacted gut. He has dreamt of a black dog kissing his lips. At first, the city spreading ahead is gray on green—then it splits into two, Cristobal and Colón, two gray patches that split again into streets, streets that split into side streets and blocks, single houses, red-tiled roofs, inset, shadowed windows. Out over the arms of the harbor he flies, turning base. A few bumboats drawing wakes, a Black Star freighter not there this morning. Turn final—the wingtip points down at the newcomer ship, slowly draws a line around it. The nuns in the back go ooooooh. Roll out on the field, in the trees back toward the Canal.

Sun flashes off the Douglas loading in front of the SACA terminal. Still two miles ahead, Forney knows all that is happening. It's the 12:30 flight to Bogotá in from Vera Cruz around 10:30 if the weather held; the smartly dressed passengers have stretched their legs, taken a cab to Colón, returned at 12 sharp with their postcards, Panama hats, seen their leather valises stowed, a happy Kraut ground crew in leather bow ties and spotless overalls topping off the wing tanks. The two blond pilots and the titty stewardess have stood smiling by the cabin door, then gone to their posts when all have boarded, shooting their uniform cuffs. Mossbach, the station chief, has checked his watch against the clock on the observation tower of the curvy camel-colored new terminal building, then nodded up to the second officer in the left-hand seat, and the starters have groaned. All this is knowable to Forney, his Tuesday run always bringing him back around this time. Mossbach, once through a memo and once personally, has told Forney he would just as soon Forney land, the field being a mile square, to the far side, so as to keep his scabby machinery far from sight of SACA passengers. SACA is currently setting Central American records for passenger miles and safe hours flown; the letters in Spanish stand for Sociedad de Aeronaves Centro-America, but everybody in the company, chairman to restroom girl, is a Kraut. Everybody knows the Germans want to take over South America, even the Indians. Everybody knows everything—this is the Depression; nothing new is possible.

The Douglas taxis downwind as Forney swishes in over the trees. He kicks rudder, skidding, so his touchdown is as close to the Douglas as he can shave it. He sees eight faces staring out the small side windows as the Trimotor settles with an obscene splat.

ACH TAXIS up to the hangar and shuts down. The structure leans to one side; in front is another Trimotor, PA–ABR, its Panama registration painted on its side. A third Trimotor, PA–ATE, hides inside, in shadows live with mosquitoes. An ambulance from the hospital waits in the shade—two drivers split a butt on the running board. In the cockpit, Forney lights up himself; he can't smoke when he flies, gas leaks in the Trimotor's corroded system, but he doesn't stop once he's on the ground. The engines tick as they cool. Behind him, the nuns lead the lepers out the rear door toward the ambulance; they talk excited French.

Forney doesn't watch them go, climbs out of the airplane, ducks under the fuselage. The portside aluminum is coated with engine oil; the engine weeps black oil onto the grass. His fingers find a split rubber oil line; what he thought.

Up comes Santos, with not much to do. He pinches one nostril shut and, bending forward as over an invisible railing, blows his nose clean. Forney points up at the nine radial cylinder heads. "Nothing left of them," he whispers.

Santos nods. "Silenders," he says. Forney takes a screwdriver out of a back pocket, bangs one cylinder with the tool's handle. It makes a flat, hollow sound. "Sounds like a tin can," says Forney.

Santos shrugs, hitches up his striped pants. Through some cousin in government in Panama City, he has been appointed airport manager, but SACA ignores him and Forney has no business. Usually, he brings the mail.

THERE ARE DEAD FLIES in the room corners, shrouded in dust. Somebody ought to paint this place, Forney thinks. Outside, on the recreation field, ratings play fungo in the heat. On the floor is a *Liberty* magazine with a cover of a curly-haired usherette seating a young couple in a movie theater. Somebody has drawn a cock and balls in blue ink, hovering over the couple like a cloud of destiny.

Here's Smiley, back from chow, banging through the screen door. He barely nods, which Forney takes as a bad sign, hangs his cap on a nail, sits at his desk, picking up a newspaper.

"So?"

"Forney," he says, dabbing himself behind the ears with repellent from a tiny bottle.

"Well?"

"Well what?"

"What do you think I'm sitting here for?" Forney's nervous, shows it.

"I ain't no mind reader," says Smiley. Forney swears —Smiley looks over the top of the paper. "I ain't supposed to say anything, that's all."

Forney's silent, breath shallow. "That's real ethical of you, Smiley, but you just did." His mind flees, to the dirty state of the room. Perhaps that's why they call it infirmary, instead of hospital. One advantage of living in the Zone: free health care for all U.S. citizens. They dug the ditch, they conquered malaria, yellow fever, although word has it malaria is coming back. Oh Jesus, thinks Forney, wincing, touching his stomach. Bugs bang against the screens. "How big is it?" he asks at last.

Smiley puts down the paper. "It ain't big at all, Forney. There's nothing there." He hesitates, takes an envelope of X rays out of a top drawer, throws it across the room. "You ain't supposed to, but look for yourself."

"Then what's hurting me, Smiley? Right now, when I talk to you?"

"How should I know? Doc says if you don't believe him, go to some hospital stateside." Forney takes out the X rays, spreads them like a hand of cards, shadowy and blurred. What is he supposed to do with them? He can't tell one body part from another. Smiley calls his name, tosses over a rum bottle. "My advice is, dose yourself with this."

Forney shakes his head. "I was trying to cut back on this stuff," he says.

TOUCANS, PARROTS screech and flap—the road is paved with flattened frogs. The fenders on the Plymouth rattle—rust oxide slowly eats them up. Cars in tropic countries rot in the same places, Forney has noticed. They're wrong, he thinks, the doctors; he'd take the time to prove them so, if he had the money. He's dying—he ought to know his own demise. Germs flow inside him, tropic germs, exotic. Some get them, some are immune; he's got them, has always, all his sad life, is dying by inches in Panama, right now. He thinks of the time he lost out on the mail route in Arizona, Tucson–Phoenix, all financed, paid for. He even greased palms; it went to a higher bidder. Germs vie in his veins: failure, bad fortune, solitude. He's tried so hard, done everything right, printed business cards, confirmed meetings by phone, taken a night-school course in double-entry bookkeeping. He doesn't drink much, piss away money on broads. Forney believes in profit, desires success. God how he has tried, time and time again, bladdered down but back to the well on bloody knees. He believes in safety wire, clean workbenches, maintenance schedules, all that's proper. He's seen assholes go bankrupt into fortunes, win hats of chips, drunk, with the other man's deck, convince the government or some rich man to finance blue sky, toilet dreams, death machines. Forney and his hoarded notions of merit and good works have been cuckolded so many times that misfortune has become tangible to him; it's changed from being simply an idea abroad in the world to something real, contaminating, a germ, something a doctor could see in his blood.

    The road ahead opens onto the airfield. Forney turns toward the SACA hangars, resolving to make one last plea. Mossbach hangs out his office window, bawling out a pilot. Forney parks to one side, waits sweating in the car until the pilot leaves. Mossbach leans on his fat arms; his suit is wet, his tie ripped open, twisted to one side. "He was late. Weather, he says." Mossbach snorts, "Then leave earlier,

I tell him—I would think that was obvious. What's on your mind, Forney?"

Forney shoves his hands into the pockets of his leather jacket. "Sell me some jugs. You don't need them anymore."

Mossbach shakes his head. "I'm not allowed to sell parts out of my inventory . . ."

"Then write off a set. Say they're defective."

"Berlin would want them back for exchange . . ."

"Oh Jesus, Mossbach—you want me to hang, do you? I'll get down in the dirt and beg—it's no skin off my ass!" And he does it, actually gets down on his hands and knees in Mossbach's flower bed.

"Get up, George."

"What the hell do I care? I got two weeks. Yepes gave me two weeks."

Mossbach looks away, embarrassed. The man's unfit for this sort of work. When Forney bought the three old SACA Trimotors at auction, Mossbach believed there was enough business for two airfreight companies in Central America. He still does—Forney's failure has not disproved it. A properly run company creates its own business. Forney's standing now, brushing off his knees. "Those aren't the same cylinder heads that came with the machines?" Mossbach asks. "I told you at the time they weren't holding compression."

"Sure they're the same. Where would I have got the money to change them?" Forney's given up on the cylinder heads, looks away. "In two weeks, somebody's going to drive out and take my airplanes. How the hell does Yepes expect me to pay him off if he takes away my airplanes?"

Mossbach is looking past Forney, over his shoulder

toward the sagging hangar across the field. The second Trimotor has joined the third inside the hangar—some men are shoving the first in at this very moment. "Who are those guys?" he wonders out loud.

Forney looks, begins to run across the field, forgetting he has a car. "Don't lock it!" he shouts. They do, six Bajuns that just shoved ACH away with the other two. They don't want to fight, but they will and stand ready, hands half-clenched. It takes a long while for Forney to reach them—by then, one of them has wrapped a chain around the trolleys of the sliding metal doors and padlocked it. Forney hauls up, too winded to speak; he turns to the Chinese in the straw boater, nailing up a liquidation sign. "A mistake," Forney wheezes. "Yepes told . . . two more weeks."

"No mistake."

"I was sitting . . . his office when he said it."

"Yepes change his mind," says the Chinese.

Forney can't breathe. He wanders away, around behind the hangar where nobody can see him. Mimosa thick as fence slats; where there's a gap, orange bougainvillea spills out and down. It's too much; he wants to scream but can't, wants to be furious but can't boil, even at this low altitude. He has the sense of watching something prodigious —snakes hatching from hens' eggs, a five-headed calf—and being the prodigy at the same time. He sinks to his knees, flops back on the grass.

No, in fact, this is fair, he thinks. He is dying by inches in Panama, that's all. He takes out a coffin nail, lights it. Stepping away, seeing him as the world does, he grudges the justice of it—he's a killer himself. Out where the jungle looms, rustlings, bugs scratching—all Panama does is reproduce. How can the mimosa stand his gaze? He expects to see only ashes, smoking stumps where his eyes sweep; he never looks backward, lest he see the car wrecks, burnt children, smashed windows he leaves behind. He's tried to hurry the disintegration, gone so far as to swallow the muzzle of the old Remington he keeps in his top desk drawer. It tasted oily, acid. That was not the way—it must happen as it should, at its own rate, and it is, he tells himself. He feels humble under the force of this process, worships it as much as he worships anything.

2

ETHEL WAKES from a dream to prickly heat, vaginal itch. The sheet leaves red spots where it touches. Ethel knows this is because the sheets are stiff with lye soap. She's seen what passes for laundry service on this boat—a teen-aged Arab gets the job, in addition to general housekeeping, boils the white things in a soup pot in the galley, stirring them with a board, then rigs a washline on deck between the kingposts. There is no intervening rinse. Ethel's hardly one to complain—she's stalked the Bowery by night, slept in tubercular adobes and dripping caves, but those who lived there had neither facilities nor inclination; she got more or less what she expected. On this ship, much effort is put into hygiene, but very little emerges in the way of results. To Ethel's mind, a thing is worthwhile only when the outcome approaches the effort expended, which Gerald once pointed out was the equation for efficiency.

Something white flashes past the porthole outside. An arm, the clang of metal, then a man's face, sweaty, topped by a sailor's cap. He pauses for a good peep—Ethel's hand covers her crotch. The man has false teeth, upper and lower, by some means is able to make them clatter in his mouth like castanets.

Ethel hurries to the porthole, flings the tiny drape across it. The bulkhead's been painted a hundred times; scratched into the last coat is the message, "This boat stinks," now enameled over but legible when the light is oblique. She peeks through a crack in the drapes—dangling past the porthole is a flexible ladder made of cast-iron links. The two men that just climbed past are not visible, lost behind the ship's curve, but below, the ladder end drops into a spotless gas-powered launch. A coxswain holds position away from the flaking hull with deft throttle and tiller work.

Ethel looks at her stainless-steel watch. She moans, starts to get dressed.

ENSIGN MCREADY used to get upset when he'd get his whites smudged by a hull plate or a greasy stanchion, then found out he could get his whole uniform cleaned and pressed for a nickel. Panama is much better duty than they told him it would be. He gave up a blue Marmon and a Baltimore poopsie to become assistant port inspector at Cristobal, oceans away from a cruiser bridge, but God suffers fools, as his father says. McReady didn't realize the nature of the compensation until his first ship, a Greek oiler. There, midships, radiant white among the pipes and dripping globe valves, he'd studied the transit applications carefully, the way the harbor master, an old commander, had shown him. The first page seemed okay—when he flipped to the second, he came upon a thick envelope clamped between the two sheets. He looked up—the Greek captain smiled. Inside the envelope was the jungle green of American money. His bosun, two paces behind him, had coughed. "Sign the papers," he'd said. In the launch heading back to the Navy pier, the bosun had explained the system. It had the legitimacy of time—he'd sent three ensigns north to fleet assignments wealthy men. McReady gave the bosun forty bucks, kept sixty, now has a whore on Front Street and a Ford Phaeton. So accepting is he of the system by now that he often takes the envelopes and signs the applications without inspecting the ships, a bad habit to get into, as the bosun reminds him. Especially tubs like this, the Black Star. Flapping at the masthead is a faded red Easy —McReady eyes it as he climbs over the rail, knocking his knee, leaving a smudge. He salutes the fantail, the skipper, his mate, both in undershirts. "Morning, Captain. Compliments of the harbor master, and could I look over your transit applications?"

The captain grunts; the mate holds out a clipboard. McReady takes it, feels the happy bulge under the clip. He's guessing how much it contains when an American woman thrusts among them, mad.

"What's wrong now, Captain? We left the fueling dock an hour ago."

The captain rubs his eye. "Yes, Ma'am, you're right on that. But now we got this inspection."

"You had an inspection in Charleston! It took half a day. Then we lost an entire day in Havana because of some fuel pump . . ."

"Feed pump," the mate corrects.

"Feed pump. Every time this ship stops, you find some reason to lose time," she cries. "Why did your company ever bother to publish a sailing schedule? I assumed that the arrival dates in your brochure had some connection with the actual dates—if I knew there was no connection, I would have taken a different line."

McReady finds her funny-looking. She's got big hands —she's wearing a peach dress with flouncy shoulders and buttons big as silver dollars. Her eyes hide behind round smoked glasses, and on her feet are ankle socks, low canvas shoes. She surely can't be told the truth, that the delay is caused by the need to bribe the port inspector. McReady doffs his cap.

"Perhaps I can be of some assistance, Ma'am?"

Ethel only now notices him. "Who's he?"

"Ensign McReady," prompts the mate.

"You see, Ma'am, the United States Navy is in operational control of the Panama Canal and the Canal Zone, and as such, has the right and option to inspect any vessel applying for transit. It wouldn't be good for a ship to break down or sink in the middle of one of the locks, would it? What if there was a national emergency?"

Ethel refuses to speculate. "Tell her about the red Easy," says the bosun.

"That's right," McReady adds. "In addition to general seaworthiness, this ship is flying a red Easy, which means, 'Attention—I'm carrying explosives on board' . . ."

"That's right. They're mine," Ethel replies. "Forty-two hundred pounds of industrial dynamite. What about it? I have all the invoices back in the cabin, as well as a notarized bill of sale . . ."

"We don't care about that," mutters the bosun.

"No, that's right," says McReady. "I'm inspecting for proper stowage, that sort of thing."

"If he don't sign us off, Mrs. Booton, we don't get through," says the captain. "You're not talking about much time. Maybe fifteen minutes, at the most."

They wait in turn for Ethel to respond. They are not exactly composed in a circle around her, but that's how

17

they look. Her worst dreams are repetitions of circles of men, sometimes assaulting her, sometimes threatening, sometimes only staring without a word. She thinks men like to do that—what can she do now but give in, surrounded by them as she is?

This is Ethel's second long sea voyage; she's come prepared, crammed her luggage with Dramamine for the storms, Alka-Seltzer for the ship's mess. She has a yellow slicker and a matching hat so she can put in her daily miles, no matter what the weather is on deck. She has purchased a number of long historical novels about vital periods in the histories of nations. She has purchased a lady's Hid-a-Way, an imitation leather pouch that straps against the inside of her thigh, where she has secreted the dynamite invoices and other confidential papers. What she has not, in fact, prepared for, is her own anxiety, the fact that she is so frightened by the whole undertaking; she is only twenty-six. She tells herself of Mozart, of John Stuart Mill reading Greek when he was four, but those stories never seem to comfort; tension has made her meals come up despite the seltzer, rendered the long novels unreadable. For three days, she paced the rolling cabin while a cold sea sloshed against the porthole. On the fourth, she saw what Havana looked like from a mooring just off the Malecon. The fifth was spent consuming a bottle of Bacardi as they crossed the Caribbean. And now Panama, suds and harbor scum surrounding the ship in rainbow slicks. Things are getting uglier the further south they go.

The line of men ahead of her tramps down the companionways, led by a Lascar with a ring of keys. Ethel has never been allowed in this part of the ship. Paint on the bulkheads flakes in layers, like a pie crust. All the lightbulbs have little cages around them—in fact, the tiny cubicles off the companionways seem cagelike, each containing one or two men, half-naked, going about some dubious task. Upon seeing her as she passes, they spin and spread apart. The footing is slick from pooled water, and it smells like nobody wipes their rectums. In a paint locker, she comes upon two black men hugging, or at least doing something to each other's backs.

At the head of the line, the skipper is reciting a list of fictions to Ensign McReady. "Our fire hoses are up to code," he's saying. "All the extinguishers were charged last month—you can look at their tags. And we had a lifeboat drill only last Tuesday—the log will back that up." The bosun stops at a red sand bucket hanging on a bracket. Blocked, Ethel must stop and watch. The bosun tips the bucket over—from it falls an old newspaper.

Ahead, the Lascar fumbles with his keys. The hatch opens; they file into the forward hold, clicking on their flashlights. The first thing that strikes Ethel is the awful smell, intoxicating, almost like medicinal ether. She feels a dampness in her socks, looks down to find she's standing in three inches of water.

"Dynamite's over here," the captain calls. McReady shines his light on the pooled water. It throws back the beam like the surface of a lagoon. "What's all this?" he asks.

"Are we leaking?" asks Ethel.

"Just a little bilge, is all," says the mate.

Flashlight beams poke around the shadowed stacks of cargo. "Over here," somebody shouts—the others gather, filing among the stacks. There they are, seventy crates of dynamite, well marked with slanting yellow stripes, properly roped off, covered with warning signs according to maritime code. Ethel's relieved to see them—last time was in a sling back at a Brooklyn dock, dropping into the hold.

"What about this water? Won't it damage them?" She's turned to the captain. He shakes his head. "Nah, that's why we put them up on pallets like that."

McReady's eager to count the money. That's the one sport in his graft—how much is actually there? A thin envelope could conceal a hundred-dollar bill, a fat one ten singles. "Everything looks regulation to me, Skipper," he says. "You just hand me those papers and I'll make my John Hancock."

But the bosun has pried open the corner slat of one crate with a churchkey, reached in, poked a finger through the surrounding sawdust until he's touched a bundle of dynamite sticks, six taped together, then tasted what the finger came away with. He's right, but then he's almost always right; he clears his throat. "Mr. McReady, I think you better not sign them papers. This dynamite's gone bad."

McReady's at a loss—winged bills leave their perch and fly away in his mind. Now the mate and captain realize the source of the awful stink. The Lascar rolls his eyes and suddenly runs off, banging into crates as he flees.

Ethel looks from face to face. "What's gone bad?"

"Jimmy, I want the ship rigged for collision," says the captain to the mate, now hoarse. "But I don't want no alarm..."

"How can I shut all the hatches without spooking everybody?"

"I don't want no panic." His voice rises. "We'll lose the whole damn crew . . ."

"What's gone bad?" Ethel interrupts, loud as she can. "For God's sake, somebody tell me!" The men all try to explain at once, roughly in a circle around her. A terrible screech trembles the ship, hull plates vibrating to the sound. Four screeches, then a pause—four more.

"Collision. He called up to the bridge," groans the captain to the mate.

"Fucking Lascar."

Ethel can hear poundings, shoutings all over the ship. There's a rasping sound, like chain through a ratchet. "They're running out the lifeboats!" hisses the mate; he and the captain both race for the hatch. "Would somebody tell me what's going on?" Ethel screams after them, helpless. "It's my shipment. I'm responsible for it. I have a right to know." Her eyes fall on McReady—he smiles weakly, places the transit papers and the bribe down atop a crate, slips away. Only the bosun is left. "Nobody will answer me . . . !" she begins. He shushes her, prying off another slat. Now he reaches in, gingerly extracts a bundle of six sticks, unwrapping their waxed-paper cover. "Your dynamite ain't stable anymore," he says, at last.

"I don't know what that means!"

The bosun clears his throat, out to be as precise as he can. "Okay, your normal dynamite is nothing more than nitroglycerine suspended safely in sawdust. You know about nitro?"

Ethel's frantic but at the mercy of his pace. "You can't drop it. It goes off."

"Right. So that's why they came up with dynamite; so

you could have some kind of explosive you could carry around and you could drop by accident with no trouble. Only if your dynamite happens to be old, on the shelf for a few years, which this stuff might, unless you have a manufacturing date..."

"I didn't buy it through a company," she blurts, then stops short.

The bosun shrugs. "Okay, so you get this old stuff hot, like in a ship's hold, and wet, like from this bilge, and the chemicals begin to break down; the nitro begins to loosen up and bubble out of the suspension." He shines his flashlight closely on the bundles. Ethel can see silvery drops coating the sticks, dew on a branch. "Smells bad, right? That's free nitro. Once it starts coming out of the suspension like that, no way to stop it. You got to burn this stuff, or at least dump it over the side."

Ethel is shaking her head. "I can't do that." Maybe this man is tricking her—she considers motives. "Maybe it's just water? Condensed water."

The bosun doesn't like to be doubted. He dips his fingers in the droplets, flicks them at the nearest bulkhead. The nitro splatters and goes off loud, like gunshots. Ethel screams.

"COME RIGHT a titch."

"Left, Mr. McReady. The tide's running left to right," says the bosun. McReady shrugs—he and the bosun are conning the *Pocono* out of the harbor. He was sent four stokers by the harbor master after the regular crew went over the side. "Get that shitpile out of here," said the blinker from the harbor master's tower, which McReady found interesting, never having seen light curse. Two hundred yards off their beam, the entire population of Cristobal lines the seawall. It looks like school has been let out—kids sit on the balustrades, dangling their legs. They all think if this ship blows, it will be a matter of a bang and some sparks, like fireworks. No, sir—this rotten hull will shred and turn to shrapnel, thinks McReady. He calls one-third ahead. The tide and wind are mild, still enough to blow the slab sides of ship down on the seawall. McReady sees a ship bearing down on them, a Grace Line banana boat, coasting toward its usual Number 12 mooring. He hoots the funnel whistle in warning. "Come right a little more," he tells the bosun. The bosun steers left, instead, yanks the telegraph handles, tells the stokers below slow ahead both. McReady feels good—his first command.

THE TAXI BOUNCES down cobbled streets, stops in a cool alley. Ethel sees a shop window filled with ladies' hats, a faded awning. *"Somos aquí,"* says the driver, pointing to the number on the scrap of paper Ethel gave him at the dock.

    She pays and walks inside. The walls and carpet are the same flat gray. There are hats all over the place, in glass cases, on stands, maroon and forest green, bundles of gauze and feathers. A dark-haired thick Latin woman is wrapping up a parcel for a couple of schoolgirls in blazers. "I hope you like it, ladies," she smiles as they leave, implying they own the hat between them. She looks up at Ethel. "And what could I show you today? A smart sunhat, perhaps?"

"I'm Ethel Booton. Off the ship."

The woman waves her hands. "Oh my God!" She heads for the nearest drapes, yanks them shut, knocking over some samples. "Don't just stand there—help me," she moans. Ethel does, going to the other window. The drapes stick on their rails. "Why, please tell me, did you come here? Please tell me that," she moans again.

"Because they told me I should if I had to. They gave me your name."

"That was simply for you to have it."

Ethel shakes her head. "Why would they give it to me if I wasn't supposed to use it?"

"Oh yes, in an emergency . . . yes!"

"Well, I don't know what you'd call this," says Ethel, ducking to avoid a hanging palm frond. "The men on the ship wanted to dump the stuff in the ocean as soon as they cleared the breakwater. I had to beg them to give me just until sunset . . ."

"Oh yes, fine, well and good. But that terrible whistle, letting the whole town know what's going on. And then driving up here, in full daylight. Don't you see how you've compromised me? And not just me, but my husband, and my children as well . . ."

She stops short. Ethel flops in a chair, picks up a hat with a long feather, something Robin Hood would wear. It's dark in the room—the heat falls off. The woman is jamming cork-tipped cigarettes into an ivory holder—she keeps missing. "You have no idea what sort of place this is," she says, inhales, coughing. "Panama. Men at the end of their ropes. Criminals, fugitives on the run. They gather here—like a constriction in a sewer. This is where they stick and rot."

Ethel looks at her fingers. Sunset's five hours off. Failure rises over the windows, shoves in at the door. The woman inhales, coughs once more. "Didn't they have a man they could send?"

"No they didn't. They sent me, so go to hell!" Ethel's shrill now; she wants to be gone. The woman draws back. "I didn't mean to be insulting."

"Well, you were. I wish you'd finish your complaining and try and help me solve the problem."

The woman nods. "Oh, yes, solve the problem. Certainly. Nobody told me what to do. I was given no instructions . . ."

Ethel has a straw sunhat made in Hong Kong, shaped like a round placemat. She's always uncomfortable around hats like these, the women that wear them. What earthly purpose do they serve? To protect? To keep the weather off? No, they are mere decoration, ribbons on a horse's mane. Take this one to her right, roughly banana-shaped, shot blue, with a huge glass jewel ringed by imitation seed pearls. How does it even stay on? A woman would have to pile her hair up, then use a number of hatpins. See how high it arches. Women can buy something, she remembers, that makes their hair stand up, but she can't recall the name. There's a hat on the floor, knocked down when the drapes were drawn, that looks like what bellhops wear, right down to the patent-leather chinstrap. On a clear plastic stand, framed by a mirror to reflect its back side, is a hat like a basket of flowers turned upside down.

The woman sits at her small desk and takes out a

phone book. "Maybe we could find another ship going south?" Ethel suggests.

"The Canal would stop it just as it did yours. Or are you suggesting a trip around Cape Horn? Do you have three weeks?"

Ethel shuts her eyes—she's sorry she mentioned it. "Here is a man with a truck," says the woman, pointing. "I know him—he does odd jobs."

"Are you kidding? I only have five days!"

"I said I didn't know, didn't I?" the woman shouts back, just as loud. Both are tense. The woman tears a sheet off a pad and draws a map. "Look—there's a hotel on the seawall called the Paseomar. It's not too unacceptable. Book a room there and don't leave it all afternoon. I'll make some phone calls and see what I can do."

"I don't want to stay in a room. I'd rather be out trying to get help . . ."

"There—you see? You know nothing about anything. Go out on the streets, as if everyone in Panama doesn't know exactly who you are already and exactly what you need. Before you do, almost."

Ethel sighs—the statement is logically impossible. Silent, she takes the map, folds it. The woman opens her desk drawer, revealing two small automatic pistols lying there, among buttons and thimbles, one blued, one nickel-plated. "You'd better take one," she says.

Ethel shakes her head. "I am married . . ."

"So what does that mean?" The woman hands her the silver one. "I myself would choose this, only because it's more attractive." Ethel recognizes it as a Colt .38 automatic. She's pretty good at guns, as long as they're out of the Colt catalog. She grew up in Hartford; her father worked all his life at the plant in the tool shop, where he and ten other Swedes cut the dies for the stamping machines. When her mother died from influenza, her father had said to her, "Well, little girl, it's you and me now." Only he became an alcoholic, violating his promise. Her father and the other Swedes always drank lots of aquavit—increasing the normal amount by only a small percentage was enough to push him over the line. She remembers long drinking bouts in their living room, she fetching the ice, Colt weapons mounted on lacquered plaques on the wall. All Colt employees had guns, bought at employee discount or received in lieu of Christmas bonus. Some hunted or shot with them—more, like her father, simply hung them up, as trophies of their life's devotion. Drunk, the old Swedes would have a machinist contest: who could file the buffalo smooth off a nickel without putting one rasp mark on the coin's outer rim. Her father, named Thorgaard, for years the champion, began to lose his touch after his wife died. The shop foreman met Ethel coming out of school one afternoon, took her for a walk by the river. Was there anything anybody could do for him? How was Ethel supposed to know—she was fourteen. She cooked soup for her father when he couldn't keep down solid food. After a while, he couldn't handle the soup and she had to quit school. He'd tell her his life hadn't turned out exactly the way he'd planned—he'd always wanted to open his own shop when the time came. His mind began to drift—he carved Ethel little reindeer out of ash blocks, the way he had when she was three. Then he died, which for him was nothing more than not waking up one morning. Thanks to an employee-contribution life insurance plan at the plant, Ethel received a thousand-dollar death benefit. She took the money and after two years graduated from Seaboard Nursing School in Boston, nursing being the single profession for which she had any experience or inclination. She did her job well and had no trouble finding positions in the Boston area, although her patients found her manner cool, her movements a little abrupt. They were always surprised to discover she was ten years younger than they thought, accused her of being a master of disguise or at least purposely drab, neither of which was true; Ethel had longed to be middle-aged ever since childhood, having found no purpose or value in youth.

NOW THE TAXI DRIVES along Front Street, its blocks of penny arcades, tattoo parlors, gin mills. In the windows are the blue eagles of the NRA. What was it the sailors on the *Pocono* said the government had for them? SOS. Same old shit. Siesta is over—the sullen unemployed drift back to the curb edge: Africans, Scandinavians, Japs, Dragomen, Lebanese, Egyptians, Burmese, all with bedrolls, torn clothes, toolboxes. They watch Ethel as she passes, but then they watch all passing cars.

Chignon—the word comes back to her. The thing women wear to make their hair stand up.

3

FORNEY SPILLS BEER over his glass rim by accident. The ashtray has overflowed as well—he's stubbing out smokes in smokes. Along the back of the bar, birds-of-paradise droop in milky jam jars. A fan swishes overhead, one of its paddles missing. That's why it vibrates so, thinks Forney: imbalance.

He's in "The Sailor's Grave," on Front Street, some blocks down from the fashionable shops. A Chinaman owns it; the bartender is a Hindu named Ben, denied alcohol by his religion. Steel shutters hang halfway down across the front portico, to keep out the slanting sun. Two SACA mechanics, Krantz and Hoffman, sing soft obbligatos to a Cuban broadcast, far down the bar from him. This is where Forney goes to drink, although he wasn't kidding Smiley; the stuff doesn't do it for him anymore. On his mind is nitro over the Andes. Nobody knows who it is that would ship nitro over the Andes in an airplane. Forney sticks his finger in the beer puddle, draws a wet question mark. More than the money, the idea of saving lives compels him. It's a mission of mercy, lives hanging in the balance, according to Hoffman, who heard it from a pal on the docks. Other pilots, lots of guys Forney has known, have flown missions of mercy: serum to an Eskimo village, food drops to flood victims, a snake-bitten kid from the desert into L.A. Hal flew one once, a telegram to stay some guy's execution when the wires to the prison were down. Hal was himself a mission of mercy, Forney thinks, tried to save Forney and fell just short. He thinks back six years to the contest—how the crowd had pushed through the police lines, run across the field. People pressed in on his airplane, looking in every window, out to swallow him up. Saving lives would be even better than that, Forney thinks. They'd carry him into town, toast his name. He imagines clippings in a scrapbook —Solitary Flier Dares Andes Horrors, Continent Salutes New Hero. He imagines huge newspaper headlines, although in Spanish, a language he doesn't read. He chuckles, now runs the heel of his glass through the beer puddle. You can't fly nitro; you'd go kabang first time you landed. Forney considers the route south—the first stop is Buenaventura, on the Colombian coast. He's been there once, as far south as he's ever gone; he remembers a broad field cut out of palms, ungraded, full of holes. That's where the axe would fall—Buenaventura. At the other end of the bar, Hoffman looks over at him. "You can't fly nitro over mountains in an airplane," he says, thinking the very same thoughts.

Krantz nods. "If there's no other way, you load the stuff on burros. Then you hitch thirty more burros in front of them, to give you a buffer. Then you lead the whole string on a pony with a fifty-foot rope, so maybe, if you're lucky, you're around a bend in the trail when the whole thing blows up."

"The Andes," says Hoffman. "Oh my God. Winds that never stop, storms that come up this fast." He snaps his fingers.

"Pan Am flies it every day," says Forney. "With passengers."

"They cross from Santiago, in Chile, where the mountains are narrow."

"They have to," adds Krantz. "To keep the mail franchise. They still lose planes all the time. That's why the French gave up. All those guys going belly-up."

A dog tied around a barrel. Forney runs the side of his hand through the beer puddle, making a new shape. Now it's a clown, flattened by a steamroller. It seems the answer to his yearnings may lie across the street, two blocks down. He's been looking for a good way to die for some years now, a way to end the process, but one short of suicide. The taste of the Remington muzzle comes back to him. Too easy—the ghosts insist on process. And then part of the reluctance comes from his Catholic mother; only God can take a life, etc., she'd tell him, actually pronouncing the *etcetera*. Although he'd grown up in L.A., Forney was born in a Pennsylvania coal town, among Poles and their many saints. Back then, what was wrong with suicide was its presumption of authority. There was only one Kree-8-tor. Forney's mother is dead now—in his sad travels Forney has found no evidence that the Kree-8-tor takes any more interest in anyone than a brief peek in the door at his moment of conception. Authority seems up for grabs after that. No, what bothers Forney most about suicide is that the act could be misinterpreted. This came to Forney that time he tried, in his office one midnight, drunk to the gills—with the muzzle in his mouth, thumb putting two pounds of pressure on the sear spring, he imagined what would transpire: Santos breaking in at the sound of the shot, maybe some SACA people running over, maybe even Mossbach himself, wearing that silk bathrobe he has with the panthers on it. Forney saw himself there, a sweet smile on his face, a hole in his scalp, his brains oozing down the plywood wall behind like thrown food. And then he realized, dollars to doughnuts, without him there to explain, they wouldn't understand why. The act would be misinterpreted—they'd say he'd had a run of bad luck, or even worse, more likely, that he was yellow, chickenshit, a weakling, that there'd always been something candy-ass about him. They'd never consider he was simply paying off his ghosts. Anger at what they'd say about him after he was gone is almost all that's keeping Forney alive at this point.

But now, down the street and across, there's a suicide he can endorse, a suicide worthy of Hal, so fine a man, who saved lives, taught love, who might have taken this job himself, and for no other reason but rescue. Forney has heard that in foreign countries the friends of a prince throw themselves on his pyre when he dies. Forney should have thrown himself on the piled wreckage of the Fleet while it still burned; he didn't, eight years ago, has been looking for another fire ever since. He wonders if he hasn't found it now —Buenaventura, on the Colombian coast. You just can't fly nitro—safe as houses, like a government bond. Buenaventura will pay off. It's just as much a suicide as the Remington haircut, but with no explanation needed. That's what he likes about it so much—everybody will fill in their own reasons why Forney took on the impossible, and every motive will be wonderful, nothing but noble. He can exercise control over his own eulogies. Forney examines the idea like a jewel, from all sides. Sometimes he can be clever, he thinks, looking up at himself in the bar mirror. Some of the silvering is gone—dark slashes across his face. He's short of stature, sloping shoulders, almost frail, hair going dirty gray. Won't see your face around much more, he thinks to himself. He squares his hat, buttons the collar of his yellowed white shirt.

A CUNA WOMAN passes with a basket on her head. The sun's so bright, the colors wash out. The two girls from the hat store cross the street, below, holding the parcel between them. Ethel turns from the balcony to the table, digs in her handbag for her watch. She swipes at a mosquito—the repellent they sold her in New York seems useless, might even attract. The table wobbles, one leg being short. The watch is next to the pistol. She feels her wallet, beside it a leather traveling photo frame which contains Gerald's hand-tinted portrait, taken when he graduated Harvard Med.

The watch says 4:10. Almost quitting time, at least for the rest of the world, thinks Ethel, who will not quit, as long as there's breath in her. It was a promise she made him, silently, one he doesn't even know of. You know how to be strong? he told her once. By being strong. That's all—the secret. You be strong, stronger than the other man, longer than the other man—eventually, he'll cave in. Gerald spread his hands. She hates pacing this mildewed room. A man with a truck. She snorts—she could find a man with a truck; that's nothing. But ten with ten trucks, maybe, or a way to sneak the nitro by train down to the Pacific end of the Canal, to Panama City, finding a steamer there, some hungry captain. She has a thousand dollars strapped to her leg; at least she could be out there trying. She's done it wrong, put herself in the hands of a useless woman she doesn't know. Four o'clock seems a good time to cancel the arrangement. She wishes she had help, a map of the town. Where would she start? The way to be not over your head, Gerald told her, is to not be over your head. There must be a hiring hall for seamen somewhere. Ethel thinks of groups of men listening, flicking cigarette ashes. If it comes down to it, if there's nothing else, she'll buy a knapsack, load it with four or five bundles, and start on foot for South America. Of course it's mad, but she'd do it, long before she'd ever give up.

She's wandered to the balcony again. Below, a man in a business hat disappears beneath the balcony floor. An old car passes, tail pipe dragging on the cobbles. She takes out Gerald's picture. So capable, sweet at the same time. The picture shows a man with a square, freckled face, squinting eyes, thick pale hair sweeping back from his forehead. Five minutes on the job and Gerald would have five alternatives, four of them good, two already under way. People respond to him; he has what she lacks: charm. Men, yes, but especially the wives of men. There's a knock on the door. That's the way they'd respond, doors knocking, phones ringing, women out to seduce him, men wanting to be his friend. Another knock—Ethel turns, crosses to the table, turns her handbag on its back so the flap lies open. "Come in," she calls, taking a breath.

The man she saw on the street enters, hat in hand. It's Forney—he regards Ethel, she him. Neither is impressed. "Where's the guy?" he asks, looking past her into the room. "The guy with the dynamite?" Forney nods—yeah. "That's me," says Ethel. "Mrs. Ethel Booton."

Forney raps his knuckles lightly against the bamboo-lathed door. "I heard this job was legitimate."

"It is legitimate. Completely legitimate, let me assure you. I'm a registered nurse, and I've been given power of attorney by a group of Bolivian relief organizations that are trying to prevent a very great catastrophe. Who are you, and what did you have in mind?"

Forney doesn't like something about her. He can't pin it down—it may be simply her, taken as a whole. "I've got an airplane," he says slowly. "I'd try to fly the stuff down." The idea comes to him he may be in the wrong room entirely. "This is nitro over the Andes into Ecuador, right?"

"Bolivia," she corrects him.

"A mission of mercy."

Ethel nods, motions to a chair. "If you'd like to sit down, I could tell you about it in detail."

Forney shrugs. "That's okay. I'll do it."

"Just like that?"

"Like what?"

Ethel's scared, afraid of this man—he's up to something dark. "You don't agree to take a job like this, just like that. Without knowing the slightest thing about it . . ."

"Why not?" asks Forney. "I do something—you pay me for it. There's a bank down the street, if you want some paper on it . . ."

"No." She rattles the chair back; she wants him to sit. "Nothing's going to happen until I know more about who you are. Such as your name."

Forney doesn't want to talk about it, simply wants to get it done, do the deed. "George Forney," he says, after a while.

"Mr. Forney, I won't go with you anywhere, to the bank or otherwise until you listen to more of what I have to tell you. You can stand if you like, or you can take this chair I'm offering you."

Forney whistles, a dying fall. Ethel, on her part, is entertaining Forney's side of the argument—namely, that she simply hire him, go to the bank, fly away, caution to the wind, but at least en route, going. She wishes Gerald was here; she hears his voice: Remember, as frightened as you are of them, they are more frightened of you. She stares at Forney.

Moments pass—Forney finally surrenders, sits, sighing. She sits across from him. "There's a town in Bolivia called Sucre, on the eastern slope of the Cordillera Real," she begins. "The mountains around Sucre have been mined for hundreds of years, back to the Incas, then for silver and gold, for tin the last fifty years or so. The mountains are literally hollow with shafts, some in use, most of them abandoned and sealed off. A terrible fire began in one shaft a few weeks ago; it's slowly burning its way through the mountain, no matter how they try to put it out. The shoring in the shafts is ages old, very flammable—if enough of it goes up, the shafts will begin to collapse, and then the mountain will start to collapse as well, and when it does, over ten thousand Aymara Indians that live at the base of the mountain will be buried in the rubble."

She looks funny, wearing a sunhat indoors, Forney thinks. He's thirsty, undoes his shirt collar, looks around for something. She's stopped—he motions her to finish.

"The only chance the miners have to put out the fire is to blast the shafts closed with dynamite. I was chosen to sail up to the States and bring back a shipment, which I did, but now there's this additional problem."

"It ain't dynamite anymore. It's nitro."

"That's right."

"Okay," Forney says.

Ethel finds no pleasure in his willingness. "You're very eager."

"Sure I am."

"Why?"

There's no dignity to this, Forney thinks. He has to make something up, simply to satisfy her. "The kale," he says at last. "The money. The mazuma. You got it and I want it. Lots of it." He's trying to sound like a businessman. Yada-yada, thinks Forney. He wonders where she's hiding it. "How much of a load are you talking about?"

"Seventy crates."

"I mean weight."

"Oh. Forty-two hundred pounds."

Forney considers. Say sixty-pound crates. The floor won't stand more than two hundred pounds per square foot without buckling. Numbers twine in his head, making patterns. "Gross on my airplane is thirty-six hundred pounds. I could take it in two trips . . ."

Ethel shakes her head. "I don't have the time. It all has to get there by Saturday, which is the twelfth." She adds quickly, "The fire will be beyond control by then."

Forney bites his lip. "I could handle forty-two hundred pounds if I had to. Figure light tanks, stripping it down, no crew, no luggage."

"And figure on my weight, since I must go along."

Forney looks up, stares. "You're not coming."

"I have to. It's part of any agreement between us."

"No it's not."

"Yes it is. That's that."

Buenaventura fades, covered by clouds. He should have known, it being a latrine rumor. He wonders whether he should go back to the bar—about now, they raise the shutters and you can watch the light dim, the clouds bunch against the mountains. The idea comes to him that he doesn't even have the capacity to arrange his own departure. He takes his hat, heads for the door.

"I'm sure it's dangerous," she calls after. "On the other hand, I've lived in a mining camp in Bolivia for the last two years. That was no picnic."

"Maybe you've lived in the Andes, Mrs. Booton," he says, turning. "You never seen them from an airplane. The peaks go up to twenty-six—the passes start at eighteen, and that's in my crapped-out airplane that couldn't hit fifteen thousand the day it rolled out of the Ford plant eight years ago. Plus I'm eight hundred pounds over gross already, and that's a gross figured on a new machine..."

"If it's all so impossible, Mr. Forney," she interrupts loudly, "then why are you going?"

Forney has to pause, remember the reason. "I told you why," he says. "The dough. The cabbage."

"Fine," nods Ethel. "If you want the cabbage, then I come along."

Forney pounds the table. "C'mon!" The purse leaps into the air—something clangs heavily when it hits. "What the hell good are you? You can't fly. You can't navigate. You're not one damn bit functional. What the hell do you think I'm going to do with a ton and a half of rotten dynamite?"

Ethel counterattacks; that much she's learned in the wards. "I have no idea, Mr. Forney. You're an unkempt man, by the color of your skin in not very good health . . . !"

"I'm sound as a dollar . . ."

"There you are, money again! That's why I'm coming. You're taking the job for money alone—you admit it. God knows what you'd do once you had an advance and were out of sight . . ."

She has made him talk himself into a corner, Forney thinks, incredulous. "I get it. You don't trust me . . ."

"And why should I? All you care about is the mazoola. You warned me yourself!" Forney is shaking his head. "I don't think you understand yet . . ." Ethel's reaching up under her skirt, into her crotch. Forney steps back, giving her all the room she wants. An imitation leather pouch appears, her Hid-a-Way. From it, she takes a rubberbanded roll of fifties, bangs it on the table. The short-legged table rocks. "There it is," she says, shrill, almost out of control. "The cabbage. The real thing! I'm acknowledging my side of the agreement—I have the money to hire you. Now you must acknowledge that you will in fact be hired, and I'm in charge, since I'm doing the hiring, and that I must accompany you and control and be in charge of everything that comes up short of the actual operation of your airplane. Is that clear?"

Forney chews the inside of his mouth. He hates her for what she's doing, intruding on his drama like this. He considers telling her more scare stories, doesn't, sensing she's the kind of person who always pushes back harder when pushed. Let her come, he thinks suddenly, his mind opening to sunlight. You're in the clear—you warned her what will happen. "Okay, Mrs. Booton. My conscience is clear. I don't think we got a hope in hell of making it. I expect to crash—I mean, with eight hundred pounds overload, that airplane is a time bomb; we're going to go blooey as soon as we touch at Buenaventura, and that's only if we make it over the trees at Cristobal. But if your coming is a part of the deal, then I guess you'll have to come."

Forney smiles—he likes the way her color fades away, slow but sure. He sticks out his hand for shaking. "Then it's a deal, Mrs. Booton." She doesn't move; feeling bold, Forney rubs it in. "Well what else do you need from me, Mrs. Booton? A blood test? Should I turn my head and cough? I'm it—I'm as good as you'll get, Mrs. Booton. Believe me, nobody's going to stand in line for this shitty job!" And to prove it, he flings open the hallway door.

Caught there, reaching up to knock, is an old one-eyed man. His pants drag—he looks like a pirate from a defeated band. "I'm Red Slovak. I'm a pilot—maybe you've heard of me," he says. "Where's the guy with the nitro?"

Forney tips his head at Ethel. Slovak turns to her, face flooding with offensive charm. "I'm your man, lady," he smiles.

4

HARD TO DRIVE A TRUCK in moonlight at two miles an hour, Forney finds. The road ruts toss it around, his foot's jiggled, the gas pedal can't help but move. He hopes the others following will be as careful, but doesn't trust Bajuns behind the wheel of anything; give them a car and they fire-wall it, full bore, in total contrast to their slow speech and way of moving. They've been told what they are carrying, but it's hard to be scared by a box. She's beside him, hands in her lap, balancing on the coil springs protruding through the front seat's leather. "She's a pistol," the mate had said of her earlier, standing midships on the freighter, watching the crates sling down into a lighter alongside. "Never saw anything like her on this ship. Brought her own food—the cook couldn't touch it; cooked it herself. The captain's afraid of her—that's where he is now, up in his cabin until she's over the side." He'd spit overboard, downwind. "How do you suppose she got that way?"

Forney was unable to guess. He's had only one significant experience with a woman, and she was not enough like Mrs. Booton to be of use. There was a loud bang; the sling with the dynamite had toppled toward the lighter. Somebody screamed—the sling had snapped to a halt five feet short of the lighter's hull and the deck men there, stretching the cable. "Tooth missing off the winch ratchet," the mate had explained. "Sometimes it will do that."

Forney's heart had pounded—it could have gone off

right then and there. "Nitro's funny stuff," the mate had agreed.
"You ever handle it before?"
"Years ago. Philippines, Borneo, around there. Them people can't afford bombs or airplanes; they got to blow each other up with something, and industrial nitro's the cheapest. You can't predict it—sometimes you hit it with a hammer and it won't say boo. Next time you look at it funny and it blows your dick off. Captain's glad to see that cargo go too, let me tell you. Sitting up in his sea cabin all afternoon, fingers in his ears, like yay." He'd grinned, to show he was kidding.

Nobody knows what to make of Mrs. Booton, it turns out. Forney thought Yepes at the bank might, being a Spanish gentleman of the old school, but Yepes had been just as flustered. She'd wanted an agreement in writing— Yepes' secretary had drawn up a form with a desktop of colored inks. "In times of great human suffering, profit and loss must wait in the wings," Yepes had said, squaring his black onyx desk set. The bank was built on Canal profits, neo-Egyptian in decor. The bank desired its loan to Forney paid off, not settled with airplanes, he'd said. How much could they get for those wrecks if they auctioned them off —five hundred at the most? No, better let Forney go turn a dollar, he'd said, combining profit and generosity. "I've always regretted your venture here in Panama wasn't more successful," he'd said. "I was hoping you could help lead our country into the new Air Age." Forney had shrugged, sorry to disappoint so many.

The secretary had entered then, bearing the completed form, complete with gold seal. The contract fee was set at

$2,500—Yepes, acting as his business advisor, had requested an advance on payment left for Forney in escrow. Mrs. Booton had balked—a dispute began. "What difference could it make to you, Mrs. Booton?" Yepes had asked.

"She thinks I'll dump her on the beach in Colombia and come back, and we'll split the money, or something," Forney had explained.

Yepes had put his fingertips to his lips. "Is that true?"

Ethel had smoothed her dress. "Something like that. You two are acting very chummy."

Yepes had stiffened at the accusation. "Yes, Mrs. Booton, I suppose we are. It is called human decency."

SHE DOESN'T TRUST THEM still, wishes Gerald had read the contract, fears Forney has put one over on her. Ethel crosses her fingers, concentrating on Gerald as though he was hung on the walls of her heart. How she wishes he was there, although not there, specifically in the truck's front seat; she would not wish him in danger for all the world. Gerald would have handled the problem differently, so much better. That's how they had met, handling a problem, back at Mass General. Gerald was in first-year residency, low man on the totem pole—they'd given him a scut job, liaison to the nursing staff. The senior nurse was a fat old queer, getting girls in trouble; Ethel had attacked her head on, with what little say she had, was about to get fired for her pains. Gerald, it turned out, had been working for months on the same problem in his own quiet way, much more cleverly; he simply designed a new organizational table, the staff voted it through, and the senior nurse was booted upstairs to a promotion. Ethel had felt so awkward, so rudimentary beside him. He'd smiled over his coffee cup in the cafeteria—it was all theater, everybody had a role to play. If Ethel hadn't done what she had, brought the fight out in the open, the change might never have happened. Ethel blushed at the praise, doubted it. She rented a tiny room in a mews off Beacon Hill—he lived with his mother on Foley Square. The family had had money once, didn't now, it turned out. They'd run into each other walking to work, make plans to walk each other home. One day he turned up with a handbill, some meeting of the Young Socialist League. It turned out he was mildly political—he took her to a lecture. Ethel was surprised to find young people speaking so responsibly about major ideas, about how to run the world; she had always assumed the elders held all the power. Some of the speakers droned; some were forceful, emotional—they could get her blood going. Famous minds were quoted—it seemed inevitable to many of them that a workers' revolution was about to circle the world. She found herself wanting to be a part of it, read Marx, Engels, the anarchists. There were meetings every night if you wanted one, wine parties, demonstrations at B.U. Soon, she was more active than Gerald. I've loosed the juggernaut, he'd say, laughing. She'd chide him for dragging his heels, tell him of the great things about to happen.

She loved him; he seemed to like her, certainly saw her often, sent her gifts. There were other girls, she knew, but what of it? She felt he'd come around; men had less feeling for the inevitable than women. Both said they were tired of Boston; reading the Sunday *New York Times* one day, they came across an ad for doctors and nurses wanted, three-year contracts at good pay tending mine workers in Bolivia. She decided to go that instant, rash, full of her youth, taunted and wheedled him until he agreed. Ethel was ecstatic—Gerald alone for three years on an Andes peak. She remembers the boat trip south, a coaster out of Galveston with a deck cargo of automobiles. Everything smelled strange, birdcagey—the fresh water had a fine grit to it. Gerald found out that ship carried cargo south, guano north, from the Chilean islands. Blown guano was the grit in the water. What's guano? Ethel had asked. You know, guano, Gerald had replied. No, I really don't know what it is. Bird shit. Ooooh, Ethel had said.

The trip was monotonous, tasteless dinners with the captain, who slurped food on his clothes. Gerald had snickered, nudged her; she had snickered too. The night they crossed the equator off Ecuador, the crew scraped up the energy for a party. Half-filled balloons were Scotch-taped to the salon bulkheads, the captain told some jokes—then a slender, dark-eyed sailor dressed as a woman flamenco dancer appeared and sang some sad *faenas,* too realistic to be very funny. In the harbor at Arica, the ship was surrounded by rowboats, each with a number painted on the bow. Ethel chose 14, her lucky number. The train took them across a barren coastal desert. In the mountains, there were tunnels and plunging ravines, rushing streams. At 8,000 feet, the trees stopped growing—they pulled into a station outside La Paz and saw their first Aymaras, breaths misting, noses dripping in the cold. The mine was at 12,500, reached by automobile. According to the newspaper ad and the Parillo Bros. rep in New York, the mines had modern, well-stocked facilities. This was not true—the mine at

Cerro de Pasco had a dispensary in an unused adobe shed, stocked with aspirin, rags for bandages, an old *curandero* who resented their presence on professional grounds. Ethel's impulse was outrage, writing letters, making angry calls, bringing Parillo mines to their knees. Gerald laughed it off and started doing what they'd come for, tending the sick. They worked well together—the miners called them black and white, *blanco y negro,* not because of their color or even their personality, but by way of expressing a concept of opposites in harmony.

THE TRUCK LURCHES—Forney shifts, grinding gears. The dark trees have fallen away—ahead Ethel sees a large structure, out of plumb. It's a hangar—the airfield, she realizes. Two men stand, waiting as they slowly near—one wears a double-breasted gabardine suit coat, the other a faded sweatshirt with YALE across it. Forney climbs out, walks past them with barely a nod; the three Bajuns down from the flatbed follow. "Where you prefer we deposit all them, Mr. Forney?" asks one, meaning the crates. Forney's unlocking the door with the key Yepes gave him. "First help me push out these airplanes." He puts his shoulder to the sliding door—the others lend a hand, but the door is frozen on its rusty tracks.

Ethel hauls her suitcase out of the cab. The fellow in the sweatshirt has gone over to lend a hand. "Name's Queen," he tells Forney. "We heard you were hiring. I've got four thousand hours—never flown a Trimotor, but just about everything else." The door gives with a screech—they run it open; Forney steps away, wiping rust off his hands. "You heard wrong," he says, crossing to a wall, throwing a switch. A dim bulb lights three Trimotors, waiting. "Why's that?" Queen asks. "You already have crews for all three?"

Forney shakes his head. "Only one's going."

Queen squints, not catching on. He's got red hair, a gap between his teeth; Ethel notes he limps. "If you want, you can wait in there," Forney tells her, pointing to a glassed-in office against an inside wall. He ducks as a wing strut passes, ACH being shoved outside by the Bajuns. The other man, the one in the gabardine suit, hovers near the doorway. "You two guys together?" Forney asks him, meaning Queen. The man snorts. "Never saw this guy before in my life." He looks like an alcoholic to Ethel—a red nose, bleary eyes. "Like I say, there's no work here," Forney says. "Too bad you came all the way out." Ethel lingers, wanting to hear the outcome of all of this. "Go inside, Mrs. Booton, I'll handle this," he tells her.

Ethel hesitates, complies after a moment; it's his business. She feels her way through the darkness, trips over something, a 2 by 4, reaches out to steady herself. She steps in a drip pan, slips. All around her are cold machines, mud-stained, oozing oil, metal dented, tires frayed, the cord showing. Entering the office, she stops short—she's caught Slovak, the one-eyed man, in the act of scraping a crust of old beans from a pot on Forney's hotplate. "Excuse me," she whispers, retreating outside.

"Sure, toots, you're excused," calls Slovak—a moment later he emerges, wiping his mouth. "All yours," he says, snaps at her nipple as he passes, gnashing his teeth, laughing when she trips backward. Ethel clutches her arms—

who are all these men? She turns, following Slovak back outside through the airplanes.

Forney and Queen are arguing about something as she nears. "What do you even care, Forney? It's our necks..." Slovak's interrupting, shouting. "Listen to this, Forney. Instructions to Mechanics. One—top off all tanks after any engine operation. Two—check tire inflation daily. Report all cracks and signs of leakage." Ethel sees he's reading with his good eye from a chart tacked to the studs ten feet away. "What's this all about?" she asks.

They turn toward her voice. "He's got three airplanes, and we're all pilots," says Slovak.

"You don't want to fly these airplanes," says Forney. "I haul lepers in them."

"Any flying is better than no flying," says Queen.

"Lease them from him, lady," Slovak shouts. "We'll fly them for you. I sure as shit know how to find Bolivia. You go that way." He points south.

"If you took all three machines, Mr. Forney, wouldn't that mean you wouldn't be so heavily loaded?"

Forney takes her arm, turns her firmly around, far enough so he can whisper. "Mrs. Booton, you don't want to get involved with these guys. They're on the beach—they're desperate..."

"They don't look that different from you," she whispers back. "What's your objection, Mr. Forney? Dividing the fee?"

Forney is insulted; he can't explain, doesn't even want to. It's a matter between him and Hal—these men have nothing to do with it. Let them find their own pyre, he thinks. He looks up—around the corner comes Mossbach himself, the first appearance he's ever made this side of the field. "Who are all these men, Forney? I thought you were taking one machine."

"That's right, you tell her," Forney says, using him, pointing to Ethel. "Tell her ABR and ATE are run out. They're death traps."

Mossbach considers. "As I remember, all three had about equal engine and airframe time. I would be hard-pressed to find a difference between them."

Forney has had it, throws down his hat, yells at them all. "I'm in charge of this—I hire. I've made my decision! Why the hell doesn't that mean anything to anybody?"

The three men regard him curiously. The man in the suit finally shrugs. "Fuck it—I ain't going to beg," he says, walking off. After a moment, Queen sighs and follows. Slovak glares at them, stamps off at last.

Forney grunts, heads in the opposite direction, toward the Bajuns loading ACH. Mossbach hands Ethel what he's brought for her, a leather flying jacket and a pair of fleece-lined pants. "Here. They belonged to a very small aviator."

"Thank you," says Ethel, surprised.

"There's a privy in back where you can try them on," he says, striding past to catch up with Forney. He's already leaning in the airplane's door; Mossbach, bending over him, sees the seats have been removed, the crates stacked as high as the low cabin roof, snubbed down with ropes lashed to the fuselage channeling. There's barely an aisle up to the cockpit. Mossbach sniffs the air. "You can smell it, in this small space."

They back out of the way of the loading crew. Mossbach looks the machine up and down, lightly kicks the treadless starboard tire. "Too much over gross. By a thousand pounds, at least."

"Everything I fly is over gross," says Forney.

"So romantic. Why are you so anxious to sacrifice yourself?"

"Since when do you give a shit?" That's too harsh; Forney's sorry he said that.

Mossbach stiffens anyway. "Any airplane crash affects me, in that it affects the progress of the industry as a whole." He pauses. "I've known guys like you, Forney, guys looking for some hopeless cause, some sacrifice. Mostly German guys, to be honest. Why, Forney, what's your awful secret? We're all exiles down here—nobody comes to Panama because they want to."

Forney chuckles self-consciously, shaking his head. From far-off, there's a woman's scream.

Out behind the hangar, Ethel has found the privy, opened the spring door. Inside is a young kid crouched on the seat, scratched and bleeding, wearing a Navy jumper inside out. "Don't worry, lady—I ain't armed," he says, to reassure her.

THE NIGHTLY CLOUDS have blown west, as they always do. Kinner's in the office, gobbling a bread sandwich. "I don't know," he's saying, mouth full. "Maybe Argentina."

"You'd be a fugitive," says Ethel.

Kinner shrugs. "I could be a gaucho, maybe. I know how to ride. The thing is, I really got to get out of the Zone."

"What sort of trouble are you in?" He doesn't look dangerous: a moonface, baby fat, pudgy hands.

"I sell things, little things, back in the jungle. I had this deal with two gunners off the *Arkansas* to sell some lube oil. The leathernecks found out. Other guys run off, but they caught me. I'm telling you, them brig Marines are rough cobs."

Forney enters, lighting a smoke. "He wants to come along," says Ethel. "He claims he's an airplane mechanic."

Kinner's stripping off his jumper, turning it right-side out. On the sleeve is one embroidered chevron and a blue propeller. "See? A-double-M. You ain't got a mechanic with you."

"I am one," Forney replies, glancing at Ethel. "You ready?"

"I thought you were waiting for dawn?"

"No point," says Forney, looking at his watch. "The moon's out—we can follow the Canal and the coastline for a couple hours."

"He's apparently in some sort of danger," she says.

"Sure he is. He busted out of the brig."

"That's okay, lady," says Kinner. "I got other ideas. I'll be okay." He motions her to follow Forney as he leaves. Ethel hesitates; he motions again. She leaves, finally outside, into the air grown thick and moist. She drags her suitcase to ACH—Forney helps her through the cabin door, stows her bag in a crack between cases and the rear bulkhead. She can see a small point of light far down the field. Mossbach is walking up to them, his pipe-coal glowing. "I paced off three thousand feet and marked it with the lantern. If you're not off the ground by then, you'll go into the trees." He sees Ethel, there in the doorway, looks her over. "So—off to rescue the Bolivians. In my experience, the Bolivians are always getting into danger and somebody is always having to rescue them. Have you noticed that?"

"The jacket and pants fit fine," she says. "Thank you."

"You realize you are exploiting a desperate man," he replies. Forney snorts. "C'mon, Mossbach." Mossbach keeps his eyes fixed on Ethel. "It's terrible what men must sometimes do to make a living," he says.

"If it is, Herr Mossbach, it's the fault of the economic system, not me—a system, you'll agree, that's been proven not only unworkable but dehumanizing, given the current state of the world."

"Oh oh. One of those," says Mossbach.

"Yes, one of those. And a humanitarian. And I look forward to a world where Mr. Forney will not be victimized by unfair competition such as your own, and ..." She thinks, Help me out, Gerald. "And where Bolivian miners are not endangered by mine disasters caused by unsafe working conditions."

Mossbach claps his hands loudly, three times. Forney shrugs; it's all the same to him. Mossbach turns, relighting his pipe. "All right, fine—go, since you have to. Watch out for the mountains."

"You can't miss them," says Forney. "They stick way up in the air." He shakes Mossbach's hand, his last handshake, Forney thinks. Up the cabin aisle, he squeezes past her, touches her as well, soft, smell of fear, all them glands. "The cockpit's mine," he tells her. "Find space for yourself back here." She looks around—the only clear space is a few square feet against the plywood bulkhead, by the door. She curls there, bracing against her suitcase.

Forney edges up to the cockpit, takes the left-hand seat, buckles the leather harness. There is no point in consideration now, taking time. Outside, Mossbach is priming the port engine—he locks the plunger, steps back, raises his thumb. Forney checks mixture full rich, cracks throttle. There's a mag booster plug on the right side of the panel—he puts the plug in the hole with a number 1 scratched into the black crackle finish. He switches on the port starter—the prop turns in jerks, palsied. When five blades pass, Forney cuts in the mag. The engine coughs, swallows, spits out blue smoke, roars. Forney gooses the throttle and the airplane rocks on its wheels.

Ethel can see the engines, between crates, out the side window. The one under the other wing fires now. It's like being in the stomach of a hungry animal; she realizes how loud the trip will be. A third engine—she can see the aluminum prop flashing through a fragment of cockpit windshield forward. All three engines thunder now, even louder. Ethel holds on to the crates. Louder still, then a sudden lunge—they're rolling. The airplane waddles on its widespread wheels, over ruts and clods. The crates dance from the vibration, no matter how tight the lashings. The hangar slowly passes. Kinner stands there, waving, Mossbach as well. Forney's turned on a landing light for taxiing; all that passes through its beam is flattened grass. The plane rumbles downwind, along a border of mahogany. Ethel realizes that trees surround the field. The machine slows—she can see Forney tugging on a lever like a gearshift between the two pilots' seats. Brakes squeal—time for a garage visit if this was a car, she thinks. The thought she may be dead in a few minutes occurs to her, but she decides if she's going to deal with that every time they take off and land, the trip will be unendurable. The airplane slowly turns into what faint wind there is. Ethel looks forward, for a sign of Mossbach's lantern, but it's hidden behind the nose. How has she gotten here, Ethel thinks, then remembers. She thinks of Gerald, kisses him, passionately, tongue in his mouth, running up under his lips.

Forney sees the lantern fine, just outside the nose engine's propeller disc. Controls are free, trim set, primers locked, throttle friction tight. Fuel on and sufficient—on and sufficient, he repeats, by habit. He runs up each engine to 1,700 rpm, grounds each mag in turn, checking for rpm drop. More drop when he opens the carburetor mixtures. His chest is tight, but it always is until safe in the air. Mossbach stands by the hangar, dim, distant. He's hesitating, Forney thinks—up run the three ganged throttles together. Grass grips the wheels, but the propblast is too strong—the airplane edges forward, begins to roll. With a nice big elevator, Forney can usually get the tail up quickly. He tries now, but it won't rise; the overload, he thinks. They rumble down the field three-point for a long time. He's holding on to the wheel with both hands. The lantern draws closer—only now does the tail slowly rise. The thick wing slices the damp air. Forney swears he can hear the lift building, a sort of high-pitched squeal. The airplane bounces less as the wings take up the load. They're not going fast enough; the slop of the controls tells him that. The plane's light enough to begin a drift to the left, skating across the grass, caused by the newer right-side engine turning a few more rpm. The trees at the far end have branches, the branches leaves. He doubts they'll make it, seeing how close they grow. The lantern's at what—three thousand feet? How long would it take to slow down, loaded this heavy? A long time—to turn away would bend the gear, ground-loop it. It's definitely a problem. Forney eases back on the wheel but the airplane still brushes the wet ground, unwilling to fly. Is it any faster now? Yes, says the airspeed needle, a little, if you trust it. Forney pulls back harder on the wheel—the machine won't budge; it's flying now as high as it ever will. Here comes the lantern. Zip, there it goes. Ahead is dying, curtains, if Forney wants it. All he has to do is allow it. No, he decides with a gasp, his appointment's at Buenaventura. He chops power, drops his hand to the brake lever. He can't hear the shoes over the slipstream, but the nose pitches down; they're biting. Can't pull hard or the airplane will nose over, like a tripped man. The trees fill the windshield. If he doesn't get the tail low, the wings cocked high so the lift spills off, he'll never stop this thing. He lets the tail thump hard on its heavy coil spring. The plane shudders—the crates strain against their lashings. Forney lets it track straight ahead, afraid to swerve even at this slower speed, all the way to the trees, stopping just short so the nearest branches stir from the sound alone of the nose engine. He lets out his breath; aft, Ethel opens her eyes, peers around the stack of crates up the aisle toward him. He feels the pressure of her regard.

FORNEY REFUSES to go where Brown sleeps, still in his suit, among the limed pilings of a banana wharf outside town. Kinner rouses him instead, pulling his toes where they protrude beneath a blanket. Brown swings at Kinner with a plank he keeps for self-defense, thumping him good. Kinner goes rolling in the sand but sits up good-naturedly, pointing to Forney's Plymouth as he relays the message.

Kinner likewise fetches Queen, where he sits in the tiled lobby of the Washington Hotel, playing blackjack with three Elks down on convention. They wear Panama hats with PANAMA stitched across the crown in red thread; they're reluctant to lose their companion. "You can't take this boy! You can't take Queen away," they cry. "Why, he's the most fun since..."

"Since what?" prompts his pal.

"Since your ass."

Queen blushes at this left-handed praise. "Fellows, I must. The sky beckons."

"The sky beckons," mimics an Elk. "I love this guy. Jesus, stay with us, Queen. We'll feed you, if that's all it is."

"These guys don't know poo about playing blackjack," Queen explains to Kinner. "They keep drawing face cards and aces, over and over, in total violation of the laws of probability."

"Never seen anybody lose like him," says one Elk. "He could enter a competition." They laugh—Queen raises his hands, pulls out a dime. "Heads I stay, tails I go flying, okay?"

"Give it a good flip, Queen," says an Elk; Queen does, catches the coin, flattens it on the back of his hand. He looks underneath—it's heads. The Elks laugh; Queen stands anyway, grabbing his leather jacket. "I'm only lucky in airplanes," he says; they hoot him out the bead-draped front door.

Slovak's the hardest to find—nobody knows his trail. Front Street at night is jammed and lit, even this hour before dawn—pinballs ping little triplets, sailors bellow, jazz spills down from arcade trumpets. The oldest house in town rests above a tattoo parlor; thin double doors hide a stairway up. A line of close-cropped ratings in their whites wraps around the corner, mostly two- and three-stripers, since the old-timers know the lines dwindle near dawn but the girls do not, shifts at this particular plant changing at ten, two, and six, just like Dr. Pepper. Past the line drives Forney and the others—Queen shouts. There's Slovak, stomping the sidewalk in front of the tattoo parlor, wearing a sandwich board on which is painted a dusky couple wrapped in tropic sixty-nine, another girl lounging legs-high in a champagne glass. Beside them, it reads "Club Caribe. Known the World Over. Dine. Dance. Girls." Forney pulls to the curb, starts to yell, turns to Queen. "What's his name?"

"Slovak."

"Slovak! Hey!" Slovak turns, fists clenched, expecting a fight. He's surprised to see Forney and the others there. "You want a job or not?" Forney asks. Slovak regards them, hesitates—then lifts the sandwich boards high over his head, throws them in the glistening gutter. "Move over," he grunts, as he opens the rear door.

5

PUFFBALL CUMULUS in long streets out to the horizon; I won't see those again, thinks Forney. Below, the ocean is dull, like velvet. Goodbye, goodbye; Forney is saying goodbye to his world like a host in a doorway. A seagull passes five hundred feet beneath. The airplane seems strong, full of purpose in this harsh morning light—the air is thin, cool. He won't see this light again, breathe air at altitude. Ahead, clouds boil, billow on billow—there will be rain soon, warm-front weather. No friend comes to mind—the face of a man in a bar, seen once, face only, not the name. Forney's bad on names—neighbors, teachers, the guy who taught him to fly. Even his name blurs: Gus something. Parents—sometimes Forney has to remind himself he ever had any, that anyone in the world he moves through was born of woman, ever sucked a breast.

Hours to Buenaventura, though not that many. He looks aft; the crates jiggle like spit on a stove lid. All that agitated nitro, looking for release, he thinks. Goodbye smokes, stomach. Out one window, ABR hovers a quarter-mile off; ATE is spaced the same distance off the other wing. Forney has split the load three ways, each machine carrying 1,400 pounds. It's enough—it's all the same at Buenaventura.

KINNER'S HAVING a great time, loves all these guys at first sight. They circled tightly over the airfield as Queen and

Brown took off last, in ATE; heading south along the Canal, he could see Queen far below slide open his side window, flip Cristobal the bone. Kinner smiles, makes a fist, stiffens his forearm muscle, out of Slovak's sight, something he does forty times a day. Now he stiffens his calf muscles, holds them until they tremble, lets go. Kinner believes in self-improvement, home study, push-ups; by mail, he has enrolled in courses on chinchilla raising, mail inspection, greeting-card sales. He has completed none yet, but only because nothing has stolen his heart. It has cost him hard bucks—one body-building P.O. box kept his dollar and sent back only a slip of paper that read "Lift weights." Nothing gets him down; Kinner has a low center of gravity, like one of those rubber clowns with the sandbag feet.

He looks up—Slovak is shouting at him over the engine's roar. "I want to switch tanks! Figure out how much I got in the mains!" Kinner looks around. There's a mechanical pencil, stolen from the paymaster, in his pocket. An old gasoline invoice lies wadded beneath the rudder panels on his side—he bends for it. On the panel is a dial face labeled "Fuel gauge." "You got that," Kinner shouts back, pointing at it. Slovak shakes his head. "Don't trust them! Figure it out—you got the departure time! Forty gallons per hour!"

Kinner looks down at the paper. Forney bought 150 gallons three weeks ago in Panama City, it tells him, not at all useful. He was never much good at math, his favorite subjects being history and geography, especially the lives of the great explorers, Magellan, Cortez. A lust for travel sent him to the fleet. He doesn't remember taking this pencil, often thinks of himself as a victim of his hands, bigger and smarter than the rest of him, with their own heart and brains. That's why he so often finds things in them he has no memory of obtaining: wire rope, canned fruit. He usually gives the stuff away, how he came to give the fifty-five-gallon drum of lube oil to a marine.

"When you finish that, figure out the landfall at Garaché," Slovak is yelling. Kinner turns to him—Slovak shoves the chart in his face. "Jesus, kid, get your thumb out of your ass!"

Kinner looks the chart over. It's a map of the northern half of South America, printed by the *National Geographic*. Hundreds of town names, all in the same small print. Most of the land is green, but on the left side, the Pacific side, it turns brown, darker and darker shades pyramiding up and blossoming into sudden white, a broken white vertebrae that follows the curve of the coast all the way down to its bony foot, which is what Tierra del Fuego actually looks like, a foot. The white part must be the Andes, Kinner thinks, the mountains they'll fly through, white being snow. There's a red line drawn from Panama south, along the coast, the route they're on, most likely. He studies the Panama area closely, smiles—it was just like that. Cristobal, Balboa. Those dots are the San Blas islands—they had gunnery practice out there when he was just a seaman, deck division on a four-stacker. The bay at Portobelo—they swam off the fantail until somebody saw a shark fin. He traces the red line south, paralleling the Canal, then launching southeast across the blue gulf toward a landfall at Cape Garachiné, north of the Colombian border. If they took off at 5:40 this morning—Slovak made him write it down on the back of his hand—how far must they be by now, at

7:14? It seems knowable, although barely. He looks at the airspeed indicator—95 it says, 95 miles per hour, if it's accurate; Kinner remembers something about their being affected by temperature and altitude. The mileage scale on the map is misleading; it goes 10——0——10 and then up to 100. Does that mean distances are different in different directions? How is he supposed to know where they are this minute, over featureless ocean? It's impossible—he can't do it, never will. He decides to guess and be corrected. "We'll hit land around noon, roughly," he announces.

Slovak runs the figures through his mind. "According to your calculations, that gives us a ground speed of twelve miles an hour."

"Let me try again," shouts Kinner, but Slovak rips the map away. "God knows what you are, but you ain't no mechanic!"

"I am too!" Kinner shouts back. "AMM. I just got out of the Fabric School at Coco Solo." Slovak is silent. "You know, cover a wing, patch a fuselage..."

"I know what fabric is!" Slovak bellows. "There ain't one square inch of fabric on a Ford-fucking-Trimotor!" Kinner grins weakly.

Slovak suddenly snorts out loud. "Bullshit everybody, huh?" He looks Kinner up and down. "Fabric School." He reaches over, punches Kinner in the shoulder.

Kinner's glad Slovak isn't too angry. "What do you think's really going on here?" Slovak asks him, his one eye cunning. Kinner thinks—before he can answer, Slovak shouts, "It ain't no mine on fire—that's for damn sure! You can tell that's all bullshit. And there's supposed to be nitro in those crates, but I ain't never seen any!"

Kinner nods, agreeable. "Me either!"

"So what do you think it really is? Gold? Not gold—silver, if you ask me. What else do they got in Bolivia?"

"Tin," says Kinner, remembering his geography.

Slovak snorts again. "All this trouble ain't for tin, that's for one damn sure!"

"I really had to get out of the Zone," Kinner says.

BROWN LIFTS a rum bottle out of a zipper bag he's stowed between the pilots' seats, takes a long gulp. Queen's noted he's killed half a bottle since they took off. "I bet your buddies like to fly with you at night," he yells. "They can fly formation on your nose. Hawww!"

Queen laughs like a horse, Brown thinks. He sticks the bottle between his thighs, takes the wheel again. "They told me I could ride out the Depression in Panama on pennies," Queen continues. "They didn't tell me where to get the pennies!" Brown doesn't respond—it's an old joke. He cranks in a little elevator trim. Cumulus is thickening high above; miles in front, it slopes down toward the horizon, the wedge of a warm front. He's too good a pilot for this job, he thinks, then checks himself by pointing out if he's so good, why is he here? Brown hates being where his name's not known—if this were the East Coast, Floyd Bennett, Lambert Field, Philadelphia, nobody would be cracking wise. These men may never know who he is; Forney thought at first his name was Braun, like a Kraut, that he was from SACA, maybe. Shit, he shot Germans down. He wonders where his scrapbook is now, decides it's with his sister in Memphis. That scrapbook could tell these people who he was, but what's he supposed to do, carry a scrapbook wherever he goes?

The airplane rocks as they plunge into the front—the light goes dim, rain spreads on the windshield. Brown looks out the side; the slanting front has driven them lower, now only fifty feet over the water. Heavy rain whips the surface into a lather. His eyes go back to the compass, bobbing in its alcohol bath.

SEE HOW THE CRATES vibrate, thinks Ethel. If she stares, their very edges shimmer. She can barely make out Brown in ATE, dim in the gray downpour. Their crates must be just as loose—even as she looks at the other airplane, it could explode. She imagines the sight—a white flash, metal shredding. Would she hear the explosion, or would the wind fling it behind? And why does she even think these things? She's always had this morbidity, stares at old men on gurneys in corridors, old ladies with ulcers on their legs, tuberculars coughing, then coughing no more, just like that. That's how her daydreams go: walking down a city street and seeing a car crash, a cop shoot a burglar, some jumper go splat at her feet. She waits for the tightrope walkers at the circus to fall. So death won't take her by surprise, Ethel's made a study of it, made it her profession even.

Water leaks into the cabin along the wing roots in fine sprays everywhere. The rain hammers on the skin, a tropical sound. She made herself a thermos of coffee before daybreak—while Forney fetched the others, wanting stimulation for the trip. She's alert now to the point of urination. An hour earlier, when she opened the tiny door to the lavatory aft, she found it occupied by three more dynamite crates. She squeezed her angry bladder shut, feasible as long as she sat still; now on her feet, the need returns.

It's loud, smelly, colder in the clouds. She wraps the jacket Mossbach gave her tighter. Her mind pauses on the short aviator. Water puddles on the cabin floor, disappearing through cracks in the plywood. Will the airplane rust, then? The idea comes to her that what's puddling is in fact overflowing nitroglycerine, welling up from their bundles. She tastes it. Oh God, it doesn't taste like water, not at all—it's dirty, or is that just from having touched the floorboards? Her bladder clenches—she hurries forward, down the aisle.

Forney's got the control column between his knees, checking his chart, doesn't hear her coming. Ethel finds it even louder here in the cockpit, wetter as well—water flies in everywhere through cracks in dried weather stripping. When Forney finally turns, Ethel sees he's wearing goggles. She cups her hands. "Where are we?" she shouts, cupping her hands.

Forney's thinking about other things. "Here," he points at some random spot in the middle of the Gulf, just to shut her up, although when he looks at it for a moment, he decides it's about where he'd guess they are, ten miles northwest of the Cape.

"When will we reach land?" Ethel shouts now. "Eight minutes," Forney yells back, not a bad hunch assuming a 100-mile-per-hour ground speed. He wipes the water off the windshield, sees only rain and ragged cloud ahead. Truth be known, Forney navigates better than he flies, having some flair for angles and predictions, some unsought talent for the mathematics of aviation. Forney is always hitting distant fields or landmarks on the dot, even after long blind legs in clouds or darkness. This facility is more valued by passengers than fellow pilots—they tend to care only for the act itself, spontaneous, anarchic. Forney almost got into a fistfight over this once, in his Alaska days, during a blizzard, snowed in at an airport bar, no more than an abandoned freight car propped six feet over the tundra on cinderblocks. The storm had gone thirty hours—nobody could drink any longer, cabin-feverish. For some reason, Forney started arguing with a pilot named Bowen over which was more important, the going or the getting there. Forney was surprised to find himself alone in defending the idea of arrival. All the other pilots said going up was better. Getting there was judged secondary, almost sissy. What mattered was the act of leaving earth, scaring the shit out of yourself, and only then, when your fuel was gone, night coming on, the weather closing down, condescending to land. They ragged Forney, all of them; it turned out they didn't like him much, hadn't for months, and took the occasion to say so.

 Now he thinks of Buenaventura ahead, wonders if he wouldn't like to stay aloft forever, like the dream of his Alaska chums. He can see ABR to one side, ATE to the other, gray on gray, still holding position. Flying formation in clear weather is hard enough, airplanes being like blocks of ice, hard to get moving, hard to stop. Pitch and throttle, pitch to slow, pitch and throttle to gain ground, in cautious bursts, moving great weights together at inches per second. Even harder in a Trimotor with rust and frayed cables, dried grease clogging the pulleys, huge thick wings that take their own sweet time to budge. That Brown and Slovak can keep up at all means they probably have Trimotor time, as they claim.

Faint daylight ahead, to the left. Six minutes to landfall, by the panel clock, which still works. Now all at once the clouds pull apart like interlocked fingers, revealing a point of land, a green cape ringed by small clouds swelling over its beaches. Dead on, Forney thinks.

"Where's the airport?" Mrs. Booton is shouting.

"What airport?"

"You said we were landing in eight minutes!"

"*Hit* land in eight minutes. Buenaventura is three hours south," he yells.

The woman presses her hands to her gut, makes a face. There's a string of bangs outside—she flinches, frightened. Forney richens the port mixture a hair, being a matter of too lean a mixture, rainwater up the carburetor. He turns—she's fled back to her hole. Below, the beach flashes under the wheels, a stripe of ivory between azure and dull green. Goodbye, ocean. Flat jungle, sallow serpent rivers, cloud shadows. He wonders if there was a turning point, a choice, if a mistake was made that sent him down his dolorous road? He can't remember one, far back as he goes. Years unspool through his mind, flashing sparks like pinwheels. It will not be so bad, he tells himself. Compared to where he's been. He realizes this is his last chance for nobility, to take on a task and do it right, the way he's always tried to. He smiles—he's not afraid; that pleases him.

THE FRONT'S behind them—the clouds gradually thin. For the last hour, they fly through rainbows; a final rainbow marks the town. Buenaventura is rust-colored, a lagoon of feverish water, crocs, no breeze, bamboo huts on rotted stilts. Forney finds the field, the cleared space behind town, waterlogged from recent rains. No telling how deep the ground lies beneath the water.

Hand out the window, he motions the others to circle until he's down. He sets up a long, flat approach from three miles out, nose high, dragging it in with power. Farewell 1,500 feet. Each division on the altimeter face is like an old friend departing. Farewell the striving, scheming life as a Yankee man. Farewell missed chances, headaches, rashes at the damnedest times. Forney kneels like a gladiator, glides downhill toward his termination. Nitro in the starting blocks. All the men he hated, he forgives. He turns loose his grudges like pigeons from a loft. He thinks of his will, but there is no estate. He thinks of a last statement, but what could he say to anyone else that could be of use? He reaches out to Hal, locks hands on wrists. He will be there, Hal will grab his shoulder, take the offering, welcome him home. Images of darkies, white robes and wings. He chops power, trims for a glide at seventy-five indicated. Tanks empty, the airplane floats nice and lightly. Forney is light too, likes that feeling. Fifty feet high now—the pooled water on the field reflects the rainbow. Oh, so many flashes now—kids on trikes, birthday ponies, beach picnics, Kansas wheat for a hundred miles, flying under the bridge at Sacramento, drunks, crashes, funerals, tears, envies that tore him open. Ten feet—the starter's pistol raises, he starts to flare, pulls the wheel slowly back into his middle, shuts his eyes, waits for contact. One second, two—so quiet, the airplane hushed near the stall. Three seconds, four.

One wheel kisses the film of water, like a maid's foot, then the other. Forney feels the earth up through his legs, the machine settles, gear slowly spreading wide, twin wakes rising as the tires slice through water. It's only inches deep, the water; it acts as a cushion, even a providential brake. The tail descends as the speed bleeds off—the airplane slows on its own, without Forney even having to touch the brake lever, comes to a gradual stop.

He lets out his breath. Perhaps I'll die in Ecuador, is his first thought. His second is one of anger, building anger. What has happened? He kept his end of the agreement, flew to his appointment at Buenaventura. He had a business deal with three-quarter tons of nitroglycerine, and he has been, incredibly, cheated once more. He took care of his end, made his preparations, did it right—for Christ's sake, his life passed before his eyes. Still there he sits in an airplane, alive. Is he so much an asshole, so insignificant, so eternally minor that even nitroglycerine mocks him? What is going on here? What world has he entered, what border crossed, where even nitroglycerine won't take its responsibility?

Through the windshield, he sees Brown flare from a flat approach, waddle to a soft touchdown. Slovak's a mile behind, lined up well, but a rain cloud has drifted over the field's end—Forney thinks it might shake his concentration. He's right—Slovak rounds out too soon, too sharply: the airplane stops flying five feet high. It drops hard, like off a table's edge—the metal groans from the stress, the compression struts bang against their stops, a fountain of brackish water billows around the airplane, hiding it for a minute. When the curtain drops away, there is ABR, whole and sound, dripping muddy water like a naughty dog.

Part two

6

FLECKS OF SUNLIGHT everywhere, on the sloped ceilings, the bamboo walls. Through a window, Ethel sees Forney out by the gas pit where the airplanes stand, yelling at the barefoot crew. The hoses don't reach the wingtops—they have to fill five-gallon cans on the ground and pass them up. Sullen, unhappy little man; Forney suffers in comparison to Gerald, but then so do most. She's in a better mood since they landed, glad to be on her way, back in South America, no matter what lies ahead.

Two Indians play cards at a corner table, a game they seem to be making up as they go along. She cleans off her table, a beer glass with a dried circle of foam, half a coconut with a cigar crushed inside it. She wonders if Forney cares for coffee; she's boiling a pot for herself at the bar stove, having found nobody who would answer as bartender. She sniffs the thick vapor. No harm in letting him see she can be civil, as long as it's not misinterpreted. That was always the difficulty with men prior to Gerald, the question of interpretation, what was really being said, what really sought. She can be pretty, she knows, even more than merely pretty—a matter of externals, handicraft, brushwork. Somehow it always used to go askew. She'd gone to a Socialist dance in Chelsea with her best friend Marygrace Stern, a dance for the E.V. Debs Defense Fund. She'd refused to buy a dress simply for the occasion. Marygrace had loaned her her best, a black number, daring for a nurse. Where'd you come by this? she'd asked. Ethel had fixed herself up, a good job of it too; they'd splurged on a cab. How eyebrows went up as they entered the hall—Marygrace Stern, yes, anything was possible with her, but was that really Ethel Thorgaard? They tickled her, those stares, how they looked, her chums, boys from the factory gates, girls fresh from pamphleting downtown, all in stiff suits and flattened hair. She'd looked for Gerald—he'd said he might come, although he was not a very public man. There was also the matter of night duty. All of them had danced, joked, gotten a little tipsy. Then two strange men had arrived, Harvard boys by their class rings. They'd foxtrotted with some of the girls, better than the girls—perhaps they'd learned at college. They'd seen Marygrace and Ethel standing together, made some sly, adolescent move. There was a car outside, a proposition was made, a sum of money mentioned. Ethel broke out crying, fled for the ladies' john, where she proceeded to scrub her face with Bon Ami from the dispenser. Marygrace forced her way in—Ethel was red-faced from the scrubbing, wearing her coat only, Marygrace's dress hung carefully over a stall door for safekeeping. Marygrace calmed her, said a friend had arrived. Ethel peeked into the hall; there was Gerald, leaning against the wall with one heel braced. She ran to him, threw her arms about him. He hushed her, stroked her back—it was a mistake, funny when she heard it. Some Harvard professor had told his class all Socialist women were dialectically free lovers. Gerald had sent the boys packing; Marygrace had stuffed their pockets with pamphlets.

He'd taken her home, been scrupulous. They'd necked on her bed, tiny, but almost half the size of her room. She said things she'd never said to a man; she'd asked for a definition of their relationship. He hadn't said yes, but what was important for Ethel, he hadn't said no. She wanted them to go so badly to Bolivia—a trial arrangement, she called it, almost cohabitation. He was hoping more for a position in a private clinic off Foley Square, posh, prestigious. It went to another intern finally, a Saltonstall, and Gerald agreed to Bolivia. How she misses him—the thought he's three days away makes her dizzy.

Forney's heading for the building. She decides to fill a cup for him, but chooses to add no sugar and provide no saucer.

FORNEY, STILL ALIVE, is pissed. He made the nitro his last friend; like others, that friend has betrayed him. The world seems blurry, a reflection in muddy water; he can't seem to focus on any one thing. Ahead, on the veranda of the airport bar, the others sprawl. Queen files his nails, Kinner clutches his knees, Slovak's down at the far end, in the only chair with any cushions left. Forney considers joining them, but there's nothing to join—they're all spread out, separate.

As Forney walks up the stairs, Brown swings his legs out of the way. Inside is shadowy; the woman is holding up a cup of coffee for him, but he can't focus on it, walks past her, bends double over the bamboo bar. On the floor behind are soft drinks in a bucket of water. He snaps one up, pops off the cap with an opener hanging on a knotted string. He swallows, then sees her arm extended there, holding the coffee. "I don't drink that stuff," he says.

"I'm sorry," she says, putting the cup down on the table. "I didn't know that."

Forney's preoccupied; it takes a while to hear her. "That's okay," he says, at last. "You wouldn't know." The apology comes too late—Ethel has retracted her offer. "I'll remember in the future," she says, looking away.

He runs his hands through his hair. "Look, Mrs. Booton, I apologize. I don't like coffee."

It sounds almost sincere; Ethel would like to believe so. She softens a little. "I probably should have noticed you didn't drink any this morning."

"Maybe so," Forney says. "Next time, pay attention," he adds, gratuitously, still thinking about the nitro.

"After all, the rest of the world knows Mr. Forney doesn't drink coffee," Ethel continues, her voice reviving. "They speak of it on the streets of Zanzibar—the poorest beggar in the Hindu Kush, outside of his Koran, knows Mr. Forney of Panama doesn't drink coffee . . ."

"Oh c'mon!" he snaps, cutting her off. How she loves to argue, he thinks. Outside, there's a rumble—a squall descends on the field; the roof begins to seep water. "I'm sorry," he shrugs, making an end of it. "I don't have much practice talking to women. The kind I hang around with, you pay." He turns away; she stiffens, hearing the same old accusation, made by the Harvard boys, other men now, in some new obscure phrasing. Each believes the other crazy, flees, Ethel for a far table, Forney for the door. Two cripples trying to tango, he thinks. His mind flies to the whores of Cristobal, their sullen looks, flaccid breasts. They were small comfort to him—women aren't; she's not. Many jokes refer to the Canal as one long snatch; much of Zone politics is described as fucking and raping.

Outside, the rain hides the field, so heavy it falls. The

others, before spread out, have gathered together for shelter on the veranda stairs, beneath the one piece of thatch that still sheds water. "How long since you've been back, Slovak?" Queen is asking. The old man shakes his head. "I can't go back. The Feds are after me—there ain't a state I'm safe in."

"What did you do wrong?" Brown asks.

"I run a thousand gallons in every night from Cuba." Slovak nods. "I was king of the rumrunners—ask anybody in Key West. One night there's rain like this—I'm out of gas, put down on a beach, hit a log, the airplane goes ass over tit, the booze tanks break. Twenty thousand seagulls lapping it up, staggering shitfaced around the wreckage . . ."

They chuckle at the thought. Forney leans in the doorway behind them, taking in his world. Brown is killing a bottle of rum. Out there, his three wrecks drip rain. An anger is building, beyond his control—he grabs Brown's bottle away, suddenly throws it out into the downpour. "If you're going to work for me, do a man's job," he shouts at Brown, at all of them. "That stuff's out. We still got six hours of flying left today!"

The men look at him curiously. Queen hides a smile. Brown watches his bottle gurgle into a frothy puddle fifteen feet away. "I need that stuff," he says. "I fly drunk."

"Want me to get it?" asks Kinner, eager.

Brown takes another bottle from his bag. "Nah—I got more."

"What happens if you fly sober?" Queen asks.

"I'm afraid to look down." The other men chuckle. "I'm not shitting you," Brown insists. "I always fly drunk.

I learned to fly drunk. If I ain't drunk, I get scared. I can't look down."

"I knew a guy like that," Slovak begins. Fuck them all, Forney thinks, pushing through them, down the stairs, striding out into the rain. He shouts at the gas pit crew, waving his hands, trying to be heard over the storm.

The men, rubbing shoulders, watch him for a while. "What an asshole," declares Slovak, finally. The others nod. "What he needs is a good enema," says Brown softly.

"Brownie's right," says Queen. "We ought to give him a nitro suppository."

"What's that?" Kinner asks.

"Two drops up his wazoo with an eyedropper. Slap his cheeks together. Whammo!" They all laugh at that—Queen laughs hawww.

BROKEN CLOUDS OVERHEAD and underneath. The tops swell into ragged canyons—Brown in ATE twines through them, following Forney in ACH. When a wingtip slashes through the billows, a slit opens, melts back together. Sunlight slants down in round shafts.

Forney is climbing—Brown adds power, to keep up. Not much point, he thinks—over, under, Forney's not going to work around this storm, it being the same damn front all day long, all the way out to the horizon, they just trailing it south. "Tumaco at 2:45," he writes on his chart, next to the hook of land. The nose punches into cloud, like a boxer, plunges into another white room.

Beside him, Queen stuffs a pipe with Prince Albert. He

does a funny thing: bends over and strikes a kitchen match against his ankle. Now he catches Brown's eye, smiling.

"Wood?" Brown asks.

Queen pulls up his pantleg, showing a wine-colored limb. "Straight-grain Philippine mahogany!" he shouts. "Designed the socket myself." He puffs on the pipe to get it going.

"How did you lose it?"

Queen leans back. "Took a married woman flying one night in a New Mexico sandstorm! Said she wanted to see the face of God!"

"Did you?"

"Nah, we crashed!"

Brown grins, checks the lubber line, takes his rum bottle and hands it across. Queen wipes the mouth with the heel of his hand. "Where are you coming from?" he asks Brown.

"Hollywood!"

Queen is intrigued. "Making movies?" Brown nods. "Wonderful! You know any movie stars?"

"Who's your favorite star?" Brown asks him back. Queen thinks. "It's a funny sort of question. Ronald Colman, I suppose. He reminds me of an uncle."

"I was Ronald Colman!" Brown shouts. Queen doesn't get it. "*The Squadron of the Damned.* I was Ronald Colman. He played a limey—you know; he'd get in the plane, they'd show him taking off, and then he got shot down by the Heinie. That was me, crashing the airplane."

Queen understands now, pointing with the bottle. "You really were Ronald Colman!"

"He was scared of airplanes, any shit like that. I did

a lot of that stuff. They'd pay me two hundred bucks to crash a plane!"

"Why'd you stop?"

"People got tired of airplane movies. They stopped making them."

Queen passes the bottle back, nodding thanks. "There was a Brown in the war," he says, tentatively.

Brown nods. "That was me." Ahead, Forney's gliding down through a break. Brown figured he would, sooner or later, put down and let the storm blow past. Queen looks up as the power comes off, peers over the side. "I don't see any field," he shouts. Brown motions ahead to the wide beach just in view as the clouds spread. The wind whistles past the windmilling props; with a free hand, Brown stuffs the bottle in his bag, zips it shut.

THE STARS COME OUT for the first time. Kinner looks up through the cockpit roof, smiles at Deneb, Vega, learned a year back from an old CPO, his division flaked out on the boat deck in their hammocks one hot night. Everybody's gone to sleep except Forney, who sits out by a fire that sputters in the wet wind. The others don't like him, which Kinner accepts but doesn't understand, since Forney seems to be what movies and comic books say he should be, namely aloof, apart, not one of the boys. Kinner likes all his new friends, thinks they're real fellows—the Navy, the best of the Navy, was all assholes and misfits like him. Slovak's aft in the cabin, sleeping atop a row of crates. "You can't get far enough away from this shit to make a difference," he'd said. Imagine, asleep on top of nitroglycerine. Kinner has no brothers or sisters, the experience of his own birth, a precarious one, him emerging left foot first and bright blue, being enough for his parents. He'd never have thought of sleeping on nitro—he puts it at the feet of having no brothers, a father who spent more time on the other side of town. Kinner has a secret—he forged a birth certificate to join the service; he's actually fifteen and a half. When he thinks about how he'll solve his problems in Panama, his mind goes blank. Something will happen, he tells himself, amnesty, maybe Congressional recall, a Christmas intervention brought about by his mother. He looks away from Forney on the sand, out the overhead glass once more. The stars fade behind a curtain of cloud.

FORNEY DREAMS he's drowned and died, awakes to confirmation. It's pitch-black—a storm drenches him where he lies, doubled up beneath a palm. He raises up on one arm, coughing rainwater, looks down the beach. Barely visible, the Trimotors rock in the wind blasts, hauling on their tiedowns. He coughs again, his stomach really hurts now, bones ache; his side is cramped from lying funny. He wants to cry, to kill. This is as far as he can sink, not Panama—he left Panama with a plan. Cold feet, wet fur, like some backyard dog. She wouldn't let him sleep inside ACH, forced him out here, in sight of the others. How he hates her, them, her for how she treats him, them for letting her. This is rock bottom; he doesn't know whether to cry, maybe laugh, a crazyman's laugh. Cry or kill, shit or go blind.

He resolves if nothing else to be dry. Forney stands, leaning into the wind, breaking holes with his fists, struggles upwind toward ACH, pants dragging with water and sand, rounds the tail, bumps his shin on the elevator, gets blown down on the cabin door, and pounds at the handle. It's locked from the inside. He bangs on the door with his fist. He looks around for a rock, a tool, but this is a sand beach. He takes off his shoe, light as a feather, open tropical weave, pounds on the handle. The wet shoe shreds. Forney goes berserk now, grabs the handle with both hands, puts one foot against the rippled fuselage, then the other, raises himself off the ground, cantilevered out from the door, a mass of angry vectors and tensions. The handle breaks off; Forney thumps onto the sand on his back. He gets up, pries the door open against the wind's force, spills inside.

Out of the rain, his legs tangle with others. There's a light in his eyes, a flashlight—he focuses past it. There's a gun in her hand, silver, very stylish milady. Oh Jesus, he thinks. "I know how to use this," she says, firmly. "Damn you," he hisses. "There's a hurricane outside."

Ethel bends past a crate to look out a side window. She's wiping goo from the corner of her eye—Forney realizes she just woke up. She sees the storm, hears it rattling on the roof. "That doesn't matter," she says. "You'll have to find some place outside."

He shakes his head. He'd sooner die than answer, providing her with what she likes most, an argument. He shuts his eyes, leans back, waits to see if his head goes splooey like a dropped watermelon. What exactly does she think he'd do, he wonders, answers himself with a chuckle. She flatters herself; she's homely and he's wet. "I'm simply taking precautions regarding the amount of cash I'm carrying, Mr. Forney," she says. He won't budge, won't twitch.

A moment passes. "It's the reason you're here, Mr. Forney. You made that clear yesterday..."

He stops her by merely opening his eyes. "Maybe I want to save Bolivians. *You* want to save Bolivians." He lets that sink in, curling up, head into his armpit so the light can't bother. A moment passes; Ethel, unsure, clicks off the light—then turns it on again. "It's hard for me to suddenly think of you as an idealist, Mr. Forney," she begins. He says nothing at all. "You said you were desperate." Forney shifts, extends a leg. In the small space by the doorway, they touch whenever they move.

Ethel sits ready, uneasy, gun in her hand, light on. Forney's chest rises and falls; water collects under his nose tip, drops to his chest. He is waiting for her to sleep, she thinks, for her guard to drop. No, he's asleep himself now—his lips quaver; she's seen enough sleeping men to tell a fake. It comes to Ethel that she's misjudged him. That's a new sensation, at least one she never admits to—she wonders whether to trust it, the alternative being to do as she's doing until dawn, at least until sleep undermines her. She wavers, drawn to one argument, then the other. An hour passes—the batteries dim, the light turning yellow. Her eyes smart. After three hours, the bulb filament barely glows, but no matter now, since the rain has stopped and outside dawn spreads over bowed, wet palm trees, dripping loudly.

7

THE LANDMARK IS Pedernales, only a village by the print size. Queen looks west to the coast—no sign of life in that boggy land. By dead reckoning, forty-two miles south of Esmeraldas. The second hand stands straight up. Queen takes out Brown's rum bottle, unscrews the cap, pours an inch or so over the pilot's head.

Brown's startled. "What's that for?"

"We just passed the equator," says Queen. "We're in the Southern Hemisphere."

East, mountains collect in the haze. The white coating the tops is snow, the Cordillera Occidental, most northern archipelago of the Andes, slanting in from the Colombian highlands to meet their course. Cotacachi just past, Cotopaxi to come, smoking, still alive, and down toward Guayaquil, Chimborazo, 21,000 feet. Not today, the mountains, but starting tomorrow, Queen thinks.

Dull flying, limp cloudless sky, nothing but noise and glare. Queen searches for a sign of life, a road, a boat wake out to sea. Even with Brown, he feels lonely. He looks straight down, tries to sense what Brown says he feels when flying sober. There, he does a bit, a sort of vertigo, a welling fear he has no business here, that he sits legs over a ledge, on a rug about to be yanked. A flying carpet, Queen thinks —haww. Why fly at all? It's what I do, he thinks, but it's a bad answer; there are other things. He could fall, he supposes, the cockpit floor could give way, the fuselage open and spew him like so much roe. What would he think about on that wild ride?

THEY POUND SOUTH all morning; Ethel sleeps soundly, curled aft. North of Guayaquil around noon, they find the river and follow it to a broad floodplain, rising ten feet to the mile toward the far-off mountains. They stooge around over the city, looking for the cemetery that marks the airport's edge, then swing inland in line, point into the offshore wind, settle to their landings.

A gas truck bounces out to meet them. Forney handles the refueling, gives Kinner a few bucks for *empanadas*. He wants to keep flying, to Chiclayo, maybe even Trujillo tonight, three hundred miles farther. Brown strolls around each airplane, touching the engines. He doesn't like any of them but number one on ACH is the worst—practically no compression when he pulls the prop through. "You got oil coming out the head, out the exhaust. I bet you got no pistons left in there, or at least no rings." Forney shrugs. "Yeah, well, if we had the time and the parts, I'd do something about it, but we don't." Tank caps go down, safety-wired shut. Kinner returns with chow, doors slam, starters grind, engines cough and catch, gather rpm's, taxi downwind.

Forney wishes he had instruments on number one now. Brown's right—it's hunting for an idle, vibrating in a funny way. Forney can hear it when he puts his ear to the fuselage channeling. He looks aft—she's braced for takeoff, in her crate cubby. What would she do if he shut down, said they had to tear into an engine for a day? Pull out that gun again. Shit on that—Brown, alongside in ATE, wags his ailerons, ready to fly. Forney waves him ahead. He revs the throttle on number one, flicks the mags. Not ignition. He studies the prop track, the way the engine trembles on its shock mounts. Brown's away, hunchbacked airplane lifting. Slovak taxis into line, looking at him. Forney waves him on as well. The pistons or the valves, he thinks. Maybe he'll hunt up a heavier oil tonight. Go or stay? A moment: go. Three throttles forward. Ahead, Slovak just breaks ground, Brown a quarter-mile ahead, both climbing. Forney does what all pilots must do on takeoff, trust to the machine.

ACH gathers speed—the tail lifts, the wheels rise off the ground. The cemetery flashes below, baroque crypts, white picket fences around marble stones. Forney begins a shallow left turn, rising over the town. There's an abrupt hiccup of flame—two cylinder heads blow off number one, filling the air with ragged smoke, shredding the fuselage with hot metal. Forney tastes blood from somewhere. He can't see through the smoke—the horizon starts to slide away to the left. The engine's on fire, the oil, the gas line, all of it, streaming orange flames.

Ethel hears the explosion, sees the fire's tail out her window. She stumbles forward, but the airplane is heeling more on its side, and the floor becomes the right-hand wall, the left-hand wall now the floor. She sprawls across a pile of crates, flailing for purchase, looking straight down into fire; below the fire, the streets of Guayaquil grow.

The airplane is banked into the dead engine, wants to die there. Forney has full opposite aileron, rudder, full high power—he even leans toward the up wing, but he's fighting inertia and three tons sag the other way. The city swells—in one direction, a high gashouse, the other a cathedral, twin bell towers, tiled dome between. Forney hears a strange new sound and realizes it's him, shouting.

Above, two planes circle, crews watching helplessly. ACH slants off toward the city, black smoke behind. Oil fire, thinks Brown. Take half the city with it. Queen can't look; Slovak forces himself to, part of the continuing test of his manhood. "Can he pull out?" shouts Kinner beside him. Slovak won't dignify the question.

Forney's head hurts. Things have slowed down, thank God. He sees where the fire started, same damn oil line. It should burn away in a minute, he thinks, being only some dried-out garden hose he found behind the SACA hangar. There—the fire puffs out. The controls are sloppy, silly in their feel. The heeling turn has pointed him toward the cathedral. He can see the street life now: some commotion, people fleeing. Fleeing him, he realizes. A lady sells peppers, red on a blanket; a man herds mules, looks up. Cross-controlled, near a stall, Forney shoves the nose way down, do or die. The airplane roars at the cathedral stairway, flat, fifteen steps, give or take a couple. Forney feels a little lift, keeps the nose down, it being no time for premature soaring. Mrs. Booton drops backward into the cockpit, tangles up in the rudder pedals. Forney nurses his airspeed like a Yankee miser, one increment at a time, hand over hand, like climbing a cliff. The shadow of the plane rises to meet them, flopping and leaping over rooftops like a salmon. The cathedral doors are opening; a mass is letting out. A nun raises one arm—Forney smiles, not being above childhood Catholic mischief. Now he lets the nose come up as it wants to, inches at a time. Despite all arguments, the airplane craves to fly. The shadow rises, flashes up the side of the cathedral, over the roofs, the dome, practically kisses the dangling wheels. Forney lets the airplane wallow there, feet over the city, gathering speed, getting its wind. Slowly, he lets it climb now, the two good engines thundering. Mrs. Booton untangles herself, struggles into the empty seat. Her mouth is moving, but she's wordless. Fifty feet gained, Forney banks gently back toward the cemetery and the airfield beyond. The windshield is crazed from shrapnel, the view ahead fragmented, up and down. Over the cemetery is crosswind, he thinks, but this is no time to circle. He skims over the pines that mark one border. "Wires!" she shouts, pointing. Beyond the road, power poles, bordering. He dips a wing right, skids over them. He's home, back on the power, letting the airplane sink slowly, feet a minute. Ethel pounds his shoulder, pointing again. Something ahead on his side of the field, a brown swarm. The wheels rumble on. Goats, he thinks.

Forney kicks rudder, left, right, fishtailing to dodge them. The goats scatter in every direction, filling his view. One slams under the nose, another crunches under the right wheel. Metal snaps; the wheel soars like a hat at a home run. The bare right axle digs into the turf—with an awful lurch, a scream of tortured metal, the airplane groundloops, plowing dirt, throwing back a wake of divots, rising up vertically onto the right wingtip as if to turn turtle, poising there for a long second, then slamming down on its gear once more, enough to bend the wings almost in two.

Forney yells "Out!" throws off his harness, reaches up,

yanks the red T-handle. The ceiling hatch falls loose; he kicks, gains the roof, sprints down the curved thirty-five feet of wing, flings himself into space, hits hard, bangs his head, lies there, wind lost, guts to the sky, in the field's middle.

It's still. The Trimotor rests askew—oil drips slowly onto the good left tire. A moment passes, then the cabin door opens and Ethel emerges. She looks about, staggers over to where he lies. She strips off his jacket, wads it into a ball and puts it beneath his ankles. She unbuttons his collar, feels for a pulse.

He rolls his eyes back. "What are you doing?"

"I'm treating you for shock." She looks at her watch.

"What the hell's the matter with you?" She shakes her head, counting with her lips. "We just ground-looped a ton of nitro!" he cries.

"So what?"

"Mrs. Booton, you just crashed in an airplane!"

"All that's important is that we both seem to be all right . . ."

He screams out loud, to drown her out. ACH reflects sunlight, at peace. He wrenches his arm away, gets to his feet in disbelief. Sweet God, what is it waiting for? What does he have to do to it? A trembling sweeps over him—he's nauseous now, looks for a place to york. It gushes up his throat, gets diverted into his nose and sinus, where it stings.

A crowd of Indians in black suits too short in the sleeves and pants has gathered around ACH the way they would a fallen meteorite. Forney pushes through them, to the starboard gear. Blood and hairy patches of skin coat the main strut. The axle has augered into the dirt—Forney scoops turf away with his hands. Exposed, the backing plate is bent sideways, like a pie tin run over. He drops to his knees beside it.

"Can you fix it?" Mrs. Booton has come up beside him. Sounds pierce Forney's head; it's hard to think. "That's a solid American steel forging, Mrs. Booton. You'd need a foundry and a milling machine to make it straight. There might be one in Quito. I don't know—I'd have to ask around."

"How long would it take?"

"I got no idea." He whispers; it hurts to talk. "A few days."

"I don't have a few days. What else can you think of?"

"There's nothing else I can think of!" His forehead burns; blood drips into one eye. "You're going to lose a couple of days," he whispers. "This old equipment, Mrs. Booton—there's a limit to what you can ask from it. I tried to make that clear in Panama." He's getting louder. "There are limits to what a man can do with it. There are limits all over the world; men know that—men go out into the world and get their heads kicked in. Women don't—women sit at home, dream up things. I think I'll fly some nitro to Bolivia tomorrow . . ."

Ethel is shaking her head, unimpressed. She did not misjudge him last night, a relief; she mistook his threat. She thought him dangerous; he's not—he's incompetent. "Mr. Forney, you thought you could take off from Cristobal with a full load. We couldn't. You thought we'd blow up at Buenaventura. You've done nothing but predict doom and destruction from the very first moment. And," she points at the landing gear, "it's becoming clear to me that if disaster doesn't come about naturally, you're willing to cause it yourself."

Forney opens his eyes wide. His fists clench; he speaks slowly. "Mrs. Booton, that was an Act of God!"

"Nonsense. You landed on a goat!"

"Hawww," says Queen. The others have landed, now sift through the ring of Indians. Coming upon the bent axle, Brown whistles out loud, pokes it with his toe. Around the other side of the nose, Slovak is looking over the number one, oil-coated, the stumps of two cylinders spread like flower petals. Kinner stares up at the fuselage, just below the rim of the cockpit window—the metal's riddled, one jagged hole just behind the pilot's headrest. Slovak nudges him, leads him around to the other side.

Some ground crew approaches on a tractor to haul ACH aside. "What happens now?" Queen asks, as they make a circle. Forney creases his hat; he won't look at Ethel. "Double up on the two good machines, probably. I'll take one, Brown the other."

"You! How come you?" Slovak is mad. "You stay—why should I eat it?"

"You'd still get your share," Forney begins.

"Screw shares! Sure, you guys want to ditch me, go off together and split the gold, or whatever it is." The men look at each other—nobody can fathom Slovak's delusions. "I'm not satisfied with Mr. Forney's opinion about the extent of the damage," Ethel tells them. "I'd like you all to look it over and give me your best idea how to repair it."

The men suck their teeth, dutifully examine the axle. Queen finally looks up. "No way to fix that short of a foundry." Brown nods. "That's right, Mrs. Booton. That's an American steel forging."

Now Forney laughs, though it hurts over the eyes. See how they stand up for each other, Ethel thinks, blushing, turning and walking off, no idea where she's going. "I thought I had rotten luck," Forney calls after. "This is rotten luck on a cushion. It's almost too rotten for me, Mrs. Booton. I wonder if any of it is yours?" Her hands clutch behind her; she thinks of Gerald, wishes she could materialize him here in the middle of this weedy field, to pummel Forney, thrash him into competence.

Forney's lighting a bent cigarette from a crushed pack. "I'll stay here—when you show up, we'll shift the load into the two good airplanes." Slovak spits at the ground, in contempt. "I was waiting for this, Forney, only the joke's on you, isn't it—I was too good for you." Before Forney can answer, he turns, angrily stomps off. Kinner hesitates, then follows after.

Brown watches them leave. "How come she can't wait while somebody takes the axle up to Quito?"

"She doesn't seem to have the time," says Queen.

"The mine's been burning for weeks. Couple of days shouldn't make any difference." He looks to Forney, who shrugs, no help.

By now, Kinner's caught up with Slovak, heading down the road into town. He throws his arms around the old man's shoulders. "Well, so much for Argentina. Too bad for me. I see some oil wells over there by the water—maybe they got work for Americans on oil wells . . ."

Slovak pries his arm off, shoves him away. Kinner almost falls. "What's that for?" he wonders.

"What are you trying to do?"

"I don't know. Cheer you up."

"Putting your hands fucking all over me." Slovak screws his face up. "You don't even know me, Kinner. Touching me. What the hell are you, a fairy or something?"

"Hey, Slovak, you want to know the truth?" Kinner grins. "I don't think there's gold in this or anything else. I think it's all just flying the nitro."

Slovak spits at his feet, a wet gob, just shy of his shoes. Kinner's eyes water; Slovak stomps off alone. This is his one flaw, Kinner thinks, uncontrollable tears at the worst time, a holdover, like baby fat, a habit no weight lifting or mind-over-matter course has ever altered. "Well up yours, mister," he says to Slovak's back, but too softly for him to hear.

THE BAR IS SIGNLESS—Queen and Brown find it only by the men sitting on its stoop, the guitar music. It's lit inside by candles despite the afternoon hour; on the walls are crossed red flags, banners, matched portraits of Lenin and an Ecuadorian with tiny eyes. *"Viva Leninismo,"* it reads, on a white sheet. Not that it was noisy, but it falls even quieter as they enter, sitting at a table half carved away with initials, knife hacks.

Queen looks to Brown for advice. Maybe twenty men in dusty suits stare only at them. It seems dangerous, dangerous to stay, possibly just as dangerous to leave. Brown smiles, raises a fist; *"Viva Leninismo,"* he says, with a bad accent.

"Viva Leninismo," somebody shouts back, in response. A sigh fills the room; there's a scraping of chairs as

men turn back to their drinking. A kid comes over with a towel in his belt—Brown lifts his bag up, takes out a rum bottle. "*Dos mas como this,*" Brown extemporizes, making up his Spanish. "Rum. *Ron.*" The kid nods, leaves. Queen's impressed with Brown's savoir faire. "You don't believe that guff, do you, Brownie?" Brown shrugs. "It got us served."

The kid returns with two sealed liter bottles, two chipped glasses. "*Dos scuderos,*" he says. Brown takes out a handful of coins, lets the kid hunt through for what suits him. "Wait a minute—let me get one of these," says Queen, taking out his own handful. The kid leaves; they pop a cork, clink glasses. "Well, Brownie, now when somebody asks you what happens when you lose an engine on takeoff in an overgrossed Ford Trimotor, you can tell them," Queen says, and Brown nods yes, that he can.

FORNEY CHEWS BREAD in the shadow of South American aviation. He's alone in the adobe restaurant behind the airport terminal—covering the walls and ceiling are names, signatures in pencil and ink, extroverted splashes of colored paint, names with dates, names in boxes, names enough to almost hide the whitewash, all pilots, every man who's ever flown through here. Forney slowly looks around and overhead. Some of them he knows: Frank Tomick, Augie Pedlar —knew him in Alaska. Lots of these guys have gone belly-up, Forney thinks. Mermoz the Frenchman, the first one over a lot of these Andes routes.

There's a picture frame against one far wall, simply the wood frame with nothing in it. Forney takes his beer over to look, stepping quietly as in a shrine. The frame surrounds an unassuming signature: "Charles A. Lindbergh." Forney pictures him, knew Slim, that not meaning much, pilots in the Midwest in the Twenties tending to run across each other. He'd helped him time the OX–5 in his Jenny, a hot day in a wheat field, dogs chasing rabbits, hawks circling overhead. Slim made it hard for the rest of them, Forney thinks; people expected a lot more out of pilots after Lindbergh.

He searches the walls closely, window frames, corners, low to the floor, name upon name, now finds what he thought might be there. "Hal Moxey." Hal had come through here, some Army goodwill flight in the old days. Goodwill, Forney thinks. Hal was supposed to rescue him, would have with time. Where did Hal come from, what cloud, magic boat? There he was, one day in Wichita, 1928, standing over Forney where he sat pounding the kinks out of a Travelaire's drag strut. "Hello—I hear you got some idea about endurance contests," he'd said. Forney had: solo endurance, an air-show category, flying around in circles as long as you could stand it, something Forney felt right up his alley. He had an option on an old Stinson, figured on gutting it, building new tanks for the cabin and wings from flattened gallon cans soldered together. Hal had listened, fiddled in the dirt with a stick—he was no formal engineer, but there weren't many in those days, just men with a good eye, a feel for weight and moment arms. Look how much better a cg you get by building the engine out another foot, he said, drawing a new engine mount in the dirt, then and there. They sat in the shade beneath the wing, picking grass leaves, talking. When the sun sank, they walked downtown to Hal's hotel, picked up his wife Virginia, went out to a steakhouse, big pan-fried sirloins, heaps of fried potatoes. He liked Forney for some reason. Forney was candid, reeled off all his sad stories; Hal laughed them away, said that adversity had only made him ready. You're just ripe for a change, he told Forney, slapping his back. Hal slapped backs, hugged—big, bulging eyes, broad hands, booming voice. For three months they worked on the Stinson, fifteen-hour days, trimming every pound, batteries out, instruments, cushions on the seats, insulation, trim, hardware, even drilling out the tubing here and there for the mere weight of the shavings. Best days of Forney's life, cold beer, smokes, pilots dropping by; Hal knew everybody, showed off Forney like his new best friend. Night work, late hours, on a scratchy radio Major Bowes and Eddie Cantor, moths pinging against the work lights. Exhausted sleep, up at daylight full of beans. "I figured out a way to brace the wingtanks." "*I* figured out a way to brace the wingtanks." Solder puddling on a hotplate, tinned irons. Forney shuts his eyes; three months, all it was, ninety days, against a third of a century. Look what he did to him. How many chances do you think you get?

He swallows a lump of bread. There's a grease pencil resting on a windowsill. His gaze finds a blank spot for his name on the wall. He snorts, heads back for his table; no sir, he's a working stiff, average Joe, knows his limits, as he told Mrs. Booton. Forney sees chasms everywhere, drops and pitfalls, watches others plummet, stays far from the edge himself, as close to the ground as a flier can. Lindbergh was a hero, Hal as well, but that was years ago—this is now, in the middle of a worldwide Depression.

ETHEL HAS WALKED the streets aimless for an hour or more. The old South American feeling rushes back; women with braids stare at her from beneath their derbies, kids race around her legs. She wants to touch them, then again does not. Sometimes she hates her white skin, the skin of Pizarro and Cortez. Boys try to sell her fried fish, glass-eyed, on sticks, potatoes in some awful sauce—her stomach growls, but she doesn't dare. Down at a street's end, she sees an airplane resting, knows she's circled near the airport again.

Around a corner, there's the field's north border, a drainage ditch piled with junk, old airplane parts, wing ribs. Beyond it a shantytown spreads, shacks of scrap lumber and cardboard cartons. The faded cardboard sides show water staining and many famous American brand names. Somebody sits nearby staring out at it: Kinner, the fugitive. Ethel calls hello, buttons her sweater front, strolls toward him.

Kinner nods back; he's been watching some kids play soccer in a flat space with a ball stuffed with rags. He wishes they'd invite him across, an old dream of his, getting chosen to join things; it never happens, having something to do with his eyes, his soft skin. Who takes Kinner, you or me? he hears over and over, all his life. He's a joiner for that reason—the Boy Scouts, the Navy, mail-order clubs—but his fate follows him; Sunday hardball games at Coco Solo are no different. Now he's odd man out with this bunch as well, typical. He moves over to give her room as she sits. "Bad luck," she says. He just shrugs, lowers his head to his knees. He doesn't want to get a job in the oil fields—truth be known, he didn't want to be a gaucho down on the pampas. If he had the chance, he'd go home to Tucson and play high-school football, but that won't happen. What is he left with? An entire foreign continent around him. Everything he sees looks ominous, even the ditch, the shanties which God knows he's seen enough of in the States. The southern sun doesn't seem to be setting right, some combination of low angle and heat. He tries to buck himself up, tries to recall some stanzas from Rudyard Kipling's *If*, a poem he once memorized line by line as part of a self-improvement course, but hard as he ponders, all that returns is the single word of the title.

"I'll be okay," he sighs. He thinks back to the black-cat ring he had once, then lost. Land-on-ur-feet, it read. "You don't see many women doing the kind of thing you're doing," he says. "Messing around with nitro."

She shakes her head. "No, you don't."

"What does your husband think of all this?"

Ethel feels flushed at the thought of him. She sees Gerald smiling, one hand on her shoulder, another in the pocket of a white lab coat. "Naturally, he worries. He realizes I have a life of my own, my own commitments—he can't say much but be careful."

"He's a doctor?"

"A very well-known young surgeon in the Boston area. I'd show you a picture of him, only I don't carry one." Kinner shrugs. "I don't wear a ring either, you'll notice. We don't believe in a lot of the traditional trappings of marriage."

"Sure," Kinner nods, as modern as the next guy. There's a shout—the soccer ball arcs over the ditch, bounces nearby, and stops against the metal wall of a hangar. The kids yell to him, something—not to come and play, surely. "They want their ball," Ethel translates. Kinner stands, fetches it, looks through a hangar window, beholds a workbench, shelves, a mechanic calling someone he can't see. Slanting sun through the hangar doors outlines two airplanes. Parts on the workbench reflect light; a box label reads "Wright Aircraft Corporation, New Haven, Connecticut." The kids are yelling—Kinner boots the saggy ball over the ditch, hisses for Ethel, motioning her over with great sweeps of his hand. He points at the boxes inside, rows of them, neat on metal parts shelves. "Are those for our engines?" she asks.

"I dunno. I think so." The mechanic inside turns away to his pal again—Kinner times his move, raises the window, reaches in an experienced arm, and comes out with a small, flat box bearing the Wright logo. Pressed flat against the hangar, they open it—out come thin metal rings, split for expansion, coated in grease, wrapped in waxed paper. "I better go find Mr. Forney," says Kinner, taking a step, but Ethel's hand stops him.

"Why not?"

Ethel shakes her head, thinking, silent. Kinner strains against her hand. "Just a minute," she says. Moments pass, Kinner standing there. "Let's not tell him," she decides, finally. "He'll only say no."

Kinner eyes her. She scratches the back of her hand. "It's my trip."

"They're his airplanes . . ."

"Do you want to fix the airplane and fly to Bolivia or not?" she asks, a little shrill. Kinner can't argue with that.

"Go into town and bring back the others, fast as you can," she tells him, shoving him in the right direction.

KINNER FINDS SLOVAK downtown, sitting in a bandshell on the Malecon, looking out at the sunset. He's tearing up a sandwich, eating half, throwing half to the seagulls. Kinner loops around so as to approach him in full view, not wanting to startle the old man. He shows him the box—Slovak slips the metal loop over his wrist, like a bracelet. "Piston ring for a Wright J–6," he says, considering.

The two of them hunt the others, up and down silent streets of flush windowless houses. In the distance, somebody sings "Red River Valley"—they home on the voice, around corners, growing louder. Brown and Queen are pretty lushed. Queen waves farewell to his audience in the dim bar, raises his fist. He gets a room of understanding fists back, working-class solidarity.

Kinner leads them all to Ethel. The sunlight is gone, the hangar now dark. They peer over the windowsill—Brown sees a row of J–6 cylinders on a shelf, finned, double-eared. They're sublime, thinks Queen, taking an aesthetic moment—how delicate the finning, firm and true the lips and flanges. Beyond the parts shelves, lit by one hanging bulb, two single-engined Fairchilds rest, nose to tail, high-winged cabin monoplanes, each with "Guardia Civil de Ecuador" on the side in flowing script. "Ecuadorian Air Force," Queen deciphers. "Perhaps all of it."

"Well?" Kinner asks, eager.

"Well what?" wonders Slovak.

"Well, you know." As a klepto, Kinner is reluctant to pronounce his own vice.

"They shoot you for stealing down here," warns Queen. "Life's cheap below the equator."

"Life's not that great above the equator," Slovak mutters.

"We'd have to get everything done in twelve hours," says Brown. "Daylight comes, they'll miss this stuff."

Queen considers. "What good does it do to fix the engine and not the wheel?"

"That airplane has a wheel," Kinner suggests, pointing at the nearer Fairchild. Slovak punches him. "So does your baby carriage—that don't mean it will fit. Trimotor takes a big forty-inch high-pressure tire. That's—I don't know—twenty-six, twenty-eight inches."

"Could you make it fit?" asks Ethel.

Dream up an adapter, thinks Queen. "Smaller wheel. It means the airplane would lean to one side . . ."

"I say we try it," Kinner declares. The others shrug in time, one by one. Nobody thinks of telling Forney—it doesn't come up. Brown bends down, rubs dirt on his fingers. "Stay put," he tells them, heading off to reconnoiter. Kinner looks at Ethel, winks, excited.

Brown slinks back a moment later—they huddle together. "There's one guard with a Mauser, but he's sleeping. We can go in through this window and he'll never see us. You and Slovak watch him, okay?" He's pointing to Kinner. "If he moves, make a sound."

"Like what?"

"I don't know. Some kind of animal." Kinner does a talent-night chicken. They giggle; Brown shushes them. He tiptoes to the side window, hooks his finger under the rim, pulls up. It won't budge.

"Somebody locked it," says Ethel, helpfully. "It was open before."

Brown looks around, stymied. He edges forward toward the front of the building; the others follow, bunching at the corner, peering around it. There are two guards instead of one—the newcomer has poked his pal awake; both argue about something. Brown swears. "Well, hell, what now?"

Kinner clears his throat, makes two fists. Before anyone can stop him he steps around the corner. "Nice night," he says aloud to the guards, who turn, fumbling with their rifles. Boldly, he strolls past the horizontal prop of the lead Fairchild, hands behind his back. "So you guys are still flying these old things," he says, sympathetic. "*Norteamericano?*" says one guard to the other. Kinner nods. "Right—*norteamericano*. And you guys must be, what? *Souteamericanos?*"

"*Sudamericanos,*" one guard corrects him.

Kinner's gotten both to turn their backs to the corner, obviously his plan. Brown and Queen take the cue, now skitter into the shadows. Kinner is showing the guards how to stitch a wing envelope, his one actual area of competence, drumming the Fairchild fabric to make a point. Behind them, Queen has swung the side window open; he hands Slovak cylinders, pistons, valves, plugs, all in a hurry. Brown's levered one of the second Fairchild's wheels a few inches off the concrete, placed a crate under the jack point to hold it high, now attacks the wheel, popping the dust cover, snipping the cotter, taking a large wrench to the hub nut that locks on the wheel. He hums, spinning his wrench counterclockwise like a majorette's baton. The oily wrench slips out of his grip, arcs flashing through the air, end over end, bounces ten feet away with a clang.

The guards at the hangar doors freeze, look past Kinner into the darkness. Trembling, Kinner asks, "Where would a guy like me go in town for a good time?" They ignore him; the sound has their attention. At this moment a woman appears from the darkness, walking across the field toward them, holding a carton and a small boy by his pinky: the first guard's family bringing him dinner. The man turns when she calls his name. Brown has just slipped the wheel off its hub; he passes it out the window to Slovak, now muscles out the window in a hurry after it. Queen still prowls for parts. The married guard is leading his family around the corner of the hangar, seeking a private moment. Slovak sees them coming, hisses to Brown—they scoop up the loot and run for cover in the drainage ditch. "Where's Queen?" Slovak whispers. Beneath the open window, the wife spreads her poncho smooth. The baby lies down, sucking his thumb—the guard yanks it out of his mouth.

Inside, Queen sees he's cut off. He hears footsteps on the hangar floor: the other guard, still tracking down the clang. He inches backward. At the rear of the hangar is a false plywood wall, a storage area beyond. He slips through an open door, sees starlight beckoning through a window feet away. His shin knocks a hollow metal pipe off a scrap pile—it clangs louder than the wrench, like an organ down a stairway. Shit, oh dear, thinks Queen; he bangs open the window, spills outside, onto the dewy grass.

THE CLOCK on the restaurant wall reads seven; none of them back, thinks Forney, not at all surprised. The cook is lighting candles in sconces on the wall. The radio plays an Ecuadorian love song about suicide. He will do the work alone, he decides, as always, the only man he knows he can depend on. He heads for the door through the gauntlet of names.

Outside, the air is thick and moist, ocean air. The airplanes rest white in the moonlight on the far side of the field. Halfway across, he hears running, feels it too. He stiffens, glances left, right, hearing his heart rouse.

Instinct says flee—which way? Who is it, loud like an army around him? From the black emerges Slovak, rolling a wheel like a hoop, laughing like a madman. On the other side is Queen—he's cradling a J–6 cylinder as he runs. "Where'd you get that?" Forney hisses. "Go long!" Queen yells to Kinner with a whoop. The young man runs a short pattern, ten yards down, spins, gets hit on the number with a bullet pass. "Where did you get that?" Forney cries. "Go Kinner!" shouts Queen. "Best midnight mechanic in the Ivy League." Brown appears with a gunnysack over his shoulder; it clanks as he jogs. "Such a nice night, we decided to overhaul the engines," he grins. Forney runs arms out in front of him, forcing him to stop. "Where did you guys get that stuff?"

Brown looks past Forney's shoulder, smiling. There is Mrs. Booton, catching up, prying a pebble out of a tennis shoe. "Over there," she says, pointing to the Guardia Civil hangar.

Forney's mouth drops. "They shoot you for stealing down here." Ethel nods, not disputing that, continues on. They don't care, Forney realizes; he stumbles after, swept up in the wake of their passing.

8

FORNEY KEEPS HIS HAND TOOLS in a rice sack, Brown his in a mahogany five-drawered toolchest, dovetailed joints, each drawer lined in green felt. The two of them stand on ladders, working on the blown number one. Flashlights are baling-wired to the struts; more light comes from a campfire burning out beyond the nose, tended by Mrs. Booton, at this moment raising her skirts to let the heat rise beneath. On the other side of ACH, Slovak and Queen fit the new wheel; they've sent Kinner off to change the spark plugs, a job his speed, 2 per cylinder, 18 per engine, 162 plugs in all.

Forney's still shaky, shows it; his fingers tremble, juggle a nut and lock washer that fall to the dirt below. Swearing, he climbs down after them, searching the darkness for the raid he's sure will come. He pictures cruel Latin faces, gold teeth, cardboard hat brims, puttees. These people have no idea where they are, the land they're in, he thinks. It's deceptive, South America, seeming slow, diffuse, but for all that, they've perfected punishment down here. For all he knows, they leave things like cylinders lying about to prime the retribution.

He climbs back up with a gas can; they're pouring avgas through the crankcase now, flushing out the shredded metal. He hears her voice, looks down—Mrs. Booton's just passed a cup of coffee up to Brown, offers some to him. Typical measure of human concern, he thinks, for her to forget his aversion in one day. He takes it rather than start that all over; the hot cup burns his hands. Oh yes, now she's the hostess at this affair, suddenly the mastermind. Look how Brown smiles at her; Slovak's wanting a refill. It takes no brains to steal, Forney thinks; crime's always there as an alternative, sheer grabbing what you want. Thank God most of the world rejects it, or where would we be? He could have led them to this, as well—we're going to simply swipe what we need from that hangar, he could have told them, it requiring only the nerve to say it, no great insight. And then what if they got caught? Had they thought of that, any of them? What could he say to them then, as the man responsible—what could she, and did she ever stop to wonder? Forney imagines a dictator's cupboard: caged rats, branding irons, acid clamps.

Whang, whang, suddenly, loud; Forney spills coffee on his arm and pants, too scared to feel the burn. The men all freeze. Forney looks about for a glimpse of troops converging. But the sound has come from ABR, barely in the fire's verge, where Kinner sits astride the nose, pulling plugs on the number two. "Kinner, you asshole!" Slovak shouts, coming around the nose of ABR. Brown is outraged, horrified. "Jesus, Kinner, ain't you got no respect for the metal?"

From the dark comes a faint reply. "This thing wouldn't budge . . ." Forney, breathing deeply, realizes what happened—a plug froze in its socket, Kinner laid a wrench on it, committed the workshop crime of using another wrench as a hammer. He'll get it now, Forney thinks.

"Jesus, Kinner, I thought you said you was a mechanic," Brown shouts. "Fabric mechanic," mutters Slovak, close at hand. They turn to him—Slovak's shrugging.

From the darkness comes a voice, stammering. "I had to get out of the Zone, that's all."

Brown pauses, then climbs down to his toolchest. From it, he takes a rubber mallet, a can of penetrating oil, hands them to Slovak. "If he's going to work on engines, go show him how," he says, and Slovak nods, heading off into the darkness toward ABR.

Forney is surprised, jealous as well. How does Kinner rate? Such charity was never shown him when young; his instructors were all pricks. Brown is getting his cup refilled —Forney climbs down as well, crosses to the fire. She's there, rubbing her hands. The reason he doesn't steal is that you get caught, he's thinking. If not now, later. His mind goes back to Alaska, Twelve-Mile Field, his DH–4, unflyable with a cracked wing spar. One night, this guy in a bearskin coat shows up with a hundred-dollar bill for the man who'll fly him to Fairbanks. Forney says no—Augie Pedlar says hell, he will, asks Forney to loan him the DH. Forney says no again, the broken spar. Augie leaves—Forney hears the engine firing outside, runs out to see the two of them taking off into a blizzard, his airplane simply stolen. Turns out the man was Parker of Alaska-Parker Lumber, made Augie his personal aerial chauffeur at a thousand a month. Augie's high on the hog in Fairbanks for six months until the two of them buy the farm one day. Forney takes that as the getting caught, the paying, but to be truthful, he's wondered what it was like for Augie those high six months.

See how she stretches, across the fire. They make us do things, Forney thinks, fight wars, lay waste to cities. He clears his throat. "I knew that engine was going bad this morning," he tells her. She looks up; he nods. "They get a sort of wobbling sound before they go."

"Why didn't you say anything?"

"You were in a hurry. Time's important." He edges around the fire until he's beside her.

For a while they're silent. "I ever tell you I won a contest?" he says. It sounds out of thin air to him; he plunges on. "St. Louis Aerial Exposition of 1929, First Prize in Solo Endurance. Fly around by yourself; fifty-two hours, twelve minutes. That's how I bought these airplanes —there was a ten-grand purse."

"You had some luck."

He shakes his head, thinking no. He pulls out his wallet, takes from it a newspaper clipping, two columns wide, ripping along the crease. Ethel sees a picture of Forney, arm in arm with another grinning man. "That's me. I was World Champion."

"I've never met a World Champion."

"Yeah, well some limey broke it ten days later." She smiles; he shrugs. "Guess what I did with the extra money?"

"You bought the airplanes." She doesn't know what he's getting at.

"The money I had left over. The airplanes cost me eight grand. I gave you a big clue," he says. "I told you the year."

"Nineteen twenty-nine?" She thinks. "You put it in the market?"

Forney spreads his arms, radiant in his bad luck. Ethel looks at the flames; she could match his bad luck, but won't, how she had a little left over from the policy after she'd paid off her nursing school, lost it all in Florida land. Queen swears—a wrench has slipped off a bolt head, tearing a knuckle. The Fairchild's backing plate doesn't match the Ford stud pattern, so they've had to cut new bolt holes with a hand drill and files alone.

CLOSE TO DAWN NOW. The number one engine sits closed up, topped off, wiped down. The men concentrate on the wheel now, fitting, cut and try, fingers sticky with machine oil and shavings.

Once more, a foreign sound makes Forney stiffen. Not again, he thinks—oh God, they waited until we were tired. The others grab up tools, stand ready before the airplanes. Moments pass—into the firelight drives a young man on a girl's bicycle. "Hi, you guys," he waves, uneasy at the sight of the tools raised. "I heard about your accident. I was meaning to get down earlier, but I got this bellhop's job, and I don't get off until midnight."

Nobody has a reply. "I'm Vern Kephart," he continues. He has an argyle sweater, socks to match. "I go to school down here, and I string for the wire service off and on for my mad money." He shoves down his kickstand, walks over to the damaged wheel. "Bent it all up, huh?"

Brown clears his throat, standing. "We brought all these spare parts with us."

"Well, I guess you'd have to, because where else would they come from?" Kephart touches the wheel with his toe. "I usually come by the airport in the afternoon, see if anybody interesting comes off the Lima flight."

"Nobody interesting here," says Forney, unwinding,

motioning the others back to work. But Queen is intrigued—he stuffs his pipe, strikes a match. "Does anybody interesting ever come through on the Lima flight?"

"Oh sure. I met Ronald Colman six months ago. He was on vacation."

"That's nothing much. Brownie here was Ronald Colman," Queen says, pointing with his pipe stem. Forney looks up, puzzled.

Brown shrugs. "In Hollywood. I was Ronald Colman when he got shot down."

"Yeah, well there's been a lot of them stunt-pilot stories in the magazines lately, so I don't know if they'd buy it." Kephart knocks aside a divot with his heel. "Actually, I flunked out of school a few months ago. All the courses are in Spanish. I sure could use a drink." He moves the same divot back to the hole it came from. "I was hoping there was some kind of story in the accident. They pay me by the word, and if you guys could find your way clear to spare me a couple hundred . . ." His voice fades, helpless.

The men glance at each other. Queen finally stretches and yawns, arms to the sky. "You're in luck, Vern," he smiles. "The airplane you're standing next to is as stuffed full of nitroglycerine as a Christmas goose."

Kephart flinches. "No shit!"

"No shit indeed. We're taking forty-two hundred pounds down to Bolivia to put out a mine fire—you probably heard about it."

Kephart shakes his head. "That don't mean nothing—news travels by snail down here. You mean when you guys crashed today . . ." Kephart's mind races, unfettered. "You could have wiped out the town."

111

Queen smiles modestly. "Let's say we could have altered its appearance for the worse."

"Nitro—jeez," says Kephart. He touches the Trimotor's belly, gets a sooty hand off the nose engine's exhaust pipe for his pains, wipes it off on a hanky. Now he takes out a notebook and pencil. "I flew over from Chile two months ago in one of them new Douglases. We barely made it. Had to suck oxygen through little rubber tubes."

"Oxygen gives you gas," says Slovak, not looking up from his work. Brown nods. "We never fly high. You miss all the scenery."

"You mean you guys do this kind of thing all the time? Like an airline?"

"Fuck airlines," says Brown.

"We're no airline, Vern," Queen explains. "If we were an airline, we'd have blue uniforms."

"And some puss in the cockpit," says Slovak.

"And life insurance," adds Forney, joining in. The men chuckle at that. Kephart's writing furiously now, fired up. "Life insurance," he repeats. "You know, this is terrific stuff, you guys. They might go for it."

"Actually," says Brown, "privately, we call ourselves the Panama Suicide Club."

The others pause, taken by surprise. Queen is overwhelmed. "Brownie, that's wonderful!" he cries. Brown smiles, pleased himself.

"PSC," says Kephart. "I'm abbreviating." He looks up again. "No kidding. Well, if you guys want to kill yourself, I guess this is a pretty good way to do it."

Queen shakes his head. "Oh no—we don't want to die.

We dare death to kill *us*. That's the point of the whole thing; that's our motto: *Mortus Ficam.*"

"What's that mean?" asks Slovak.

"Fuck death."

"They'd never print that," says Brown. Queen is putting an arm around him, lifting him to his feet. "We all live together on this estate—never mind where, Vern. All of our needs are taken care of, that you can bet on. We're like brothers, maybe even closer. You dare death with a guy for any length of time, you see the bottom of his soul. I don't think there's a thing you could name we wouldn't do for each other."

Kephart is silent for a moment. "You know, you hear about these things . . ."

"It's getting light," Ethel says, clearing her throat, speaking at last.

Kephart nods. ". . . wouldn't do for each other," he's writing, now looks up. "Hey, listen, I'm grateful for what I got. This is terrific stuff—you guys done me a real service. One last favor." He hands the pad and pencil to Slovak. "Pass this around and write your names down. That way, they won't get misspelled."

Slovak squints, prints carefully. Queen signs with a flourish, then Brown, even Forney, snorting. Kinner stands to one side, across the fire, hesitant. "C'mon, Kinner," says Brown; Kinner hurries over, writes his name large. Kephart shakes hands all around. "Me for the cable office," he cries. "Good luck, you guys." He lifts his bike in a one-eighty, pedals off rattling toward town.

113

IT'S LIGHT long before the sun appears, it taking an hour to top Chimborazo to the east. At 5:30, a Hispano-Suiza rumbles over the cattle guard onto the airfield, turning toward the Guardia Civil hangar. In the backseat are two Ecuadorian officers, a tall Indian pilot with huge hands, and his navigator, an Andalusian, in riding boots and spurs. They're splitting a smoke; as they bounce past the Trimotors, they nod to the men there, the navigator touching his cap bill with his plaited riding crop.

"Dawn patrol," mutters Slovak, bolting on the new wheel. Forney paces behind, lock nut, cotter, safety wire, sharp ends scratching Slovak's hands as he braids it. "Done," he says, standing, wiping his hands on his pants —Forney nods, motions them all to their machines. Cabin doors thump closed, starters moan, waking engines cough stale air and condensation. Sluggish oil stirs, coursing through ports and gaps as eight engines run up together, shouting and snarling.

Forney in the cockpit of ACH can't get his number one to start, no matter what he tries. God, what did they leave out of it, he thinks, squirming. Once more—prime, crank it to draw the gas in, starter now, flywheel spinning up to speed, engagement—the engine shudders, backfires, wheezes dead. Forney hits the throttles with his hands. Somebody's running over—Brown, from ATE, slashing a hand across his throat. Forney cuts ignition, throws off his harness, bangs back down the aisle. Ethel huddles there, worried. He jerks his thumb. "Get up there and do what I tell you," he shouts, shoving her out of his way as he pushes past, hard enough to make her gasp.

The metal doors are just tracking open at the Guardia

Civil hangar. Mechanics roll out the lead Fairchild; the Indian bends over, tears off a clump of grass, lets the wind take it, noting where the leaves fall. "*Asi,*" he says, marking the wind direction with his hand. Two orderlies are fetching heavy leather fur-lined jumpers, made-to-order in Spain.

Brown and Forney pore over number one, hands dancing. "Could you get off on two?" Brown asks him. "Fuck that—I tried that yesterday," Forney cries. Brown suddenly runs off. "Hey!" calls Forney, then turns back to the engine. The ignition leads are tight, everything looks proper. Here it comes, capture, traps closing; he was right all along, simply premature.

"Why won't it start, Mr. Forney?" Ethel calls, head out of the cockpit over him. Forney ignores her, wiggles the carb linkage. Brown runs up panting, with a small tin can. "What's that!" Forney asks.

"Liquid ether. If this don't fire it off, nothing will." Brown pulls the cork, pours the contents down the carburetor throat. "Choke it with your hand," he tells Forney, stepping back. Forney shouts up at Ethel. "Okay—listen carefully. Switch on! Push the starter button, wait for five or six prop blades to pass, then engage it, and you might have to goose the throttle a little until it catches!"

Ethel has a panicked look. "I don't know what any of that means!"

Brown runs off again. Forney tries to explain: "Goose the throttle; kind of move it back and forth." The plane rocks—behind her, Brown is stomping up the aisle. He flings himself into the cockpit, leaning over Ethel, hitting switches, giving her no chance to get out of the way. "Just stay put," he shouts, squishing her against the armrest.

Outside, number one cranks over again. Forney begs, man to metal, head inches from the hard steel prop. The engine hits on dry cylinders. Forney looks across the field —they've moved the lead Fairchild outside, have gone back into the hangar for the second one. "C'mon!" Forney yells at the engine, as if it's teasing. He covers the carburetor throat with his hand, trying to choke the ether down the manifold. Brown comes off the starter—the prop slows, impulse magnetos clacking. His face shows helplessness. "Again! Again!" Forney yells. Brown hits the switch once more. *Kabang,* the engine fires, with a tornado of smoke and noise. The smoke clears; there's Forney, singed, deaf, grinning. He runs around to the cabin door, meets Brown hurrying out. They wedge in the doorway for a second, giggling, Keystone flying.

  In the Guardia Civil hangar, the sergeant lines up his ground crew behind the Fairchild wing struts. On his command, they push together. Nobody notices the tarp covering the left-hand wheel—the plane rolls a foot forward, collapses on its left side with a scrape of steel on concrete. One of the Indians nudges the soap crate that had been holding up the axle. Behind them, far across the field, three Trimotors taxi toward the wind, one listing slightly to its right-hand side.

9

THREE CHILDREN STAND in the awful wind, hair, clothes, skirt hems streaming like pennants. They're holding crucifixes made of tied sticks—Ethel wonders why they wave them back and forth so, tracing lazy eights. Aymaras? Or are they, this still being Peru and not Bolivia yet? She motions them into the hangar, out of the blast, but they shake their heads, no. So stubborn, she thinks, like their parents. They'd rather stand in the wind.

Sand gets in her eye—she pulls the lid down to flush it, in the approved manner. Her watch says eleven—Forney went off with a Chinese lady, it seems an hour ago. Out on the line, a crew of Indians struggles to refuel the machines. The wind whips the gas hoses about like cobras—see how the men lean into the wind, almost depending on it. Lashed down as they are, tie ropes anchored to oil drums filled with cement, the airplanes still strain to lift off and fly away. Something gets in her throat—she coughs, brings it up. It has a bloody taste; a bug she thinks, shuddering. The men sprawl behind her, clustered at the back of the hangar, farthest from the wind. Loose siding bangs. They don't want to fly in this, that's clear. She'll have to make them somehow. She dreads it; don't they realize she's not that strong?

Ecuador changed to Peru this morning, an hour out of Guayaquil. So did the land—no sooner did they pass the farthest west, the continent's pregnant bulge, then the jungle stopped short, almost in a line perpendicular to the mountains, with only small salients daring a half-mile's advance here and there. Then a desert of copper and bronze, flat, traced by roads, erosion limbs and branches, telephone poles half-buried in sand. The Desert de Sechura, she remembers being told on the boat down with Gerald. Spoken of in awe, this land—rain perhaps twice a century. Hours of wasteland, dunes and broken hills, the only change at all the mountains, edging closer every mile south.

Three hours out, the plane began to jiggle, now and then, a palsied little leap, strong enough to startle her, irregular enough to make her tense. The leaps grew stronger, closer together—at times, the machine would creak loudly in response; the nitro crates would rise as the bottom fell out, banging together when it rose again, coughing sawdust clouds like blackboard erasers slapped together. She tried to do a crossword, couldn't, one jolt slashing her pencil across the grid. Finally, she had squeezed forward down the aisle, leaned into the cockpit as far as her shoulders. Forney was steering with one hand, slowly leveling the wings once the bounce was past.

"Is there something wrong?" she'd shouted.

"Windy around here," he shouted back, pointing ahead at the Andes. "Comes over those mountains."

She'd nodded; her eyes had fallen to the empty co-pilot's seat. For the first time, it had enticed her, not only more comfortable than her space to the rear but brighter, airier, for all she could tell, less bouncy, having some connection with being nearer the wing. She'd considered sitting down, despite what Forney had said—then decided no, gone back aft. The bouncing had gotten continuously worse; the land had slowly risen beneath as the sea grew more faint to the west. They were heading inland, she realized—below now were arroyos, bunched foothills. Out the side windows, ABR and ATE, a quarter-mile on either side, rising and falling like leaves on pond ripples.

Landing at Chimbote was interesting—the planes had stopped almost as soon as the wheels touched. The head wind, she'd guessed, so strong. Forney had trouble taxiing in—she could see him fighting the wheel, jamming the brake lever one way and the other. Climbing outside, the wind had snatched her breath away—Forney had pushed her toward the open hangar while he, goggles on, and the Indians moored the airplanes, then had staggered off toward a shack marked *Officina,* leaving her there, the others as well.

She motions the Indian children inside once more. They shake their heads. She can handle them this age, innocent, not responsible—it's when they grow up that they become recalcitrant, purposefully stupid, unable to see the course of their own welfare. Part of it's habit, part of it the Church that oppresses them. See how they wave these feeble crucifixes. The smallest boy finally makes a sound: brumm, he says. Ethel realizes the sticks are in fact airplanes.

She looks up—here comes Forney and the woman, hands over their faces, running past the gas pit into the hangar. The men stand, gather around. "She says it's always like this this time of year," Forney tells them. The lady nods. "Lost two planes last month. You want my advice, wait until midnight tonight. Maybe be lucky, the wind dies for two, three hours."

Ethel shakes her head. "We can't afford to lose the time."

The Chinese woman resents another's contradiction. "Sure, go ahead. You don't want my advice, go any time you like. It's a free country."

The men look from Forney to Ethel. "Any other way around the pass?" Queen asks.

"No other way," says the Chinese woman. "Worse out to sea. You get the hot west wind off the ocean. Cold east wind off the mountains, from Huascarán." She makes a swirling motion with her hands. "Chimbote is where they meet."

Ethel brushes dust off her sleeve. "We worked very hard last night to get here. It would be a crime to stop now."

"Ha! You work for a mean boss." The Chinese lady laughs. "Even the airlines fly at night, and they got good machines and pilots—not junk like this." Her arm sweeps past the airplanes, unkindly includes Slovak where he sits.

"You saw what the turbulence was like coming up," says Forney to Ethel. "Figure ten times worse in the pass."

Her stomach clenches at the thought of only twice worse—still she calls to herself for strength, believing herself to be the last repository of it, sensing all around her the men falling away. "I didn't think it was that bad," she smiles. The Chinese lady shakes her head. "You crazy—goodbye!" she says, ducking, stomping toward her shack through the windstorm. An old newspaper follows her, trying to catch up.

Ethel turns to them. "Are you going to let her get away with that?"

"Away with what?" asks Queen.

"Calling you those names like that. Those airplanes junk."

"They are junk," says Brown. "Even the airlines don't fly in the daytime..."

"You're not an airline," she snaps. "You said so to that reporter last night."

Queen shakes invisible pom-poms. "Boola-boola," he says.

Forney sighs. "What do you expect us to do, Mrs. Booton?"

"I expect you to fulfill a commitment." She's standing now. "You're aviators, aren't you? Aviators take chances—just going up in the air is a risk. Why are you suddenly so cautious, especially with all those lives depending on you?"

"Nobody takes any more risks than they have to, Mrs. Booton," says Brown. "That's why we're still here."

"Still where?" she shouts. "Panama? Where's that? Maybe you should have taken more risks when you had the chance?"

The men eye each other with uneasy smiles. It's nothing they haven't thought of themselves. There's something at odds in the notion of a safe pilot, they know. If it were safe, everybody would do it—there'd be no pilots at all.

"Don't think of me," Ethel continues. "I'm not. I'm thinking of a little boy called Hiribierto. I'm thinking of an old man I know named Ramón, a poor crippled old man who lives in a village under that mountain. They can see the smoke pouring out of the galleries on the upper face, but they won't move, no matter how much we warn them, because they don't trust us—they're poor and they're ignorant, and they think if they move off their land, the soldiers will come in and take it away. There are ten thousand like them, and when the mountain collapses, they'll die where they sleep or where they work in the fields or where they're eating . . ."

She's talking too much. Who's in charge here? Forney thinks—who talks the most? "I'm willing to give it a try," he says all at once.

They look at him. Forney's unsure where the words came from, out of what orifice. He waits for them to scorn him but they don't, to his surprise, don't say anything at all, nor does Ethel. The silence must be filled—the most uncomfortable fills it. "We got this far," Forney adds. "Give it a try. We could always come back if it got too rough."

"Downwind, in a narrow pass? Not hardly," says Brown. Queen's cheek is bulging—Forney realizes he's stuck his tongue in it. "Put it this way," Forney says, louder, committed by now. "I'm going—anybody who wants to can come along. You don't feel like it, Queen, you wait here."

Queen blushes—the tongue drops from his cheek. "Hell, I'll go if everybody else goes. That's the question—is everybody else going?" Nobody seems to say no; if they are all mad, they at least have the solace of the same distraction.

Ethel looks up, thrilled. "Are we going?" All around her the men are getting to their feet, stretching. She's overwhelmed; it's worked, what Gerald told her, to say whatever she had to say to get her way. A chill runs up her back—she reminds herself there actually is a Ramón, some truth behind that awful speech she made. Brown's zipping up his jacket. "If it was up to me, we'd go through that pass anesthetized."

"If we make it through, I'll buy you all the liquor you can hold," she says.

Brown looks up, studies her. "You hear what I did?"

"Must be the altitude," says Queen, gathering up his gear. Slovak kicks Kinner and they head out into the wind, toward ABR. Ethel feels light-headed, but she doesn't think it can be the altitude—the sign on the airport office reads *"Chimbote—Alteza de 1,800 metros,"* which only works out to 5,800 feet. One hand to her sunhat, the other to her bosom, she hurries through the wind after Forney, toward ACH.

Inside, he climbs forward—she prepares her spot. She hears a whistle—Forney's in the cockpit doorway, motioning. "Maybe you better sit up here. Back there, you'll bounce off the walls." Ethel nods, accepts the offer, climbs up to the second seat. Her breath is short; it occurs to her once again, she is getting what she asked for, which has so often been the problem in her unsettled life.

THE MOUNTAINS SEEM a long way off, low on the horizon. The chop is not too bad, even here at 12,000 feet. A sense of portent comes to Ethel; she wonders if it comes from sitting forward, where the controls are. She glances over at Forney as he flies, feels, to her surprise, a sympathy. How he slouches, in total defiance of his spine. It's not fair to measure him against Booton though she finds herself constantly doing so, simply by dint of the thought. It would be interesting to compare their backgrounds—probably not that different, when she thinks of it. Forney is the child of proletarian parents, but so is Gerald. A strong argument for nurture over nature; see what one man has done with his chances, another not. What Gerald had to go through to finish medical school: night jobs, day jobs, reading on streetcars, in alleys, delivery truck seats. The difference between a man who follows a star, and one who doesn't. Could she have talked Gerald into flying into this wind? Probably not, and a significant difference; Gerald would weigh the arguments, make up his mind, stick to it, right or wrong. Thank God Forney's more arbitrary, open to influence.

She clears her throat. "Do pilots have affection for their airplanes? I mean like sailors do for their ships. Calling them she?"

He's been thinking of how the earth curves—her question brings him back. "What are you talking about?"

"Nothing! I merely wanted to say hello."

"What for?"

"No reason at all. I was trying to be pleasant!" Forney nods, finally understanding. She watches how his hands work for a while, how he moves his feet, just the tiptoes. "Why don't you show me a little how to steer it?" she shouts. "Maybe I could take over while you stretched, something of that sort."

Forney looks at her, thick glasses, sweater spread back over her shoulders. Her hair is rusty, metallic, in snarls like wire at the bottom of a toolbox. Ho ho, he thinks, but shouts instead, "Why not?" and guiding her hands onto her wheel lets go of his.

Ethel feels a thrumming, like putting a finger on a struck piano string. She looks out along the bottom of the high wing, sees the starboard aileron twitching, a fraction of an inch up and down. A sense of the system comes to her —they're like boat rudders, making the wing rise or fall. She looks past Forney, out the left-hand window—another aileron, interconnected obviously, since it twitches down when the first one rises. The horizon is tilting—she wonders why. Forney taps her—the left wingtip is slowly falling off toward the ground, she waits for him to correct it, but he folds his arms, smug. Ethel tries to turn the wheel the opposite way. It's like levering stone, beyond her strength, growing worse. The engine noise rises, the wind hissing past the nose and through the windshield cracks. "Mr. Forney!" she shouts. The nose is plummeting now—a line of parallel ridges below begins to slowly rotate to the right. "Mr. Forney!" she screams, loud as she can. He pretends not to hear, perhaps honestly can't, so loud now do the engines roar. Those hills are upside down—they're corkscrewing, spinning, whatever they call it—oh my God, diving nose-down, for the ground. She knows what makes it go up—she pulls on the wheel, hard as she can, back into her chest. The hills fall from view—a gray haze sinks over her eyes and she feels her jaw spread as if pried open with a lever, arms pinned to her sides, her bottom flattening into the seat. She wants to yell but no sound can rise against so much gravity. Ahead, the nose climbs into blue sky—the windshield discovers the sun; she squints to keep from permanent retinal damage. The wind sound has fallen off; the engines have slowed, grind with a futility. Now the airplane comes to a stop, pointing high, hanging there.

"You're stalled," Forney says, soft in the relative quiet.

The nose drops through like a board diver. Ethel screams at the top of her lungs—her vision grows red. Those same awful hills appear, the horizon to the side cuts vertically. Diving—no, the nose rises once more; she feels her weight double once more, triple. This is the single worst moment of her life—she shuts her eyes to it.

The weight subsides. She looks—Forney flies again, slouched, one hand on the wheel. The plane lurches in chop. As her blood finds its levels again, so does her anger. "That was a rotten thing to do!" she yells.

"You thought you could fly this airplane, Mrs. Booton!" he shouts back. "No man would have the nerve, not unless he had a thousand hours under his belt and a half of them in multi-engines. You think all it takes to fly is saying you want to? Lots of people *want* to—lots of men in the world think it would be swell to fly a modern, multi-engine airplane, but damn few of them can when it gets down to it, and most of them wind up with the same shit-eating grin you got right now!"

She does not take criticism well. When Forney looks over, showing his teeth, her eyes are glazed, like tiny lakes. "What are you crying for?" he shouts.

"I'm not crying!"

"Sure you are. Your eyes are all wet!"

"All right, they're wet. Eyes get wet!"

Forney senses he's gone too far. "Take the wheel again," he shouts. She won't. He reaches over, plops one of her hands on the wheel rim. "Lightly—with your fingertips." She turns her head away. "Look, lady, you better turn around and fly because I just let go of the controls!" She looks—it's true; the nose is wandering already. Her other hand leaps to the wheel—she blinks, staring ahead. "Lightly! Watch where that engine cuts the horizon—that's straight and level! Don't worry about how the controls go. Move whatever you have to move to keep that engine on the horizon!"

Ethel tries. It's like a penny arcade game. The wheel forces are heavy, not bad if you catch them in time, bad very quickly if you don't. "You're dropping a wing again," he yells. Ethel glances past him—the same damn ton of metal, dropping off. She twists the wheel over, watches it grudgingly rise. Looking forward, the nose engine's three inches above the horizon. This and that, interactions, influences. She tries to relax, leans back a bit, lets go the tension in her forearms. The airplane seems to ride easier for it. She lets her back curve. The most comfortable position, for the purpose of control, she finds, is a sort of slouch.

"That was smart what you said back there," he says, after a moment.

Ethel wonders what he's referring to. "What was?"

"Telling them you'd buy them booze on the other side." He nods—she follows his indication. The mountains, in the future minutes ago, are now in the present. The airplane begins to wallow, creaking in protest. Ahead, splitting a stone wall of mountains, is a slit, a narrow valley; she can make out green fields. It looks alpine, Swiss postcardish—she can't imagine danger from anything so lovely. Wham—the plane shudders like it's run into something. Ethel gasps, the wheel rips away. Forney takes over, levels the wings. "Chimbote Pass," he yells.

"It doesn't look so bad."

"Yeah, well, wind's invisible, isn't it?" he shouts. Ethel feels foolish.

IT'S WORSE, as he said it would be, ten times worse or more. Climbing into the pass, the plane snaps left, drops a hundred feet before it finds rising air again. Ethel wheezes through her nose, forgets how to breathe for an instant. Wham—again, the airplane rears, engines racing like a ship's screws out of water. She looks for a vortex, a mouth, some source for all this violence, sees nothing but calm brown mountains, quiet sunlight.

In ABR, Slovak grits his teeth, hunches down in his seat. The nose lifts—he jams the wheel forward just as fast, treating the wind personally, not about to be fooled. Out of the corner of his eye, ATE, Brown and Queen, skids across the sky toward him, tucking in just feet away. Queen's hand hangs out his right-side window—he's sending code, the old military trick, fist for dot, palm for dash, against the fuselage side. "What's he saying?" Slovak yells at Kinner, eye on the horizon, then swears at himself for forgetting—the kid's no navigator. He steals glances at ATE. Palm-fist-fist-fist. Palm-fist-palm-palm. Fist. Bee. Why. Eee. Bye. "Bye to you too, shit-for-brains," Slovak screams into the windblast. ATE waggles its ailerons, banks away, spacing out for the pass itself.

The three airplanes climb together, points of an arrowhead. In ATE, Brown cinches down his shoulder straps until they hurt. Queen's been looking over the side—there's a series of parallel ravines, each with its own alluvial fan, converging at the open mouth of the valley; on the side of one, he's spotted something shiny. Another glint on another ridge as they cross the sun more, silver fragments in a broken cluster. An airplane, Queen realizes, both of them. How many wrecks hide below, gone aground in this strait? He taps Brown—Brown looks, nods somberly. "Kind of makes your ass pucker!" he shouts, reaching for a bottle.

ACH wallows in the turbulence, breasting the wind. Bad, thinks Forney, due to be worse once they reach the valley mouth. It seems far off one second, rushing toward them the next, as the land climbs steeply. ACH staggers, loses a hundred feet, gets one-two'd from either side, loses a hundred more. The controls are rigid in Forney's hand, no purchase against such a force. The windshield buzzes from vibration—loud whipcracks against the fuselage, he recognizes, as rudder cables banging in their fairleads, on their way back to the tail.

They frighten Ethel, the whipcracks; she's worked her way aft, fetching her small aviator's flying suit. They're both feeling the cold; she drags it forward, along with Forney's heavy fur jacket, helps him into it, one arm at a time. Trying to climb back into her seat, she runs aground on the brake lever. They hit an awful waterfall now, spill over the brink and plunge, ballooning her weightless and screaming, pinned to the cabin ceiling. Forney hauls her down, flings her into her seat, more to clear his vision than any gallantry. It's nightmarish, worse for Ethel than any roller coaster for someone who hates them to begin with; even roller coasters have a safety record, a fixed duration as well. She tries to measure her fear against Forney's, hoping to find him at least tranquil and thus able to laugh herself off as a green hysteric, but while his face is rigid, his eyes are wide and dilated, which means clinically he's just as afraid as she is, her hysteria wholly justified. The valley widens, a parquet of farms, rough fractured cliffs enclosing on either side, higher than they are. They seem to be sinking constantly—she can make out a farmhouse now, a chimney streaming smoke. Once more the plane drops. Rather than scream, she bites her knuckles until the blood flows, any screaming would not be heard, even in her own ears. Forney's jammed on full power, all three throttles forward in their quadrant; it's almost silent, so loud is it, silent because there's no sound in the world save one.

There are witnesses to their passage, all farmers, Chimbote being fertile, semitropical, fed by Huascarán's runoff. Near the south end, an Indian looks up from his wooden plow—the wind whips his hair, bends the windbreak cypress almost sideways, but he's grown up with that. What's novel is the airplanes, three of them, directly overhead. Few come over in daylight—he hears them at night, engines faint over the wind's howl. How pretty they look, calm and birdlike. He takes off his hat and waves, for the sheer joy they give him, holding it tightly so the wind won't carry it away.

In ACH, Ethel puts her fist to her mouth, about to vomit. "Out the window," Forney is shouting. "I don't want your bananas all over the cockpit!" The word bananas is the trigger—she flings back the side window. The windblast snaps her head against the bulkhead; when she blinks back to consciousness she notes her nausea has been swallowed. The nose jerks up, down, left, right, like a victim in

a fit—Ethel has no hope of calm air, barely a memory of it. Forney points ahead, where the valley pinches, against the base of a sharp pyramid peak. "That's the far ridge!" he shouts.
"How far is it?"
"Three miles."
"Will we make it?"
"Want to see something funny?" he asks.
"What?"
"We ain't moving!" he shouts.
Ethel looks overboard. Nothing moves below—she might as well be standing on a cliff, a tall building. The farmer has called over his brother to see a remarkable sight —three airplanes hover overhead, pinned there, engines roaring, not advancing a foot. The Indians assume it's a feat of science but can't imagine what end it serves.
This is real bad, Forney is thinking, trying to remember a worse fix to distract himself from this one. Very bad, he repeats, knowing this is the way death comes to a pilot, easing into a bad situation like this one, it growing worse and worse, the pilot repeating very bad, very bad until the final repetition. Forney has crashed once or twice in an airplane—you see it coming in advance, are never really taken by surprise, do what you can to save yourself, say oh shit and fly into something. So his mind works, swirling in circles like the wind itself, passing time. Balls to the wall, no power left in the overheated engines. Mrs. Booton is pointing to the airspeed indicator. "It says we're doing a hundred miles per hour!"
Forney nods. "So is the wind, in the other direction!"
What else can he do? Not turn back, that dumb prom-

ise at Chimbote—running with a gale this fierce is surrendering to it altogether. He can't land—the fields below are too small, split by stone fences, full of rocks anyway. The wheel kicks in his hand; rudder pedals thump against his shoes. There's a ripping sound, metal banging—somewhere skin is tearing loose. It's one of those moments, he thinks, very bad—and then is suddenly outraged at that voice, so calm and manly. It doesn't speak for him, never has, for all he's wanted it so—his true voice is a screech, a wail. It's lost inside him; he tracks it down, wants to tear at his throat as if that's where the constriction is. This is not just bad; it's terrifying, paralyzing, final. See how far he's fallen, letting his engines do the screaming for him.

ATE is a hundred yards off and behind—Forney signals to them now, wagging his wings, rolling left, leveling out, rolling left and leveling out again. In ATE they wonder, with Queen finally figuring it out. "He wants us to bank toward the rocks."

"What for?"

"I don't know. Maybe there's a lee there!"

Brown shrugs, doubting it, but starts a left turn, gingerly letting the nose quarter into the wind.

"Isn't it more dangerous near the cliffs?" Ethel is shouting, both of them watching Brown's turn. "Maybe it's calmer," Forney shouts back. "How should I know—I'm guessing!" "You see Slovak?" She glances around—he's bobbing a quarter-mile behind to starboard, farther out in the valley. Forney reduces power, letting Slovak catch up.

To Kinner in ABR, it looks as though Forney is drifting back to join them. Slovak barely looks—he's sweating, the one eye red from the strain. ACH hovers between Slovak and the cliffs—Ethel has her hand out the window, pointing toward them.

"He thinks there's a lee," Slovak shouts. "There ain't no lee—there ain't no shelter anywhere! We'll just get blown down on the face!" Still, he starts a turn; when he does, Forney starts his own. Pitching and bobbing, the two machines wheel slowly around. Slovak lets his upwind wingtop rise too high—a mistake; the overwhelming wind reaches under it, lifts, forcing it higher. Slovak tries to shallow the bank, but it's him against the tempest.

"Where is he now?" Forney shouts, fighting the crosswind. Ethel looks behind, goes pale—the bulk of ABR is skidding toward her, oil-streaked, gear dangling, filling her window.

Slovak knows what's happening; seconds slow down, stretch out, the way they do. He's got full right aileron against the bank, Kinner adds his muscle for what it's worth, but they're prisoners of the wind, sliding toward Forney, all three tons. "Turn more," cries Kinner, hauling back on the yoke. Slovak knows they'll spin out if they do; better hit and take their chances. The kid is pulling hard on the wheel; he'd take it on the chin. Why not, thinks Slovak, with no future, nothing to live for? As opposed to him, Slovak. Slovak considers what he in fact has to live for, now concludes—revenge. At this moment, it seems unworthy of what he spent his life trying to be—he lets go the wheel. Kinner's strength prevails; at this low airspeed, the wing broad on the wind, the plane rears like a charger and slides up and over the top of ACH. Forney and Ethel duck, the light goes dim as the huge tires cross inches above the cockpit glass. ABR falls behind, stalled out, doing what

Slovak knew it would, sighing off into a left-hand graveyard spin, nose straight down.

Forney strains to see, banking for a view. Ahead, near the cliffs, there are Brown and Queen in ATE heading up the valley, making slight headway. Maybe there is a lee there, Forney thinks, two out of three ain't bad. He goes cold—oh my God, I'm sorry, Slovak, I didn't mean to write you off.

Slovak wouldn't argue. The valley floor is a muddy blur—bangs aft, things crunching and snapping. He peers back, ducks as a shit-storm of dynamite bundles rains down the aisle and into the cockpit, liberated from splintered crates set loose when the ropes snapped under the g-force. Sticks are all over, in free fall, jabbing at him, filling his vision like snow, floating to the cockpit floor, wedging where the control column meets its torque tube. He bats them aside, considers the spin, sets about to correct it, stomps right rudder hard as he can. Something crunches, a dynamite bundle he realizes, fouling the rudder—the pedal slams to the firewall stop. No response from the airplane. Aft center of gravity, air over the rudder, he thinks, floating outside, looking things over. Throttles full forward, a last resort; it increases the airflow over the rudder, but it likewise tightens the spin. His eye hurts, so do his teeth, an old cavity aroused under the stress of his clenched jaw. One and a half more turns—the spin stops abruptly with a bang, flinging him off the cockpit side. Now a dive, speed picking up so fast—he hauls back on the wheel, but he's too damn old, screams for the kid to help. Kinner lets go of the seat rim he's clutching, grabs his wheel —it's like drawing a paddle through concrete, he thinks, although grateful to get his hands on the controls at last, it always having been a dream of his, thwarted by the officers and enlisted pilots at Coco Solo. The nose starts to climb the terrain—Kinner is blacking out but he keeps hauling blind.

There is a band of calm air near the north face—Forney circles tightly there, in the shadow of the cliffs. A mile back, he can see ABR, clearing the ground by barely twice its length, climbing for a rock pile of boulders against the cliff face. To Forney's horror, ABR now rolls slowly right and hangs there, knife-edged, wing low, parallel to the cliff face and sinking toward the ground again.

Slovak in ABR talks to himself: good boy, atta boy, easy, keep up your airspeed. They're his own words, but the voice he hears is Oliver Shenson, his instructor at the Curtis School when Curtis wintered at San Diego. The Flyer they learned on was a killer: one speed, 40 mph, for climb, cruise, and glide, only it wouldn't glide at all, would hardly turn without tucking a wing and heading for the trees. No two seats either—Ollie would say, go up, try some turns, keep the nose up when you do. Slovak's keeping the nose up now, but it feels all wrong, Ollie. Something's wrong and it scares him. "That ain't the horizon you're on!" Kinner is screaming, trying to wrench the wheel left. Slovak won't let go—out Kinner's side window, the fields climb toward him.

"You ain't lined up on the horizon! We're sideways—you're lined up on the mountainside!" Slovak feels suddenly weak—Kinner muscles the wheel around; the airplane flops level, ungracefully, packets of dynamite, clustering on Kinner's side of the cockpit, now sliding to the floorboards.

The chop's unbearable this low, where the rocks shred

and grind it; they're slammed down, over, and over. Slovak is dabbing at his good eye with his thumb. "Can't you see?" Kinner yells.

"I see fine! Call out the airspeeds!"

Kinner bends forward—the instrument needles tremble and shake. "Sixty-five," he shouts. "Sixty-three. Sixty. Going down!"

"How am I supposed to get out of these rocks?" Slovak sees more spires ahead, on both sides.

"Fifty-eight. Fifty-five."

"Aw, shut up—you're no help to me!"

"You're putting us into the rocks, Slovak."

"It all feels the same to me. All sink—I can't find no lift anywhere!"

Something is settling alongside, large and dark. Wheels, fuselage, wings, into view thirty feet off. It's Forney in ACH; he's doubled back out of the safe air. His hand's out the window, pointing across their nose, at the rocks. "Maybe it's calmer closer in!" Kinner shouts. Forney thinks so—he's waving his fist now. Willing to cede all responsibility, Slovak banks left, toward the cliffs he's been trying to flee. Does the air begin to smooth, or is he just worn out?

Beyond and above the valley, over the far ridge, ATE circles—Brown and Queen have dodged the wind all the way up the north wall, like hikers under a waterfall. They search back down into the valley for the others, see neither plane. "Think we ought to go back?" shouts Queen. Brown shrugs. "We might never get out again!" He looks at the panel clock. "Give them two more minutes!"

A mile back, the tops of the cliffs are terraced; farmers there now lean on their hoes, watching the airplanes below them. One drags its wingtip along the rock face, the other follows in its turbulence. As they rise, so does the land, machines and terrain both converging on the far ridge. There are stone huts near the ridge, shepherds' homes—one shepherd sits even now with his herd on the very saddle. There's a muttering sound, the sheep stir; the cliffs bat the sound back and forth so he can't tell the source. There—below, two metal machines. It takes a while to figure out how airplanes can fly lower than the ground he sits on, until he decides there is sky in the valley as well. He wonders how close they'll come, can't imagine too much, since such coincidences don't occur, not in a land so vast. On they come; the propellers flash silver—the wings look hunched, like someone drawing in his shoulders to pass through a narrow doorway. That's why they're heading for him—the saddle's the lowest point on the ridge, basalt knolls on either side. He's getting worried—whistles to his dogs and starts to shift the herd downslope a bit, out of their way. When he looks up again, the machines are a hundred meters off. He's frightened now—he whistles shrill, the sheep scatter. The dog howls in pain. Fifty meters off. The propellers pursue him wherever he flees, slashing the air around him, ancient terrors, sworded gods. He throws himself flat; the two planes thunder five meters above him, grazing the saddle, bursting beyond into the still air. Sheep and shepherd tumble in a storm of dirt and rocks and leaves.

 Slovak kicks away another bundle fouling the rudder pedals. "I'm too old for this shit!" he says out loud. Kinner nods—only now does he notice that the stuff in the cockpit is the nitroglycerine. He moans, flinging a bunch off his lap. "What a wind," he says, leaning back, as the planes are spewed out, into the south.

10

THEY FIND THE RIMAC two hours on, follow it to Lima, spot the golf course, land at Faucett's Field. When the engines stop, no one moves. Sound by sound, the world revives: tall grass whistling, darting birds, a train hooting from the yards along the river. Forney looks over at Ethel, unstraps, makes his way down the aisle, hands braced on the nitro cases. The cabin door opens—in comes worm smell, lupin. He steps out—his toe catches on a bent coaming never fixed, and he tumbles toward the grass. So be it, he thinks, sprawling, spreading wide his arms. He feels held up by the earth, sandwiched between the ground and the sun overhead. Lying there, he can feel his body pulse, hear his ears hiss, see air bubbles sailing across his cornea. All the smells—Jesus, his nose almost hurts from them all, so strong.

Ethel appears in the doorway, upside down. "That was very exciting," she whispers, stepping over him. Exhaustion floods her—she rolls onto her back in the grass just like Forney, but some feet apart. Her head flops to the side. There's Kinner, climbing from ABR, disappearing out of sight below the grasstops. Slovak's behind him—he stretches, heads around to the other side of his machine. Queen sits in the shadow of ACH's wing, hugging his knees; Brown heads toward them, unwrapping a bundle of dynamite.

"I got this and sawdust all over my airplane." He gives

it to Forney. "Slovak says just about every crate of his busted."

Forney touches the dynamite, licks his fingertips. He looks up, surprised. "This stuff is dry."

Brown nods. "Ain't sweating anymore."

Forney sits up. "How come?"

"I got no idea."

"But it was wet on the ship," says Ethel. "I saw it myself..."

"I can't tell you why," says Brown. "It's stable again. I guess it does what it wants to do."

Forney's amazed. "Well, come on—what did it? What do you think—altitude? Temperature, air pressure, what?"

Brown shrugs, leans back, bracing his arms. Forney has to stand now, so electrified is he. Does this explain what happened at Buenaventura? Has the nitro quailed before him? Queen's crossing toward them— "Think fast," shouts Brown, snatching the dynamite away and lobbing it to him. Queen dives for the bundle with a yelp, almost drops it, then eyes it, sniffs. "What happened to the nitro?" he wonders.

"Gone," Forney and Brown answer together. Queen cackles, jumps in the air with a whoop. "Slovak, heads up!" he shouts; the old man is just turning the corner around ABR when the thrown dynamite meets him. He bats it away, yelping from fright. "You dumb fucker," he yells, picks it up, then begins to chuckle. The others call him over, Kinner following. "All our stuff busted loose in the pass," he's saying. "Jesus, dynamite everywhere. Red here could barely see to fly. I thought we had it there until you came along, Mr. Forney, because we were flying into the rocks..."

"I knew what I was doing," Slovak mutters.
"I didn't say you didn't..."
"You were lucky," says Brown.
"We all were," says Forney.
"We were good, too," adds Queen. That statement embarrasses them, so bold; they're silent for a while because of it.

Forney's looking off at the terminal. "We got to turn up six hundred gallons of eighty octane someplace." Slovak shakes his head. "That ain't the first order of business." The men roll over to face Ethel, waiting for her to keep her promise. "The thing is, if we blow half a day here, we'll have to fly all night," says Forney.

"We could fly all night," says Brown. "Shit, if we could fly that pass." The rest nod—that's that. When they stand, they help each other to their feet.

THEY TAKE A TROLLEY into town—Kinner, excited, stands with the conductor. Forney's alongside Ethel, breathing deeply through his nose. The nitro has gone stable; there's a new fruit on a roadside tree, a new shade of whitewash on adobe walls. He feels lighter, wonders about the lessening of gravity at this elevation. They pass downtown, regal courts, whipped-cream palaces, streets of foreign cars all painted black. A man with a briefcase points out the best restaurant in town—they pile off, file through an archway flanked by marble griffins, hung with geraniums.

It's too good, that's the problem, too elegant, filled with waiters in livery, men in suits, ladies in silk dresses, sipping maté through silver straws. A shoeshine boy appears—"*Lustre?*" he asks them, until he sees their boots. The men mill, awkwardly—some turn to leave, bumping into those who don't. "Where are you going?" Ethel asks them. Forney keeps his voice low. "This ain't our kind of place." He motions her to follow, starts to lead them out.

"I think it's fine," says Ethel, not budging. The tuxedoed maitre d' arrives, looks them over, their oily pants, split nails. "*Sí, señores—una mesa para seis?*" Clutching his menus, he looks over this room. "*Lo siento mucho.* I sorry —*no ya tengo para seis. Unicamente tres y tres.*" He's pointing to two tiny tables, on opposite sides of the courtyard. He spreads his arms, helpless.

"You can put them together," Ethel says, smiling firmly at him, even as Forney pulls her sleeve. She brings two spread fingers together to give the maitre d' the idea. He looks at Forney under heavy lids, appealing to his sense of embarrassment. "What's wrong with some enchilada joint?" Forney whispers. Slovak is turning Kinner around by the shoulder, pushing him back through the archway.

"If we're going to eat at all, we might as well eat where the food is decently prepared and halfway wholesome," she replies, putting little effort into speaking softly. "All any restaurant can ask is some guarantee that we can pay the bill, and we can." The maitre d' is saying something fast to two busboys. "Why do you let a man in a dinner jacket intimidate you? Why stand up for your rights on a picket line and then hand them over in a place like this?"

"I never stood in a picket line in my life," says Brown.

"Pilots got no union," Slovak mutters. Kinner points at something over his shoulder—the men turn, see busboys hoisting one of the tables over ducked heads and placing it alongside the other, covering them both with a single cloth. The maitre d' makes a capitulating gesture, *"Cómo ustedes quieren, señores. Mucho gusto."* He bows low, remains there until they pass him. "You see?" says Ethel, as they cross the room to the table. "It's a question of standing up to them." She sits them down together. Still uneasy, Brown tests the weight of his silverware; Slovak cleans his nails on the tablecloth hem. A waiter hurries up, tiny moustache, metal glasses, pad ready. "Well, what should we get?" Forney asks. "Wine," says Slovak. *"Vino,"* Queen translates, for the waiter's benefit. "Screw wine," says Brown loudly. "Hard stuff. Rum!" Around them, tailored patrons turn, napkins to their lips. A man rises and hurries to the maitre d'. Here it comes, thinks Forney—a scene.

He's right—the man and the maitre d' twine through the tables toward them. Ethel sits erect, already counterattacking. "I'm glad you're here." she begins. "I think some water would be in order, as well as some bread to help pass the time, if you don't mind." The maitre d' isn't listening, circles around to Forney, solicitous. "You are Americanos, señor?"

"Yes, and your hemispheric partners," says Ethel.

The other man spreads the front page of a newspaper. "This isn't you guys, by any chance?" he asks, in tidewater tones. It's the Lima daily—the headline reads: *"Seis Aviadores Intrepidos Saltan Las Montañas para Ayudar Sucre."* There's a map of their route from Panama, a morgue shot of three odd airplanes in formation. *"Estan ustedes, verdad?"* asks the maitre d'. *"El Panama Sooisid Cloob?"*

Brown picks up the paper; the others cluster around.

"Six heroes, young, assaulted . . ." he begins, fumbling. Queen grabs it aways, reads. "Dateline Guayaquil: Six young heroes, risking their lives so thousands might be spared, winged through Guayaquil last night on a daring rescue mission and a rendezvous with destiny over the Grand Cordillera of Bolivia. Despite a severe mishap to one machine on landing at General Limón Field yesterday morning, the Panama Suicide Club effected repairs in an all-night race against time . . ." He looks up, howls out loud. "Brownie. The kid wrote everything you said!"

Slovak points to the photograph. "They got the wrong airplanes."

"Still, that's you guys, isn't it?" the man says. "Which one of you is Forney?" Forney sits up straighter—the man comes around the table, hand extended. "No kidding, this is an honor, Mr. Forney. We've been following you guys all morning—we heard you'd left Chimbote and we figured you might pass through. Gay Knudsen—short for Gaylord. I manage the Dos Ventanas. Say, do me the honor, all of you guys—c'mon over, let me buy you a meal. We can all squeeze in there . . ." He's pointing at a table across the room, where a bald man waves. "That's Ed Schacht, local G.M. rep. What do you say, guys?" The men look to Forney—he's not sure what the rules are. Word of who they are is spreading around the restaurant—some people clink knives against their glasses; one man is even standing and applauding. Knudsen waves his hands. "Look, belay what I said—this place will be a madhouse in a few minutes when the news gets out. Come up to the house. I'll call the families; we'll have a little potluck. All the booze you want, hot showers—one call does it all. What do you guys say?"

Forney looks around—everyone's nodding. "Sounds good to me," he says, folding his napkin and putting it back where he found it.

THE KNUDSENS' PLACE sits on a hilltop, above a cloud. It's the vast hacienda of a former dictator; the families are the American community in Lima, now drawn up in rows on the ornamental tile staircase, waving American flags as the cars drive up. Forney feels swept up the stairs by some magic wind, his hand shook, his back slapped. Here is old Mr. and Mrs. May, who export hats, Ed Schacht's family, his fat wife, Lolly, her sister down from Cleveland, Colonel Ringer, the army attaché, the Muellers from the Ford Agency, Elias Campos, the late dictator's son, his Texan wife, Honey. "We're pretty cut off down here," Knudsen shouts to Forney over the tops of heads. "Not often we get a chance to crow." A regal woman waits in the grilled doorway. "Joan, this is Mr. Forney and the men of the Panama Suicide Club." *"Mi casa es su casa,"* she smiles. Twin girls in identical pinafores curtsey, Paula and Patricia. "And this is our oldest, Sally, who's always a little shy at first," says Joan Knudsen, pulling forward a seventeen-year-old by the wrist, a smoky, long-haired girl waving her flag in slow, deliberate arcs. "Chow down," whispers Slovak.

Inside is Babylonian—Forney thinks back to rotogravured plates in a thumbed Bible, hanging gardens, velvet drapes, bowls of fruit and flowers. Mirrors line the walls; llama-fur carpets soften the alabaster floors. "Are you completely starved, or would you like something to drink?"

Joan Knudsen asks. She presses a wall button—yards of mirror pivot—revealing liquor shelves floor to ceiling. Brown blinks, Forney downs a double Scotch, just like that. The families file in, filling the room around them, eager for the drama of the pass. Awkward at first, Forney warms up, talks with his hands, this plane here, that there. Mrs. May tells a story of yorking on a SACA flight to Iquitos— everybody has their flying story, since the rich fly, as Forney reminds himself. They call him George, squeeze his shoulders—it's a magic moment; he feels at home, home at last in this palace, of all places, and he wonders how come, whether it's their grace or perhaps some latent nobility in him. Perhaps he was a rich man's child, victim of some hospital skullduggery—those things happen. He hears himself small-talking, even droll, not much like the Forney of Panama, but he loves it, thinks he could do it forever. Is this in fact his proper station in life—was he born to be rich and befriended, lord of a great house, only happy once and if he arrives there? He's had the notion all along, parts of him, childhood dreams. There was a taste of it at Des Moines— this reminds him of Des Moines, the clubhouse reception, ladies in tight hats, flashbulbs, martini glasses, voices on every side. A second Des Moines, this is, and after he gave up hope of Des Moines ever again—that's what's so amazing. See how life now and then confirms your dreams, just to keep you struggling. A servant refills his glass. He could keep struggling, he thinks, if he could count on a fix like this every now and then. An addict's contract.

    Now a bell rings and they pass into a dining hall, walls hung with shields and helmets of conquistadors. Fat maids bow, mumbling pidgin. Forney sits at Knudsen's right—

potluck is rack of lamb, corn oily with butter. "Some fridge," grins Queen. Lively talk, thinks Forney—rich people talk their own special way, talk as currency, as though beams of money passed between the rich when they conversed. He starts to use his salad plate for an ashtray, notices nobody else does. The twins stare at him—he makes them giggle by wiggling his ears. Sally Knudsen likewise stares; she don't look no seventeen, he thinks, feeling an unsought hard-on. Dark eyes under long bangs. Queen and Slovak bracket her—she's laughing at something but looking at him. "Oh God, yes, Peru's nice, but I won't be sorry one minute to leave," she's saying. "I start Wellesley in September."

"What's that?" Forney asks.

"A high-class girls' school," says Queen. "What's your major?"

"Men. First thing I'm going to do is get laid."

The pilots blush red; Joan Knudsen sighs. "Sally's read girls in the States are very liberal in their speech these days. Not having any model, she makes up her own."

"Well, you will admit my sex life is a total goose egg, mother. The locals are pretty low-grade ore," she says, glancing at Forney again.

"I shudder for the men of Yale," says Knudsen.

Queen spreads his jacket, revealing his Yale sweatshirt. "I'm Eli. Class of nineteen twenty, though I never graduated, to be completely honest..."

Sally intrigues Forney, a bold girl who speaks her needs. A rich trait, he thinks—how nice it must be to get what you ask for. Down the table, Brown is telling Lolly Schacht a long involved story. Forney only hears the punch line: "I wouldn't mind it so much, except here I am flying crap in South America and the goddamn gorilla's a First Pilot with Eastern Airlines." All laugh—Forney laughs, having earned the right. He feels something stroke his ankle beneath the table, a pointed shoe. Joan Knudsen? Sally? He looks from face to face, sees not a clue. They're good at this, he thinks, the rich—it could be any of them, even a man. That's what's wonderful about this life, the possibilities, that anything's possible. His eyes meet Ethel's, sitting silent at the far end, barely eating. Mrs. Booton, he thinks.

Ethel is slipping her napkin ring on and off her finger. What's needed is to be polite but not the slightest bit approving, and she cleaves that fine line. She knows the rich —she's seen their ceilings, walking home up Beacon Hill after work at night. She's thrown tomatoes at their limousines outside the Boston Symphony. It's all hollow, this whole celebration—tomorrow they'll all be forgotten, like a movie they see. What would Gerald say about Forney, the others? Dancing bears in the court of the czars. He says things like that, lapidary phrases, quotable. What was it he told her once: The American working class does not want to overthrow the aristocracy so much as ascend to it. Cynical, a shade bitter, but still to the point, a good description of Gerald as well. She'd drive all night to hear a speaker, he only to try a new pipe tobacco, to buy a hacking jacket on sale. She wishes he shared her zeal; he doesn't, doesn't claim to, although he gives the impression of having once, of a great heart crushed somehow. Perhaps in politics, more likely in love. Gerald is mostly a man of beginnings; he'll start the clinic in Chelsea, he'll go to Bolivia, support the work, back all the right things and causes, but in the end turn sour, let things crumble. He knows so much more than she does—my God, the books in his library, and bound, too; she owes what theory she has to his library, but it's as though he's renounced all he once found there. He'll be a doctor—what they botch, I'll patch, he says, *they* being the world's evils, but he doesn't believe in change anymore. She wonders how he's doing without her; she's convinced he does better with.

They're getting drunk, all of them, pilots, locals; the walls seem to pulse with their laughter, like a ventricle. How she hates them—oh, she could stand and tell them off, for their cruelty, their awful waste, how they live their high lives on scaffolding braced by sooty miners, pale factory girls. It would be a mistake—she'd stand revealed. Stealth and cunning—mind your mouth, keep your wits about you, she tells herself. Outside the window she can see Ed Schacht's Cadillac, cream and chocolate brown. The kind she threw tomatoes at, a silly thing to do, no doubt, but what better pastime until the Revolution comes? Oh God, could they buy her off with a green one, two-toned green, with wide whitewalls? She clutches her chair bottom, a sailor in the rigging in a high gale. Forney's laughing at something—his teeth are yellow, witness to years of nicotine. She wants to rescue him from this folly, throw him in a cold shower, scream Marx and Engels until he comes to his senses. They've starved him for years—now they feed him eclairs, and he takes it for food. Ding, ding—Knudsen is standing, tapping his water glass. Oh God, she thinks, toasts.

"I know nobody wants to hear me make a speech," he begins. "But I don't think there's anyone here sober enough to stop me." Cheers at this—Knudsen tries to look serious. "I don't have to tell you times are hard, not only down here but all over, thanks in large part to that crew in Washington, and it's very easy to get to a point of despair where you don't think the old girl's going to pull through this one. And that's why our visitors today are so important to us—because just at the moment we needed it most, they came along to remind us that the American traditions of courage and honor and bending down to help lift up the less fortunate are still alive and kicking." Hear-hears, clinks and clapping. "It's not every day you can have an authentic American hero over for lunch, much less five of them, but we have them here today, five American aviators, riding the products of American engineers and manufacturing genius, the greatest the world has ever seen."

"Hooray," cries Ed Schacht.

"You know who they are," Knudsen goes on. "You've read about them—you know how far they've come and about the terrible mountains they'll be facing. They call themselves the Panama Suicide Club, which I can't help thinking is a bit of a joke, since I'm sure they want to get over those mountains tomorrow as much as anyone else. We can't help them over the mountains, but since they came through Lima, I think the very least we can do is all stand together, and raise our glasses, and wish them the very best of luck, and Godspeed."

Chairs scrape and all in the room rise—Mrs. May helps old Mr. May to his feet. Even the twins get a finger of wine in their milk glasses. The pilots stay seated, eyes on the table in modesty. Sally suddenly leans out over the table, looking down at the far end where Ethel stands, hands empty. "Mother, look, Mrs. Booton isn't drinking. Mrs. Booton, won't you join us?"

"She don't drink," says Forney.

Vixen, bitch, thinks Ethel. What Sally's been attempting with Forney has not gone unnoticed. "Sometimes I do," Ethel replies, cheerfully. "On special occasions." She nods to a servant who splashes her glass full. When the rest raise their glasses and repeat, "Best of luck and Godspeed," she gulps it down, wincing, a dose of vinegar. It twines down her throat; a pressure descends on her head.

The others are shouting, clapping—"Speech," someone cries. Others pick it up—they applaud until Forney gets to his feet. He rubs his nose for a while, feeling dumb. "It was nice of you to do all this for us. I want to thank you ..."

"On behalf of a terrific bunch of guys," prompts Queen. Forney smiles. "On behalf of a terrific bunch of guys." All clap; Forney sits quickly. Knudsen motions—six servants enter, each carrying white straw hats. "All we could find on such short notice, thanks to Mrs. May. They're called Panamas for some reason, even though they make them here in Peru. Trade around if they don't fit." Kinner's falls over his ears—Slovak snatches it away, plops another on the kid's head. The twins giggle behind their flags.

Old Mr. May stands now, leaning on his wife's shoulder—the room quiets to hear him. "It may be out of fashion," he whispers, raising his glass, "but here's to Old Glory—long may she wave. O'er the land of the free and the home of the brave." Loud but respectful applause; Mr. May slowly sinks back to his seat. Hold it in, Ethel tells herself, crossing her legs. Now Schacht stands, likewise solemn. "Peru's nice—I'm not knocking it," he says, lifting his glass. "But there's only one God's country, and we all know where it is."

"Palestine?" blurts Ethel. Her hand goes to her mouth.

They turn to her, some laughing, some not. Why did she say that? The red haze helps explain it. Now Queen is standing—"Keep it clean," Forney whispers. Sit down, Ethel wants to tell him—eat their food and let's go. "Ladies and gentlemen," Queen begins, sweeping his glass left and right. "Since we're being patriotic, and looking homeward this afternoon, would you please join me in drinking the health of the very honorable Franklin Delano Roosevelt."

The room falls quiet. The twins raise their milk glasses, get the gist, lower them again. "I think this is a Republican airport," Brown mutters.

The families stir in their chairs. "No, I wouldn't say he's too popular down here," says Knudsen. Colonel Ringer leans forward. "Well, we can certainly toast the office, if not the particular man, can't we?"

Queen frowns, arm still outstretched. He repeats, smiling evenly, "The health of Franklin Delano Roosevelt." People twitch at the name—a knife falls off the table, hits the floor.

Knudsen looks to his wife for extrication, finds no out. "I'm surprised you'd back a scoundrel like that," he says. "I mean, politics is a private matter, but he's packed the court, he's railroaded all sorts of Red legislation through Congress, his new tariffs on imported raw materials are going to bankrupt all of us if Congress lets them pass . . ."

Queen refuses to move. Schacht tries to help, in a lighter

vein. "We call him Rosenstein down here. It's sort of a joke, but there is some fairly convincing evidence that old Eleanor is a hebe."

"I don't know much about politics," Queen shrugs. "He's my mother's cousin."

There are gasps, hands to breasts. Ethel is on her feet. The red haze is thick now, magenta, like a welder's goggles. "I would like to drink a toast," she says, surprising herself at her own clarity, "to all of you for showing us such lavish hospitality." Nervous smiles—after Queen they're wary. "Especially to you, Mr. Knudsen, and the Dos Ventanas Mine." Knudsen nods, twists his class ring. "And to Manuel Parillo y Hermanos, S.A., the consortium founded under a special secret treaty between Peru and Bolivia handing over mineral rights in perpetuity to that consortium, which happens to own almost every tin mine in the Grand Cordillera, including Dos Ventanas, in return for a sizable percentage of the profits, money not placed in the national coffers but hidden in special accounts for the sole benefit of certain high government officials . . ."

"What is she talking about, Gay?" asks Joan Knudsen. "I hate mixing politics and social events," mutters old Mr. May. "Yes, Mrs. Booton," calls Knudsen from the far other end. "What are you getting at? And how come you know so much about my business, anyway?"

Ethel closes her little trap. "Because, Mr. Knudsen, I work for you." Look how they buzz at that, she thinks, holding off a weariness rising osmotically from her legs. "I'm one of your contract nurses, working with Doctor Gerald Booton at Cerro de Pasco, the Parilla mine in the Quimsacruz. And I would like to drink the health of the

Indians I treat who are indirectly responsible for this celebration today, the Aymaras and Cachumatas who work fourteen hours in the pits, get docked for sick call, who go deaf from the blasting, blind from the dim light, tubercular from the rock dust . . ."

"Boo, boo," yells fat Mrs. Mueller, her first words all afternoon. "Sit down, sit down," shouts her husband. Schacht is thumbing his nose at her; his wife makes a raspberry. Ethel shuts her eyes—she's swaying more now, like a balancing rock. "Whose children freeze at night in tarpaper huts at fourteen thousand feet, with no school . . ."

They're all shouting now, aroused—Schacht heads for her. Ethel has her own problems, knows she won't make it. "The same Indians who have suffered under foreign oppressors since the Spanish came five hundred years ago . . ." It's mostly reflex now, memorized phrases. Why didn't she have self-control, she wonders. She's made an ass of herself—she'll be remembered in Lima not as the firebrand who planted the first seeds of revolution but as that silly woman who got drunk and fell across the table, for that's what she's doing, she realizes, in very slow time, falling toward the table and its platters of plenty. Her breasts will land in a plate of tomato halves, fitting, she thinks, the rich throwing the fruit back at her for all those splattered limos. How can she ever hope to help anyone if she's so damn helpless herself, she thinks. Oh shit—the plate rushes toward her.

11

THE OTHERS have special cigar knives on their key chains—Schacht has a miniature guillotine. Knudsen leans toward Forney with a lighter whose mechanism is sunk in a pound of quartz crystal. He puffs; they all puff, like a circle of small factories where they sit, out on the patio. "Monte Cristos," whispers old Mr. May to him. "The best." Forney nods—they all are, it all is, all of this. Oceans shift and plunge within him; he's energized, flowing. These others are drunk; he's totally clear, though he's had as much as them, maybe more—he's metabolizing things differently today, some new plumbing never used that rejects the toxicity, takes from the alcohol the sugar alone, the sweet food of the ferment. "Wouldn't call it the Panama Suicide Club, that's for sure," Knudsen is chuckling—out of the blue, he and Schacht have told Forney they intend to bankroll him in an airline. "Ed and I are always looking for something fun to plunge into," Knudsen says. Forney's not surprised; he's rolling sevens today, unstoppable. They'll make it to Sucre, all the way. He's had a vision; it came upon him earlier, before dinner, and he shoved it away, but it's oozed back since, undeniable—they're simply going to make it, almost have already. "Something with Panama in it, though," Schacht is saying. "You don't want to throw away a million bucks of free publicity." Mueller blows a smoke ring. "Panama Air Lines?" he suggests.

Forney smiles—the cigar tastes rich and manly, like roast beef, a piece of hide. He feels his blood tides; this is the way Hal lived, he thinks—sought, craved, friends on every side. Or was Hal even ever this far—does his name stop on the wall at Guayaquil, and will Forney go farther? He trembles at his own arrogance. These guys don't know shit about airlines, that's for sure, where the money is, where it disappears.

"I can't think running an airline is any more than doping out your costs," Knudsen's saying. "Your SACA, your Pan-Am—all those big fixed costs, equipment, airfields, new terminals. They're offering a luxury service in a time of tight money." Over Schacht's shoulder, Forney sees Queen driving off in a roadster with Sally Knudsen, down the slope below the hacienda, into the cloud. So she was rubbing Queen's foot, too, he thinks, perhaps at the same time. "It seems to me if somebody started a new operation based on a more realistic appraisal of what the market will bear," Knudsen says, "he might just swoop down and pick up all the marbles."

"Just might," Forney nods, out to give little away for nothing. Let them stroke their shiny machines, leather lobbies, neon-lit route maps. He stretches his legs until the knees crack, yawns. "I don't know if it's really fair to keep you this long from your fans," says Knudsen. Schacht nods. "Maybe so, Gay, but I don't think we ought to let this slide." He turns to Forney with a vatic look. "This isn't an accidental meeting. I mean, I don't believe for one minute your coming here was accidental, George."

Forney smiles—nor does he, not one bit. It all makes sense. He wonders where Mrs. Booton is, having last seen her carried upstairs by two maids. He stands, stretches, cramped from sitting. "I think I'll go up and lie down for a minute," he says. Knudsen winks. "Got the guest rooms set up for you. Take a shower if you feel like it." Old Mr. May waves his cigar. "See you in a while, Jim," he says, mistaking Forney for another man.

Forney heads off across the patio, feeling just fine. A breeze spills off the mountain, lubricates his passage. Somebody's singing a song:

> *Their mothers never told them*
> *The things a young boy must recall.*
> *About the nature of aeroplanes*
> *And how they rise and fall.*

Around a Moorish pillar, he comes on Slovak, Kinner, and Brown, all drunk, teaching the old song to the twin girls. The fourth line calls for a refrain; "mostly rise," sing Brown and the girls, "mostly fall," sing Slovak and Kinner. Brown looks up at Forney. "What were those guys talking about?"

Forney's offhand. "They want to back me in an airline."

"No shit," says Brown, impressed. "Uniforms and everything?"

"Everything. First class. One hundred percent financed."

Slovak hesitates. "All of us, or just you?"

Forney smiles down at the old man. Captain Slovak, eye-patch, natty cap, three-day stubble. "Everyone. They think we're the Panama Suicide Club."

"Did you tell them we're just five assholes from Panama?"

"I tried. They wouldn't shut up long enough." The men laugh at that.

"Maybe we are the Panama Suicide Club, after all," says Kinner, abruptly. They turn to him; his tongue's thick. "We must be. Only the Panama Suicide Club could get this far."

They can't trace the logic of it, but they like its sound. Queen, Slovak punch his shoulders. Forney heads for the stairway; the twins sing solo the song they've learned, high voices twining:

> *Now crashes have damaged their manhood.*
> *Their innocence stol'n by the sky.*
> *So teach your sons to be ribbon clerks;*
> *Don't ever teach them to fly.*

Slovak adds, basso profundo, "*Teach-them-to-fly.*"

FORNEY FOLLOWS a second-story balcony around a courtyard. A shuttered window hangs open—through an inner door in a bathroom mirror, he sees a woman's back, bent over, stops and hears choked gagging, something spewed. He stops, listens, then knocks on the bolted wooden door. A moment passes—a weak voice says enter.

Her shoes are by the bed, canvas shoes, little doughnuts of stocking beside them. The bathroom door is closed now; from behind it, more gagging. Forney knows nothing of women, nor has he ever sought knowledge. Small shoes remind him of another one, Virginia Moxey; he sees her thin hair, bottle shoulders, large green eyes, looks around that railroad flat in Wichita, laundry everywhere, cotton socks dripping on the rug, rolls of blueprints in the umbrella stand, a drafting table, T-square, triangles and french curves, all Hal's. She had one dress, polka-dot, but she didn't seem to mind. Hal told him she'd buried a first husband, opened two diners, sold out both times at a profit, run a dry-cleaning shop, been self-supporting since she was fifteen. She and Forney had talked once or twice, waiting for Hal to come from somewhere. The more Forney looked into her, the more he'd found. You could mine a woman like that for life, he remembers thinking. Hal called her his best friend; Forney remembers barging in one Tuesday afternoon and catching them screwing. Who screwed on Tuesday afternoon? He knew she never saw much in him; he was Hal's idea. Imagine how he felt, telling her the news, knowing he wasn't that much in her eyes to begin with. She'd sat there; Forney's gaze had drifted off to Hal's drafting table, onto the curves and angles of some new design there, as always letting airplanes carry him away. "Well, I can always start a restaurant," is all she'd said, silent until Forney left. He'd thought later that night of going back to her, falling abject in tears at her feet, but he'd decided against it, figuring she'd had enough of him, had skipped the funeral for the same reason. He'd lost track of her—if she'd taken up with another flyer, he'd have heard about it.

Now the door opens slowly—Ethel crosses the room, wrapped in a sheet, falls face-down on the bed. Her hair is frizzled; she's been sweating, Forney thinks. "I thought you didn't drink," he says.

Her voice is muffled by the bed linen. "I don't. This is why." Forney settles across the room in a leather chair.

"Jesus, that was embarrassing, what you did." She won't reply, pulls the blanket up over herself. "They give us the hospitality of their home. Big feast in our honor . . ."

She shakes her head, whether to illness or him, he can't tell. She doesn't compare well to Virginia Moxey; he doesn't have the same feelings about her. "They're reactionaries," she's saying weakly. "They kill people . . ."

"Aw, bullshit, you're just bad-mannered." Forney looks around the room, at the mirrors in worked silver frames, silver candelabra. "They like us. They think we're the Panama Suicide Club." She snorts into the blankets. "Maybe we are," he says, defensive. "How would you know? You patch up beaners in Bolivia—that don't make you an expert on everything."

He waits—she won't respond. "They're talking about backing me in an airline."

"And you believe them?"

"Why would they bullshit me?"

She pulls the covers over her head. Forney's getting annoyed now. "Oh, you're going to knock that too."

The covers come off. "You're the one who's always being disappointed."

"Me? Says who?"

"Says you, Mr. Forney. It's all you ever talk about. It would be a shame to see you hurt again."

"Who asked you?"

"I do it without being asked. I'm a nurse."

Forney stands—he could get angry, finds he doesn't have to, not today, paces back and forth. "Maybe they are bullshitting me. Fine. Let me tell you, the way things have been with me, even bullshit feels good."

He turns for her answer, sees her throwing back the covers, racing for the bathroom. Too fast—her feet slip on a throw rug; she spins in the doorway. Forney hears a bone crack, winces, follows her inside. On hands and knees, she struggles for the rim of the bowl. He lifts her by the waist and holds her there, bent double while she chokes and sprays. Bananas, Forney notes, confirming his prediction in the pass. Some falls wide of the porcelain, onto his shoe. Normally he'd gag at such a defilement, but he doesn't now —look who's holding up who, he thinks.

Done, she groans—he guides her back to the bed, lays her down. "You take care of yourself, lady. Don't worry about me," he says, standing by the bed, hands in his pockets. "Take care of people that ask for it. Your Bolivians. Your husband—whatshisname, Gerald."

She says something, but the blanket muffles it.

"I didn't get that."

She pulls the blanket down from her face. "I said I'm not married." Her hair's in her mouth—she pulls it away. "I'm not married. I will be when we go back home—we have an understanding."

Forney snorts.

"I used his name on the way down to prevent unfortunate incidents."

Forney looks away from her, eyes to the wall. "Well, it's working, let me tell you."

For a while, neither speaks—Forney stands there. "Well, okay, I'll check in on you in a while. Get some sleep or something." He turns toward the door.

"You don't have to go," she says, quietly. "I'm not tired." The hem of the blanket stretches below her eyes, like a bandit. "You can if you want to, of course, but I'm not going to sleep."

Forney hesitates. "Well, yes or no? Should I stay or go?"

"It's up to you. I gave you the choice."

"I don't give a shit one way or the other." He considers —a smile comes to his face. "To tell you the truth, I'm worried if I make the wrong choice, you'll take that gun out of your bag and shoot my ass off."

Her face falls—he barks aloud, taking her expression as a victory, one more on this victorious day. She turns away, taking his laugh as contempt. He feels dismissed, finds his hat and leaves, closing the door behind him.

THEY DRIVE BACK through Lima with the tops down, the long way around so the whole town sees them. Shops empty at the sound of the horns, the sight of all those flags—windows open in baroque facades, men in sleeve protectors lean out cheering. Forney waves, sees the others waving from the Cadillac behind, nudges Ethel, smirks. An open Fiat pulls alongside, matching speeds—in the back, a photographer bends over his reflex hood, waves with his free hand. Forney salutes—even Ethel smiles, tentatively.

By the time they turn toward the airport, the sun is setting over the western hills; it's dark when they get there. Queen and Sally are waiting by the airplanes, sitting on the roadster's running board. "We drove around for a while," Queen says. "We just got here." His shirttail's out in back; nobody believes him, but nobody cares. Forney puts his hand on Gay Knudsen's shoulder. "Gay, I want you to go in the terminal and send a wire to Arequipa saying we'll be coming in around four or five this morning, to put on the lights, or if they don't have any, line up some cars with the headlights on. Can you do that?" Knudsen is delighted to be of use, hurries off—Forney turns to the others. "Okay —let's dig up some crates. We're going to have to repack this stuff and lash it all down again." Moans but goodnatured ones, loyal to the skipper. The families all pitch in, scrounging crates from the neighborhood, repacking the sticks in fresh sawdust. The twins fight over a single bundle, tug it back and forth. The servants have packed a cold supper, lamb, chicken in aspic, more beer and wine—the mission is a long time getting off, it being almost midnight before the planes are loaded.

Forney stumbles through the darkness toward the terminal and its dimly lit crapper, the old flyer's tradition, lightening ship before lift-off. The others are there already, in line along the gutter, leaning over, one hand braced against the stucco wall. Some whizz, some read the names written there. Forney eyes a newly drawn medieval crest, mounted by a griffin, a winged lion—three things in the middle, and underneath, on a scroll, "*Mortus Ficam.*" The others chuckle at his reaction. "Queen's work," says Brown.

"What is it?"

"Three kiwis rampant on a field of azure," Queen explains. "If we're going to be an airline, we ought to advertise."

"In a pisser?"

"Name a better place, the jobs we'd wind up with," Slovak mutters. He nudges Kinner. "You went already—

you're just playing with it." He leads him outside, and Queen follows.

Now only Brown and Forney remain shoulder to shoulder in the quiet. A moment passes—Brown clears his throat. "I been meaning to ask. You knew Hal Moxey, didn't you?"

Oh Jesus, Forney thinks—the room dims, the temperature drops. He knows, Forney thinks, caught in mid-arc; he begins to take off his captain's robes, obediently, like an actor. "Hal and me worked the fairs one summer," Brown is saying. "Wing-walking. Must have been nineteen twenty-seven."

Forney's throat is dry. What shitty luck, he thinks, today of all days, then realizes: his luck. "Which one of you walked?" he asks, softly.

"He did. Hell, you wouldn't get me up there. Half the time your foot went through the fabric." Forney closes his eyes, can barely picture Hal, sees only the blurred face from the photo in his wallet. He remembers glasses and broad shoulders, a funny combination. Forney doesn't want to lose what he's gained this day, struggles now to save it. Yes, he flew to join Hal at Buenaventura, just missed him at Guayaquil. All admitted, but that was yesterday, before Chimbote. He's had a change of plans—he thinks it might be good to get to Sucre after all. Yes, he promised Hal a sacrifice, he remembers—there in a Lima crapper, Forney negotiates with his ghosts; will they accept in payment, instead, ten thousand Bolivians delivered? Forney pledges his neck to them, the same one offered all along. They've just got the mountains ahead, one more day. Think of ten thousand saved—who wouldn't find that a worthy substitution? Forney looks—there is no response, no sign from Hal, no flickering light, no moan in the wind.

Brown is buttoning up his fly. "I killed twelve of them myself," he says, offhand. Forney looks over; Brown's nodding. "Crashed one of them old wooden Fokkers. Tanks burst, everybody fried in their seats. One of them was that football player, Lodovic. Remember him?"

Forney nods. "Lodovic."

"The airline had an investigation board. I told them, hell, the reason we crashed is because you can't fly an underpowered airplane over the Alleghenies with ice on the wings. They found one of these in the cockpit." He taps a rum bottle in his jacket pocket. "Took my ticket away. Hell, it wasn't booze—it was all that ice on the wings. Or I don't know, maybe it was the booze. I can never tell."

Forney is quiet. "Sometimes you can't, I guess."

Brown nods. "That's right. You can't, sometimes," he says. "So what can you do?" He shrugs and heads outside.

Forney stares at the whitewashed walls. How did Brown know to say that, at that very moment? An airplane engine fires, far off. Forney thinks there must be a communication here he does not know about—he'd do well to sit down with Brown, this new friend. In his mind, a vision of a sidewalk café appears, at the end of the line, in Sucre, marble table, saucers piling up, cigar ash snakes in the ashtrays. Brown knew Hal too—what could Forney learn from him; how might Brown help pilot him out of his sad valley? Forney smiles—more destiny on a day of it, more lucky than Chimbote, even Knudsen's promise. He imagines a coin flipping through the air: This is it, the day he's lived for, when bad luck shifts to good, tails to heads. From now on, he thinks, things will be as good as they've been bad previously; that's no imposition on justice after a life like his. His heart pounds—he's getting excited again, shaking his clinkers loose, cleaning his grate. Another engine fires outside—that's what he is, he thinks, a heat engine. He walks outside, sucks in cool air, oxidizes it. Another engine roars alive, flames spurting from the exhaust stacks. Moisture in his cylinders burns away—a ring of carbon glows red, crumbles; he coughs it out. There's Gay Knudsen and Schacht ahead, by ACH, bent double in the windblast, shielding their eyes. They slap his back, shouts drowned out. Forney looks over his three engines, full of fire, just like him. "So long," he yells—they hug him, the *abrazos* of gentlemen. Queen is kissing Sally in a headlight beam—Forney bellows, waves him to his duty. Come back for that—we're off for Arequipa.

Striding to the cockpit; Ethel's there, strapped down tightly, humbly in her place at his right hand. Forney looks left, right—on either side, Trimotors tremble in headlight beams, engines throwing dirt. He puts his raised fist out the window, drops it, lets go the handbrake—the three machines roll off in line, toward the telephone poles that mark the field's end. How many explosions do his engines make, detonations per minute times three? Okay, 1,600 rpm, 9 cylinders, each cylinder firing 180 times per minute, 48, close to 5,000 bangs in all, trapped in steel walls. There are 5,000 in him as well; Forney thinks of himself out there on the nose, pulling this airplane up and over the Andes by his will alone, Forney as a Wright, Forney as a Wasp. The throttles run forward, he turns the friction lock—10,000 explosions now, and every one he feels as he rolls true, the

165

controls stiffen, the airplane begins to go light. It wants to climb—he forces the nose down, skimming two feet over the field, trading altitude for airspeed until he sees the cupola of the country club through the dark ahead and he lets go, lets the wheel bang back, and the airplane, desperate to fly, bearing all that lift, leaps up, nose high, almost vertically, tail toward earth, Forney with a cold grin on his face, glimpsing out of the corner of his eye two tiny cars with tiny flags waving, thinking to himself, damn good flag for an aviator, blue for the sky, white for the clouds, and red . . . ? Why, red for the pilot's blood, he thinks, feeling his own impelled and pounding down the ports and galleries of his body.

12

MOONLIT CLOUDS, rising in canyons. Every hour some faint light below, over a post office door, in a mine kitchen, a bare bulb hanging at a market cross. Course 129, nailed on the lubber line, altitude 10,000 feet. Off to the left unseen is Humanrazo, 6,000 feet higher. This is dull flying, long night flying—Brown stretches his eyes, dry, gritty. They close slowly—he levers them open again, reaches across and shakes Queen awake. "Take it for a while," he shouts, pointing ahead at a dim orange light. "That's Forney's exhaust. Keep it about where it is now!" Queen takes the wheel; Brown yawns, raises his jacket collar, lets his head drop.

Queen fiddles with the trim until the airplane flies one-handed. He looks out at the terraced clouds—how far from home he is. He knows how he got here; he can trace his decline easy enough, each step descending plausibly to the next, but what he can never comprehend is the total distance, the stretch between now and where he started, back on a rolling lawn with its croquet stakes. Sometimes his sense of past with its parties and promises is so vivid it competes with the present, so that his life now seems only a daydream of that small boy on the lawn. Where are all their mothers and fathers, he thinks—Forney's, Slovak's, even Brown's? Where are their families—how did they each get so far away? That's what home means to him—not location but people alone, a mother that wept, a father he could not win. He might go back to them when this is done, over, Queen thinks, not to alter things but for his own needs, to see what a decade has done. He knows he's returning to nickel apples, bread lines, no work for pilots, for sure. Still, if you have to eat shit, he thinks, it might as well be the shit of your homeland. Queen smiles—he finds that vaguely patriotic.

ETHEL DOZES in ACH; Forney is wide awake, still electric, would pace if he had the room. He's thinking of what he'll say in Sucre to the reporters—if Lima was any sign, think what will be waiting in Bolivia. What comes to him is Lindbergh-like: "Well, we just kept going, is all. There were times when I got a little worried, but those engines kept turning and I kept on saying to them, 'C'mon, just a little longer ...'" He laughs—what horseshit; what fun. He hopes the photos turn out better than Des Moines; there he was too tired to think of appearances. Forewarned is forearmed—he could dry-shave before landing, at least comb his hair.

He looks over at Ethel—she sleeps against the side window, still pale from Lima. Credit where it's due—she brought him the work, kept things going. She stole the parts as well, he admits. She's not so bad once you learn her operation. The men too—Brown did well at Guayaquil, Slovak didn't funk it in the pass. Any of them could have dug in their heels at any time. Good men, better than they look. He glances out at the running lights of ABR, glowing off his port wing. Slovak's crazy but he's done a decent job. He looks past Ethel for a glimpse of ATE. The dark sky's empty—the airplane's vanished, nowhere in sight.

IN ATE, BROWN STIRS, one eye open, then two. "How's it going?" he yawns, fist to his mouth. Queen points at the orange light dead ahead. "Just fine," he shouts. "Forney's right there!"

Brown looks, sits up straight abruptly. "Jesus Christ, Queen, that ain't Forney." He stretches forward, face to the windshield. "That's Canopus—you've been flying formation on the constellation of Pictor." He throws off his straps, scrambles aft. Queen looks back—Brown is midships, shoving crates away from the side windows, left and right, straining for a view. He hurries forward again, flopping back into his seat. "Better start looking for some kind of landmark."

"Won't see anything until dawn," Queen says. He looks up. "Sorry, Brownie."

"Bullshit sorry, Queen! You got us lost!"

Queen nods, says nothing. Brown sighs, takes a fresh bottle out of his bag, swallows down an inch, passes the rest to Queen.

THREE MILES AHEAD, ABR and ACH slide toward each other. Forney's flashing a light out his window: s-e-e-a-t-e? The answer's a while in coming back; Slovak sends Kinner aft to search below and behind. A two-letter reply: dah-dit, dah. No.

Forney bangs the wheel with his palm. "Should we turn back and look for them?" Ethel shouts. Forney shakes his head. "We'd never find them in these clouds." Forney swears at the thought of his new friend taken from him so soon. As always—what is his curse?

"They're good pilots—they know what to do," he shouts. Course 129, plunging through the clouds. "Maybe they'll beat us there, for all I know," he adds, doubting it.

THE TELEGRAPHER ENJOYS cigars, his wife does not; since the train station is their home, he smokes them outside, on the platform by the baggage carts. It's three in the morning—an ore train's due in an hour, the only reason he's not asleep like the rest of the mountain town. He twirls his cigar as he lights it, spreading the flame, slurping so loudly he doesn't hear the far-off whistling, the hiss of something shoving air aside as ATE drops toward him out of the heights. In fact it's not until the airplane is upon the town, wheels grazing the roof and Brown shoving in the power, that he's aware of it at all, and then he jumps up thunderstruck, hollering, while his wife inside grabs the baby and races out to join him. There, the roaring dark airplane is climbing over the gorge at the far end of town, raising high on one wing, higher, seeming almost to stand still in the moonlight before the nose falls through and there it is again, diving back toward them. Not having the imagination to escape, the telegrapher and his family can only stand rigid. Down it glides, silent for something so large once more, at only the last possible moment, the engines find their roar, the machine passes overhead and rises back up the canyon.

In the cockpit, both men strain to read the moonlight name on the station roof. "Cochibambi?" shouts Queen. "Something like that," Brown nods. "Look it up!" Queen shines a flashlight on the chart in his lap. His finger points.

"I got it! Cochabamba. We've drifted into the mountains. Christ, we're way off!"

"Give me a heading!"

"Try 110 until I figure it better. We got enough gas?"

"I don't know—couple of hours!"

Queen uses his spread fingers as dividers. He sucks in his cheeks. "Maybe it will be enough!" The plane banks, the compass card slowly passes beneath the lubber line. Brown levels out—"A hundred and ten degrees!" he shouts.

DARK FOG AND DRIZZLE at Arequipa. The two Trimotors twine through mountains east of town; on the airfield ahead, the headlights from a line of parked cars define a runway. They settle over them onto wet turf—the doors of the terminal open and out files a sleepy brass band in shakos and epaulets, cleaning the spit out of their horns. More locals follow; the alcalde, two assemblymen, an admiral in town on a chance visit, lingering inside until the machines actually taxi up to the line and shut down before exiting into the cold. The band plunges into Rossini—the alcalde is looking for Forney, decides it must be this unshaven man lighting a cigarette striding toward him, begins a speech, short earlier in the evening when he first arrived at the terminal, longer now from embellishments added in the course of many rehearsals. Forney cuts him short. "We're missing a plane. Has anybody heard anything?" The officials look at each other. *"Aterrizaje de emergencia,"* says Ethel, using her hands.

"No, no," says the alcalde. *"Nunca oigen. Pero . . ."*

Forney's not interested—he pushes past, into the terminal; the others follow. Nearing the door, Kinner stumbles on something, would fall but for Slovak catching him. "Jesus, you can't even walk," the old man mutters. "It's slippery," says Kinner, pointing at the ground. Slovak runs his toe over it, feels a rime of ice cracking. "Frozen, that's why," he says.

Forney's climbed three stairs at a time to the Operations room on the second floor. Teletypes clack now and then; two SACA pilots doze in a corner. Forney rings a counter bell, a clerk emerges from an inner office, knotting a tie. "We're missing an airplane that left Lima around midnight," Forney says. "You hear of any forced landings?"

The clerk shakes his head, looking over a clipboard. He has a German accent. "The problem is, it's such a large country. Things happen and it's days before we learn of it. Could they still be flying?"

Forney turns to Slovak. "What do you think?" Slovak shrugs. "Another half hour if he really leaned it out."

"When does this fog burn off?" Ethel asks. A German pilot, waking now, speaks up from behind. "Sometimes not at all, missus. At least not for days." Forney nods, looking out the window. "Yeah, the stuff's coming in, not going out."

"Then how could they land, even if they got here?"

"They could do a timed descent on the volcano," says the clerk. "That's what others do when conditions are like this."

Forney snorts. Timed descent—airline words. There's an overstuffed couch against a wall, kapok showing—Ethel sits on it, hugging her bare arms. Hours ago it was burning, desert, she thinks. Forney swings a window open, leans out into the fog. Some parts of the sky are brighter than others —it's past dawn. He can make out El Misti, the volcano that marks the city, gray against gray in the wan light. Now he hears airplane engines far off. A Trimotor—no sound like it. He turns and hurries for the stairs. "Is it them?" Ethel calls after.

They rush outside—the band begins to play, spontaneously, but Forney waves them quiet; their music dies. He listens hard, hears faint pops, far away. "Backfiring," he says to Slovak.

"How can they see in this fog?" Kinner asks.

"It ain't foggy up there," Slovak says. "Just down here."

HE'S RIGHT—the Trimotor hangs in cobalt morning sky, 13,000 feet high, 500 feet above the fog that fills the valleys and hugs the mountainsides, a flat dirty ocean broken only by the cone of El Misti. They've been homing on the volcano since dawn, like sailors at landfall, drinking rum, approaching a tropic island. It rises 6,000 feet above them, 11,000 feet above the streets of Arequipa, 19,000 feet above sea level. The engines backfire, shudder on their mounts; Brown has them leaned out as much as they can stand, gasping for fuel.

Queen's looking over the side for a break in the overcast, sees none at all. "It's down there!" he shouts.

Brown nods. "We're up here. Problem is to bring us together!"

Queen taps the fuel gauge, making sure the needle isn't stuck. "We got maybe ten minutes, Brownie!"

Brown puffs his cheeks, blows. It's not the going up he thinks, never is—it's the coming down. No problem turning into a bird—it's becoming a man again. He looks out at the weather, can see it's getting worse. Below that placid fog is an airport and friends, also basalt mountains, all randomly scattered like hidden treasure. "Let's time a letdown from the damn volcano!" he shouts. "What do I need?"

Queen already has it figured. "Head south about two-ten, four miles!" Brown banks, and the volcano slowly slides before the nose. "What I'll do is fly outbound at one-twenty for two minutes," he yells. "You time me—at four minutes, give me the cut!"

Below they can hear the engines louder now. Brown is turning, overhead, climbing. Out over the field, two swallows chase each other—nothing moves otherwise. The alcalde runs his fingernail along the gold chasings of his ceremonial staff, the admiral slaps his arms, the band turns up their skimpy collars. Forney paces—a cigarette sticks to his lower lip. When he pulls it off, a bit of paper remains. The engines pass over the field—Forney can tell they're heading for the volcano. Slovak explains to Ethel, shivering in the chill: "He figures out where the airport bears from the landmark, which is the top of the volcano, because that he can see. Okay, say it bears such and such degrees, so many miles—he flies up to the volcano, turns onto that heading, flies back that many miles."

"How can he measure distance?" she asks.

"Timing it, a mile a minute at sixty, two miles a minute at one-twenty, whatever airspeed he uses. When he's over where the field should be, he cuts his power and comes straight down through the fog."

It sounds dubious to Ethel. "Does it work?"

Slovak shrugs. "Guys have gotten away with it." He's looking up—the engine noise is growing louder again; they're passing overhead. Minutes pass—the sound is slowly drifting toward the east. "Cut them!" Forney shouts at the sky. "Cut them, Brown," Slovak says, less loudly. The engines drone on, two, three, four seconds, more. Then ten, even fifteen. Then, sudden silence. "Too far east," says Slovak quietly. "They'll come down in the mountains." The trumpet player sneezes—the trombone player gives him a dirty look.

Four thousand feet above, ATE sinks into the fog in a left-hand spiral. Brown cranks in trim to keep the speed in hand. The idling engines pop, the light fades—they're deep in it now. Things are surprisingly quiet—hear how the wind whistles through the windshield cracks. Brown watches the airspeed, the altimeter, the ball, back and forth, Queen clears his throat. "Okay, the field's at ninety-two hundred. You've got high ground to the east, peaks at eleven."

Brown nods. "We'll go as far as ten." The altimeter needle sweeps the face—Queen calls the numbers. "Eleven-five. C'mon, give us a break."

On the field, they can hear the wind rush now, the windmilling props. The fog hides everything. Louder whistling, higher in pitch.

"Eleven," Queen's saying, watching the needle.

"Talk about broads. Tell me every fuck story you ever heard."

"Did you ever fly through Elko?"

"Lots of times through Elko." With the engines idling, Brown doesn't have to shout.

"The most beautiful girl in the world works at the airport café in Elko."

"I remember her. The guy's daughter. Julie."

"Lily."

"Lily."

"Lily. Ten-seven. She was a lily, too, like a flower in a vase. Guys off the southern mail routes used to fake bad weather, just for a chance to take food from her hand."

"What are we doing?"

"Ten-four and I can't see shit."

"How'd you do with Sally?"

"I screwed her on top of the nitro. It lent a certain *je ne sais quoi.*"

"What's that?"

"She knew the stuff was going bad."

"How'd she know that?"

"After all, she grew up at a mine."

They hear them, 1,200 feet below, some great weight hurtling down, still see nothing. The dignitaries fidget. Behind them, Forney sees the terminal building, windows open, people filling them, more standing on the roof deck.

In ATE, Queen rubs a clear spot on the frosted windshield. "Not a thing. Coming up on ten, Brownie." He waits—moments pass. "Ten thousand," he says.

Brown hesitates. "We'll cheat a little," Queen twitches, a private spasm. "Okay. Nine-nine," he calls. "Nine-eight . . ."

"C'mon, shit . . ."

Queen looks up and blinks. A ragged hole just flashed past. Another shredding—and there, just above, a break in the billows, brown earth, resolving into a ridgeline dead ahead. Queen yells, Brown hauls back on the yoke, jams in power. A mass of rock slides past below—the airplane mushes near the stall. The fog parts—they fall through it into sallow light, spreading fields below, the airport a mile off, to the right.

Forney is grabbing Ethel, she Forney. Slovak dances with Kinner, hats fly, the band assaults Rossini, puffing and panting in the thin air. Beyond, ATE is gliding toward them, banking to land. Kinner hurries over to Forney. "Shouldn't we warn him about the ice?" ATE is a mile off, lined up for landing—Forney breaks into a run, slipping on the slick ground.

In the cockpit of ATE, Queen is slapping Brown. "Terrific job, Brownie! Outstanding!" Brown grins, modestly. "It worked, didn't it?" He has the wind off the nose—the field fence passes below and he eases back on the throttles. Who will be waiting here—beauty queens, film roles, world tours? "It's Forney," Queen shouts, pointing.

Brown looks—there's a tiny figure in the field's center, hugging himself, stamping the ground. He adds full power, checks the sink, lets the airplane climb ponderously away. Below passes the terminal, flags, hats waving, the color of the band. "Ice on the ground?" asks Queen. Brown nods—that's what he got. He wags his wings, to show receipt. Ice on the ground is tricky, not as tricky, however, as a timed descent. Thinking of beauty queens, Brown banks tightly, keeping the airfield well in sight. Once more he lines up, slowing it down, letting it sink barely inches at a time. He slides open his side window, sticks his face out into the raw wind so he can look down and watch the very tires touch. Here is the road again, cars parked, people standing alongside the chain-link fence, the glistening field. Ground rises to wheel, meets—the shock struts creak as the wing spills its lift, the gear takes up the burden. Many ice slicks are puddles glazed over—the wheels crush through them, ice water flying, coating the belly, gear struts, the mechanical brake cables, the shoes themselves, curling inside the wheel drums. The cables tighten—Brown adds brake lightly, the plane rolling out, still fast. The shoes pinch, but ice meets ice, with no grip. The judgment races up the twin cables, through linkages, bellcranks, up to the lever between the two pilots' seats and Brown's hand. There will be no brake. Ahead is a hangar—empty, thank God, Brown thinks, to the end concerned for flying machines. Queen looks over at his pilot, unsure—Forney, where he stands, knows, seeing the airplane racing past, unchecked. Slovak knows, now Kinner; Ethel sees and screams for all of them.

In ATE, Brown cuts the mags. The airplane plows into the hangar, screech of metal, horribly loud—the hangar collapses around it. The nitro does what it wants to—thirty cases explode with a white flash, a thunder unbearable. The shock wave flings those who stand to the ground; the terminal windows implode, the curtains shred. Screams rise from the building, people slashed by glass. A Stinson at the gas pit is on its back, a mail truck on its side. From the collapsed hangar rises a swelling orange fireball and a pillar of oily smoke.

The thunder echoes up the valley, meets itself, diffuses. Men are running from every side—dopey, Forney joins them, trying to outrace them all, for reasons he doesn't understand. A firetruck bounces across the field with only one man aboard, the driver. Pieces of skin metal still float down like iron leaves, looking for someone to sever.

There's little left of plane or hangar, a few shreds of metal wall bent over, some of the wingtips, the tail assembly, leaning on the ground. At the hangar's center is a hole thirty feet across, still smoking, rich and brown, good glacial soil revealed. The firetruck has stopped, its siren moaning slowly down—the driver sits at the wheel, not even trying.

Slovak and Kinner lag behind the others running. Kinner stops short, gags—there's Queen's wooden leg, lying off on its own, the mahogany smoldering. Ethel comes up behind them—dazed, speechless, they seek out Forney. There's no fire, barely a sound—a hole, hot metal, a billow of sawdust swirling across the field in the frightened air.

Two cars and an ambulance pull up now. One car carries the dignitaries—the alcalde is pushing through the crowd toward Forney, yelling at him; Forney turns away, not listening—the alcalde gets the admiral to translate. "Mayor say get your other airplanes the hell out of here," he says. Forney sees four men carrying what looks like a burnt wooden armchair out of the wreckage. It's Brown, Forney realizes. The admiral is starting in again—Slovak shoves him away, furious. "Tell him we're on a mercy mission," he shouts. The admiral does, gets an answer. "He say, hell with you—have mercy on us. Plenty of other places to go."

The ambulance with Brown heads off, toward the gate

to the town road. Forney looks around for a place to sit down, but where can you sit, in the middle of an airfield? He staggers off, not caring where, hears voices, does not listen.

Part three

13

BELOW IN THE COURTYARD, people sit moaning on folding chairs. Laceration victims from the terminal, Ethel thinks—bloody bandages lie everywhere, underfoot. Worse than unhygienic—septic, contagious. None seem critical, gratefully, their carotids and jugulars intact.

She turns back into the room. Kinner's weeping in the far corner; he hasn't stopped since the airport. What's left of Brown lies propped up by pillows in a bed, swaddled in gauze now brown and stiff from all that hemorrhaging, head included, wrapped like some jolly jack-o-lantern with tiny eyes, a bump nose, a jagged mouth. He smells gamey; his mouth opens and closes rhythmically, like a valve or a sea anemone, but no sound is heard. On either side, nuns bend over him spreading petroleum jelly across his chest with tongue depressors, lathering him thick, working hard like sculpture students. They're chatting in Spanish, assuming Ethel can't understand; they gossip about a young priest newly assigned to the hospital, allegedly well-hung. There's a metal sidetable on wheels and a crucifix over the bedframe —otherwise the room is bare.

Ethel feels hands on her shoulders but they are imaginary—they are Gerald's. He's looking her in the eye—I hope you're up to this, Ethel. You're a terrific girl but God knows what can happen to you on the way down, and if you think this is over your head, say so now and we'll figure out some other way. His thumbs knead her shoulder caps; his look's intense, yet sweet at the same time. I want to, she's thinking, to show you what I am. Lives hang in the balance, generations to come, whole families, a national history hinges on her—what a thrill to be at the center of history, along with him. Still, she did not think death would come this way. Look at Brown, force yourself, she tells herself, wiggling in the chair, sitting more upright. I have seen manifold death, she thinks—I'm a nurse; I work midnight shifts in a major metropolitan hospital. Brown's mittened hand is twitching, fingers clenched, spread open, clenched again—some palsy, some nerve end, synapse, flopping like a fish on deck, she thinks. Oh God, Gerald, you didn't tell me I'd know them. Gerald's beside her, hand covering her shoulder. You don't even know his first name. Last names only in the hospital—she's Thorgaard; he's Dr. Booton; the indigent patient, the wino, the cripple, Mason, Guber, Kramer, the unknown ones. Forney's first name is George—she knows that much.

Forney enters the room now, tiptoeing, Slovak behind him—she must have had a premonition. She hears a noise from Forney's stomach when he sees Brown, a moan. Slovak drifts silently over to the wall where Kinner sits. "We found a field outside town," Forney whispers to her. "We had to walk back, what took so long." The nuns eye Forney, go back to their spreading. The smaller speculates on what's in his trousers—the larger shushes her. Brown's mouth opens, lipless, dark, closes again.

"Can't they give him anything?" Forney hisses.

She swallows hard. "The doctor was in here a while ago. I can't understand what he's saying very well."

"Well, Jesus, somebody ought to do something." The door opens and a young doctor in a pince-nez looks in.

"*Hay cambio?*" he asks the nuns and they shrug. As he withdraws, Forney follows, catching him in the doorway. "What about the pain he's in?" he whispers.

The doctor has a British accent. "There's next to no pain, actually. His nervous system's so traumatized he can't feel anything—that part of him's already dead. You might see that as fortunate." His manner is cool—they are not heroes in Arequipa.

Forney lets him go; he steps to Ethel, begins to repeat what the man said. She shakes her head, having heard. "I've treated burn victims. He's in terrible pain. His voice box is burned away, that's all. He can't scream."

Slovak coughs across the room. "Shit, read his hand." Forney does—what Ethel thought was random nerve firing is in fact the flyer's Morse, same as the day before in the pass, fist and palm. The movement's repeated, three fists, three palms, three fists, three palms, three fists. SOSOSOSO. Man in distress.

The nuns are done—they cap their jars, smooth down the sheets over Brown's chest and leave, smiling at something. "How long can he go on like this?" Forney asks.

"Fuck that," says Slovak, loud suddenly. "How long does he have to? He's telling us what he wants."

Of course, to fly away, flight from the pain, Forney thinks—how could he have missed it? Only how would you kill Brown; what is there left to undo? Oh please no, not here in this room, this freezing town, this barren country, hopeless continent. I was born in Pennsylvania, he cries; his spirit flees into outer space, taking refuge behind the moon and stars. Brown's hand allows no scruples. SOSOSOSOSO.

"Well, what do we do?" whispers Slovak. "Draw straws?" Kinner finds his voice. "That's okay. I think that's fair." Forney snorts; it's obvious to him. He's killed lots of men in his mind, never with his bare hands. He crosses to the bed and snatches up a pillow from behind the bandaged head. The head, unsupported, bangs back against the bed frame. Forney looks at Ethel—she has her eyes shut, her hands over her mouth, stunned by his suddenness. "You have a better idea?" She shakes her head. "We were never allowed to. I mean, we couldn't have. It was against our oath." Forney's unclear what she's talking about; he jams the pillow, floppy, feather-filled, over the mouth and leans on it, his arms stiff.

There's no sound. Ethel, Slovak, Kinner are still. Somewhere a baby calls for feeding. A door slams down the hall; a phone rings. Brown's head flops up, down, up, down, up, then down, limp. Kinner is bawling; Forney stands and wipes his hands off on his pants, feels dizzy, holds onto the bedrail. His legs go jelly, but Slovak is there to catch him —Ethel hurries around to get his other arm.

FOG'S TURNED TO light rain—there's water everywhere, on leaf backs, tree branches, basalt and pumice. The cemetery is out of town, among volcanic rocks. Money has been paid to a gatekeeper for a plot, to these two squatting diggers for twin holes, to a carpenter for two coffins, one full-sized for Brown, a child's for Queen, needing only to contain the leg. The gatekeeper has even found an American flag among a pile of flags in his hut; it's old, having only thirty-six stars, but they drape it over the coffins to keep them dry.

They stand by the pits—three are silent, the fourth, Kinner, still weeps, a swallowed wail that barely stops for breath. The diggers are rigging slings around the coffins, lowering them down. Forney goes through Brown's wallet. A few bills, a silver dollar—he tosses what he finds in the hole. A picture of a dog, a German shepherd, head tilted to one side. "Wonder who the dog was?" Forney says. Slovak looks at it. "Sometimes pictures come with a wallet when you buy it," he says. A woman in a car, a ribbon from the war. The wallet drops in last—the diggers untie the knots, retract the ropes.

They're all looking to Forney, one at a time. He swallows—what could he ever dare to say? His voice cracks, even in the moist air. "Queen joked around a lot—he was the kind of guy who always kept your spirits up. Brown overhauled the engine—I don't think any of us could have done that." He pauses. "It's too bad they're gone—we could have used them." Forney looks up, beyond the others—his eyes are wet, vision blurry. On the road outside the cemetery, two Indians lead a llama. They're dressed in newspaper. Kinner wails still, no way to ignore it—it might even be taken for a sort of music. "That's all," says Forney; the others raise their heads.

The diggers reach for their shovels; the four head off, trudging through wet ash, porous rocks. Ethel cries as well now—Forney walks alongside, hands in his jacket pockets. Kinner follows behind with Slovak, sniffling, trying to stop his tears. "I don't like funerals," he whispers. "They remind me of death."

Slovak guffaws out loud, blushes, cuts it short. Forney, five paces ahead, grins, but hides it with his hands. Even Ethel smiles, faintly, looks back at Kinner. "Jesus, I'd like to go flying right now," Forney whispers to her.

THE ROAD ENTERS the outskirts of town, small allotments, weedy fields with a lone cow, crumpled adobes with wet walls. A square with Indians hiding under wet ponchos, waiting for the rain to pass. More people, an oxcart, a car going by. Around a corner, there's a street of shops, shiny trolley tracks. Indians run past with rolls of leaves in their sashes. A policeman in a raincoat directs traffic. The avenue widens—there's a fountain, a marble temple full of men reading folded newspapers. Businessmen flag cabs, crowds of young men stroll arm in arm, secretaries bend to window-shop. They've come to downtown Arequipa, a busy city at midday; walking through it, wet, morose, the city opens to let them by, closes behind them when they've passed.

FORNEY AND ETHEL kill an hour in a city park. Children fight for swings, scrape their knees on coarse gravel paths.
Now they walk down an *avenida,* off the main street, climb the outside stairs of a two-story building with a chipped facade and a red light. A fat whore leads them into a smoky room. There are scraps of red wallpaper, but the walls are mostly brick, hung with cardboard beer ads—a windup Victrola in the corner plays jazz. At a center table

sit Slovak and Kinner, eating beans and potatoes. Kinner stuffs his face with a big wooden spoon.

The whore comes back with two slat chairs—Ethel and Forney sit. She looks about, slowly, taking it in. Slovak shrugs. "It's the only house in town."

"She's the only whore," says Kinner, swallowing. "They had another one, but she died."

The whore now carries in glasses of beer, an odd red color. Forney sips some, makes a face. "She says when it rains like this, it can go on for days," says Slovak, taking a drink. He spits it suddenly back into the glass. "What is this piss?"

"*Chicha,*" Ethel says. "The Aymaras drink it. They chew up grain, spit it on the ground, and let it ferment." She thinks of Aymaras at the mine, getting drunk, delusional, thinking they're Incas, sleeping it off.

Kinner pushes forward a small bowl with gray leaves. "You think that's bad. This is worse. It tastes like dirt."

Ethel smiles. "You're not supposed to eat it. It's coca leaves. It helps them stand the altitude."

"Coca?" thinks Slovak, his mind to hot chocolate, snowy mornings. She's taken a handful of dry leaves, ground it in her palms—now she cups her hands and inhales the powder. A beat—then the others, one by one, try it. They lean back, silent, waiting to feel its effects.

The whore eyes Ethel, unhappy with her presence; Ethel presses her skirt between her legs. "Have you done what you came for?" she asks Slovak, quietly.

"He's been too busy eating," says Slovak, meaning Kinner. Kinner looks up from his food, glances at the whore, looks away. "What do you say, Kinner?" Slovak says, "*Sí* or *no?* Is this the night or what?"

The whore has a thick neck, spit curls. Kinner knows that bridge must be crossed some day, was hoping it would not be this soon. On liberty in Panama, his mates went to the houses, he to the penny arcades. It would be different if he had some feeling for this woman, he thinks, if he could get an erection but how can he, with his mind still thick with fire and sound and metal raining down? "You don't want to be *El Primero,* fine," Slovak says. "You can eat leftovers." He jerks a thumb at the whore and the two of them head down a hallway.

Forney inhales another coca leaf. "You feel any different?" he asks Ethel. She shakes her head no. Time passes—Forney turns to Kinner now. "Where are you from, anyway?" "Yuma." Kinner can't think of anything to add to that, although there's more. Forney unzips his jacket, stands and walks to the shuttered window. Tile roofs spread below, joining at odd angles, tiny houses warm with dinner smoke and odors. In one bricked-in backyard, a small boy bathes in a washtub, naked and lathered, singing a song of his own invention. Forney shuts his eyes. Oh my God, he thinks—feels a force throbbing, rising toward his head, wet, some sort of massive hydrostatic. He thinks it's the coca, climbing the blood. The boy shimmers, jewellike and spotless, almost transparent. Behind him, Slovak is coming back into the room, buttoning his shirt, shaking his head. "I can't get drunk. I can't get laid. I'm in bad shape," he whispers.

UNDER A SODDEN MOON, Forney and Slovak hurl rocks at the airplanes with all their might. The rocks clang off the metal skin, leave no mark. The two of them cough, out of breath in the slender air. Forney stumbles about, picks up a big one, a five-pounder, pitches it. Whang—the metal flexes, brace wires flick water, but there is no dent. Forney's howling like a dog, Slovak growls like a beast. The larger the rocks, the more physics flings them backward, and they trip and sprawl on their asses finally, wheezing in the wet grass. The airplanes stand unfazed, tiptoe on their wheels.

Forney rolls over, the world spins, and his stomach lurches; the moon leaves his left eye, reappears a moment later at the far corner of his right. Slovak nudges him, pointing up at the thick wing of ACH stretching overhead. "See them rivets?" he pants. Forney looks—he's pointing at a double line of tiny domes, joining one sheet of underwing skin to the next. "Oil around them." Forney gets his meaning—each rivet has a tiny corona of black grease. That doesn't happen when they're tight to the metal, only when they're working loose. "Like that all over," Slovak says. "Damn thing's coming apart."

Forney nods—so much for Henry Ford, so much for the voodoo of American manufacture. Even Trimotors can't cohere this high. He imagines Henry Ford spinning around this meadow, snoot full of coca dust, shredding apart under Peruvian gravity, derby, black tie, shoes, all whirling away like propeller tips busting off. Oh God, Forney thinks—he will throw rocks at airplanes, throw airplanes at the rocks. Up here it's all the same.

Slovak is trudging off, exhausted, toward the stone barn by the trees. Forney finds his feet and follows. His hot breath surrounds him in his own cloud; he navigates blind, on his own instruments, to the barn door. Inside, Slovak is making a cocoon out of two horse blankets. Kinner's to one side, buried in a wet straw pile—Ethel sits upright in a stall, legs covered by an engine tarp. He stumbles toward her, rubbing his palms, now pulls up short, five feet away. She hasn't heard him, at least makes no sign, but she's not asleep—her eyes are open, on the ground. Forney shifts from one foot to the other, making the most tentative of sounds. She turns, sees him there, arms and knees crossed. Nothing is said—Forney waits, head to one side. Ethel pulls back the tarp corner at last, barely—Forney stumbles forward, coughing, settling beside her, pulling the stiff canvas over them both. She smells him, ashtray smell, feels his bones, his boots trodding her toes, now, suddenly, his teeth biting into her shoulder, his drool—he's crying, mouth open, trembling in the cold. She tries to pull the tarp higher, touches his shirt, a button missing, then by surprise his bare belly, goose-bumped, his dusty navel. Misreading her intentions, he traps her hand there—she feels his other arm circling her, drawing her close.

"Happens to me every time," he whispers. "Same with Hal, same damn thing. World's record. Flying in circles for two days. Let's go flying in the Fleet, he says. We climb up about five thousand." On he goes, talking with one slow hand. "It's evening, big orange sun. I pull a loop—sun's upside down, Hal's laughing. I come down, roll it, another loop, another one. Everytime I lose a couple hundred feet, but that's all right—the sun's going down, and I'm looping all the way to the ground. I come out of another loop, pull a couple of g's, and hear a little ping, just barely. One of the cabane wires snapped. You know—hold the wings together. Little thing." She nods. "That's no good, so I roll out, slow it way down, slip it down toward the field." Forney coughs, behind her back. No, he's still crying, she thinks. "All of a sudden, the whole goddamn wing breaks off and curls back. We start tumbling. Hal's trapped in front, under the wing, like in a cage. I'm pulling on the wreck with my hands, but the wind keeps it flat. I get him by the wrists; he's looking up at me. I pull hard as I can, hard as I ever pulled in my life, and then something busts and there I am, out there, all of a sudden, floating in midair, me going this way, airplane going that. I can hear him screaming. I pull the D-ring, the chute pops and I come down. Fifty feet away is the Fleet, in a pile, on fire." Forney sobs, sobs and coughs now. "I flew the goddamn wings off it. I pushed too hard. Isn't that crazy?" She shushes him but he won't stop. "Think about it. It happens every time—Hal back then, this time with Brown and Queen . . ."

"I don't believe it. There isn't any connection."

Forney shakes his head violently—don't tell him that. There's a reason pilots are superstitious—look at their charts: courses, headings, here and there, from city to city, these people and those people, all joined by intersecting lines. Don't dare tell a pilot everything's not connected.

Ethel yearns to comfort him—she does that, her job, unasked—but the urge is poisoned; she's the source of pain as well. She shuts her eyes, pulls Forney closer. Oh God, she wears whites and hurts men; where's the good in that? She's drained—tell her what to tell him, you other clever men, Ramón or Gerald. His hand has slipped to her breast, looking for a ledge to hold to. She wants out of this, relief, rescue herself—she will not ask more of this man. She hesitates—yes, that's her decision; she will find some other means this last leg over the Andes, she can't imagine what—a truck, a car, another airplane even, flying it across herself. She thinks she knows the principles. Forney will be spared this last suffering. "The rain's not stopping. You can't fly anymore," she whispers in his ear, stroking his hair.

He coughs. "Sure I can. First thing tomorrow."

"How?"

"I can fly." He sniffs. "I just can't see, that's all." His body's shaking; he's laughing, that's why. He thinks it's funny. His head sinks slowly down over her breasts, into the cushion of her crossed legs. He curls up there, lost beneath the tarp completely, wrapped in his own heat and smell.

IN THE DISTANCE, a dog barks. There are voices outside, a truck engine idling. Forney opens one eye, his face in Ethel's waist. A shaft of sunlight falls across the barn floor—it's dawn. Something sticks him in the side—he reaches back, feels Slovak's knee; the old man snores behind him, teaspooning. There's a hand on Ethel's belly not his—Kinner's, sawing wood against Ethel's other side. They must have crept over during the night, Forney thinks. The cold hits his face; the corners of his eyes grind. The barn doors open now—in walk four men, all pilots, all dressed in tailored blue uniforms. Two are Krauts from SACA, one wears the wings of Interperu, the last is an American from Pan-Am. The Krauts are carrying heavy leather jackets—they hand one to Forney as he stands, another to Kinner who's just stirring. The American is pouring coffee from a thermos, prodding Slovak awake. Ethel sits up abruptly now, in the middle of a dream.

"You guys better get moving if you're going," the American says. "There's a break in the weather, but it's supposed to close down by noon."

Forney blinks. "How do you know?"

"We have a man in the shack with a radio at sixteen thousand feet," says one of the Germans. "He saw the front pass through at dawn."

Standing now, Forney turns to Slovak. "Let's go, then. Check out the airplanes ..."

The South American smiles. "We saw to that—one of our crews. They're topped off, gas and oil, both of them." Forney can't believe it all: coffee, cigarettes, hot rolls in a paper sack. Tying their shoes in a hurry, buttoning their clothes, they run their hands through their hair and stumble outside.

A fuel truck is driving off into the drizzle. ABR and ACH stand ready; two mechanics in Interperu overalls wipe off their windshields. One of the Germans hands Forney a chart of the mountains. "I drew in your most favorable route," he says, "considering your machines don't have much of a ceiling. Your compasses are all haywire—did you know that?"

Forney shrugs, sheepish. "Hell, they've been off for years ..."

"Then follow the landmarks I've marked. And if you don't have seventeen thousand by the time you reach Illimani, you better turn back. The peak goes to twenty-one thousand."

The hot coffee burns Forney's throat—he nods. "Listen, you guys, thanks for all this."

The South American looks down. "Too bad what happened to your friends." The American shakes his head. "It's the shits, ain't it?"

14

THERE'S NO THRILL to takeoff this morning, the machines more willing than the crews, Ethel thinks. The nitro has begun sweating again—crates show rosy stains at their corner miters. The stench fills the cabin, pinches her between the eyes. They climb slowly through the ground fog, surface into sunlight—the city is a faint grid below. Far overhead in a dark sky, wispy cirrus, white brushstrokes. Forney sees her gaze. "Ice clouds!" he shouts. Ahead, thicker, deeper clouds straddling the mountains; here and there an island peak rises above them. It looks benign—Ethel thinks of surgical cotton, spread by the nurses around the base of the fourth-floor Christmas tree each year to hide the wooden stand. The Andes might not be so bad if it's simply a question of traversing this sea of fourth-floor cotton. Now the clouds begin to billow over her—Ethel realizes they reach higher than she thought, much higher, that the airplane, hardly climbing, will never reach their tops, so that traversing the Andes will be in the end a matter of flying through them. She feels the grab of nausea, doesn't know whether it's fear or *soroche*, gropes in her pocket for the common antidote, a paper bag of coca leaves, a present from one of the SACA pilots. How many people know, she thinks, that the pride of the airlines fly the Andes routes under narcotic influence. Her head clears, like a night of sleep falling away; she hands the bag to Forney, tries to zip her jacket shut. It's so cold the slide won't budge. She yanks hard—a sharp edge cuts a shriveled finger. Raising her fur collar, she gets a whiff of a man's neck sweat, huddles lower in her seat. Ahead, clouds spill toward them pellmell over the ridges. The snow line passes below, sharp outcrops, dark brown, almost the color of dried feces. More cloud, cloud overhead, blanking out the sky. To one side is ABR, suspended against white. She looks out the other side and sees white alone, no machine at all, curses herself for forgetting why.

Forney notes a gorge below, a small brown finger on the chart they gave him, says farewell to all landmarks now as the clouds enfold them. The light dims, the engine note shifts higher, more frantic. One hundred and fifty feet per minute indicated, meaning a thousand feet climbed in seven minutes, the ten thousand he needs in an hour and ten. Ahead is depthless gray, not even texture. Forney lowers his eyes to what instruments he has: airspeed, compass, altimeter, needle and ball. Needle backs up compass, warning of a turn. Altimeter backs up rate-of-climb, claiming now a slow rise, the needle barely moving. Something on the windshield, bending light. Rain, thinks Forney—oh hell; the light outside drops ten lumens more. The airplane lurches, wheezes as if punched midships. Here comes the chop, he sighs. An explosion startles him, lightning off the port wing like artillery—the airplane leaps as if frightened; the harness straps cut his shoulders. Jesus, just like Chimbote, Forney thinks, Chimbote all over only worse, Chimbote blind. He sends out calls for strength, to his legs and arms, but there is no reply. Chimbote was conquered; the Andes will simply have to be endured.

Lightning all over now, neon strikes, ozone smell, no sign of ABR—on their own, Forney thinks, as he and Ethel are. Rain leaks into the cockpit everywhere in icy mists. Forney wipes his wet face, yells to Ethel for help. She nods, staggers aft through the rocking cabin, holding onto the rope lashings, brushing against the crates. Back she comes, dragging her suitcase—she fumbles with folded nightgowns, a flannel robe, cotton undies. Forney wipes his face dry with a chemise. She tries to tear strips of flannel and jam them into the window seals, but no luck. More lightning; the airplane stumbles—Ethel hits her head against the windshield framing. It hurts, terribly; she feels a swelling. "This storm ain't coming!" Forney shouts at her. "It's here! We're in it!" Ethel looks out along the wing's bottom, sees it flexing in the turbulence. Flexing, for God's sake. Everything is movement—cabin dirt floats up in grimy clouds, the rain melts against the windshield like some clear syrup, and now there are these dots, small, black, swimming across her vision like waterskimmers. She bats them away, or tries—they float back, unperturbed. Her head is throbbing, over her temples. Oh Jesus, she's suffocating, she realizes—she yells to Forney but barely hears the words herself. She flips back the side panel—air like icewater bursts over her. She gasps, ducks away, fights the window closed again, taking deep diaphragm inhales, head between her knees. There, there's some lung satisfaction, a little thickening of her breath. The spots fade, skim out of sight. Breathing slowly, more deeply, she looks over at the altimeter: 15,800 feet. That's all? She slumps back—her vision lags, still presenting her knees when her head is upright. She shuts her eyes, thinks of Gerald, but he passes, flung back like something out the side window. The plane shudders again; God how she hates the surprise of it. She tries to concentrate on something distant—Sucre, Ramón, Wallo, José, her apartment at home, her oak bed, her best friend Marygrace, the tufted cotton quilt, the corner label, "Woolsey Mills, Montpelier, Vt." All flash past, anything known, stable—there's no longer history for her, only a horrible instant that repeats over and over. All the world can be is this lurching cockpit, this man, gunfire and phosphorus outside, the incredible cold. She glances outside at the wing. A second ago, it cleaved the rain like a ship's prow; now it's opaque, encrusted. "Is that ice?" she shouts. Forney glances out his window at the pearly coating. "What does it do?" she shouts. He doesn't answer.

There are shredded gaps in the clouds—Forney sees fragments of mica, slab ridges, five hundred feet below. They're lost, oh yes. The plane is drifting, compass card turning, needle cocked left. See what happens when you take your eyes off the clocks? He levels off—another hole outside baits his eyes and he looks down, sees for a flash a frozen lake with a white snow beach. Weight in the left cheek of his ass—the instruments confirm it, needle showing a left bank again. He snatches out the map under his leg, thrusts it at Ethel. "Figure out where we are! Kidney-shaped lake!" He can't spare more, the airplane mushes on the edge of 16,000, props not biting, engines hoarse, wings nibbling desperately for lift. The more the ice builds up, the more the airfoil deforms, lift slides away, the airplane grows heavier from the load, up and over its gross again.

Ethel's searching for a lake along the pencil course. Small print blurs, pigments run together like a kid's watercolors. There's one, perhaps, kidney-shaped—she jams her finger on it so it won't get lost. Oh, that's awful, that wrench, the bottom falling out, metal creaking. The altimeter unwinds as if its spring was cut. Another wrench—the crates aft leap up against their ropes in unison, slam down. The altimeter winds up just as fast—200 feet lost, 200 feet gained back, 3,000 vertical feet per minute, trapped in a hurricane wind that hurls them anywhere it wants. The wheel tears from Forney's hands, hitting him in the gut, knees. What can break? he wonders, recalling Slovak's rivets. The engines on their mounts? If so, the whole airplane tears. Main tanks, buried in the wings, fat oval tubes on wooden cradles, held down by web straps? They're a weak spot. His mind is wandering, lost in structure—the compass drifts, the altimeter peaks at 16,200, falls back. Forney grabs the coca from her, jams his hand into the bag, crumbles some against his face, rubbing the shreds over his chapped upper lip, sniffing in. Heat wells into his facebones, eyes—not bad, he thinks. "Find that lake?" he shouts.

"I think so!"

"How high are we over the mountains?"

On the chart, the mountains are in meters—peaks are circles with concentric lines, little suns—5,940 meters, times three, rule of thumb. Ethel writes it down, mind so sluggish, zero, two, carry the one. She smiles—this could take hours; they'd be long past where they are. She guesses "Seventeen, eighteen thousand feet. There's one either side of the pencil line!" The altimeter reads only 16,450; they're either between mountains or inside them. Perhaps this is what goes on inside a mountain, she thinks, her mind giddy. What is it—altitude, cocaine? Something sharp and crusty around her mouth—ice, her own saliva frozen. There's frost on Forney's lips, too, when she looks. Oh, this is special—

she welcomes back her abstracting mind, returned slowly to her by the good services of the narcotic. Thank God she can wander now; how terrible to cross these mountains simply in the present. She can reach Gerald now—she calls to him, broadcasting herself ahead. I'm on the edge of destruction, Gerald, flying home to you like some fine bird. See me where I am, tell me if I'm not worthy. It's been hard, harder than I can even say, but give me two days' rest and I'd do it all over, so much do I believe in it. Oh Gerald, if you care for me at all, send back magic, warm air to melt this ice, clear skies to see by, fairy wings to fly us over the peaks and chasms. There's a funny smell, a new one, wet on the back of her neck. Ethel's hand touches her nape, comes away pink, some homey smell she can't quite place. Outside, something looms—her focus slowly shifts from her fingertips, outside past the blurred nose propeller to infinity, eye muscles slowly racking. It's white, sheer with a glacier spreading underneath like an apron, a mountainside a bare quarter-mile away, shining through the clouds. She hollers, points—Forney looks up from his instruments, blinks, banks hard right. The ailerons wag accordingly but the airplane takes its own sweet time in this airless cold—wings slowly grudge a turn, even as the mountain fills their vision. Cloud swallows them both again, plane and mountain, the arc of its turn now just geometry, abstract, collision a matter of vectors and rates. Seconds pass—Forney holds his breath. Two-minute turn—sixty seconds should make a one-eighty, an about face; it makes sense, only something's wrong. Forney's mind converges on it, in no great hurry, something about the engine noise, feelings in his ass, sliding sideways out of the bowl of his bucket seat.

He rolls level by feel alone—the turn and bank needle argues with him, still hard over. Forney trims for climb—the rate-of-climb needle denies it, insisting on dive. The compass is spinning, carousellike, no commitment to any course, simply off on its own dance. The instruments are dead, he thinks.

Ethel sees his face—"What's wrong?" she shouts. Forney shoves open his side window, hangs half his face out into the gale. The sleet lacerates his skin; he glimpses the instrument venturi, the horn fixed to the fuselage side below the cockpit that draws vacuum for the instruments, thick and blocked with ice. He flops back into his seat, face bleeding like a bad shave. "It's frozen, that's what!" He throws off his straps—"You fly it!" he yells, grabbing her surprised hands and clamping them around the wheel. She tries to speak—no words are at hand. He's already struggling out of the cockpit, ice-caked and woozy, bouncing off the bulkhead like some happy leather bumper-car. Hal Moxey stands in the aisle, about to say something—Forney shoves him aside and passes, no time for Hal now. He hurries aft, after a jar he remembers. Where his breath hits metal, it freezes, thin frost. The nitro crates rise and fall like a glissando of piano hammers. Forney smiles at them, stumbles, falls, picks himself up. Hal Moxey is standing in front of the lavatory door—Forney sighs, takes Hal firmly and moves him aside, fumbles with the frozen latch. He likes Hal, loves Hal, only friend his whole life provided, but he's too busy now to linger. Hal has a tolerant but puzzled look—Forney wrenches the door open, finds the jar, the one he uses to bleed the brake lines. Back toward the cockpit he crawls, listing to the right; she's banking and doesn't know it. There's an awful shudder, and crash, the worst—Forney fends off with his hands as the negative load floats him toward the ceiling. A sudden machine-gun rattle, a scream of icy air swirling around him—a seam of side fuselage skin is parting, peeling back from the structure feet from where he stands, letting in cloud. Shit oh dear—he hauls himself forward, braces his body as best he can in the bulkhead opening, begins to rip open his belt, undo his fly buttons.

Ethel has pushed the wheel away and folded her arms, lost interest in its operation, somewhat to punish Forney for leaving her like that, more for the act itself, as an acceptance of helplessness. To what end guide an airplane when there's no anywhere—why go through a travesty of intention? They will slam sideways into a mountainside, they will not; she no longer thinks she can affect the outcome. It has something to do with the narcotic, she knows, but it's hard to indicate cause, probably in the end not even valuable. Up is down—gravity seems to pull her on her head instead of her feet. It's a form of mental illness, she decides. See, look there, behind—Forney stands urinating into a jelly jar. It seems coherent, given where she is. He will stand there, pissing, she will sit there, clowns will continue to spill out of the small car forever; there will always be another clown squeezed in somewhere. Forney is shoving the jar, lid on tight, into her hands—it feels warm, elemental. "Tie it over the compass!" he's shouting, struggling into his seat. Ethel laughs, delighted—Forney has a huge nose, red greasepaint streaks on either cheek. No, actually it's blood streaming—her pleasure fades. He's got her by the clavicle, shaking her hard—her head snaps backward, off a fuel line.

"C'mon, move, tie it up there!" He's pointing to the centerpost between the windshields, over the compass.

"With what?" she shouts back.

"How should I know! Your shoelace!" The altimeter reads 15,400—they've lost a thousand feet through her indifference. Forney takes another great handful of leaves, smashes some, eats the flakes. Power rises through him—his mouth goes numb, like novocaine. "Mrs. Booton!" he yells, trying to wake her, but the word comes out funny: Mffbooln. She bends slowly, raises her foot, begins to draw the cotton lace from her shoe. Now she ties a loop around the jar, bends forward, elbows braced on the shaking panel, fumbling with a knot. The thick liquid splashes and foams. She wedges the jar bottom against the top of the compass, wraps a couple of turns around the centerpost. Wham—the plane leaps; she hits her head again, swears, lets go by accident. The jar doesn't fall—the knot holds, thankfully; she slumps back. "What is that for?" she shouts.

Forney's grinning. "It won't freeze over, that I'll guarantee you!" With a free hand, he's sliding the shoelace down so it circles the jar even with the level of the liquid. The plane lurches again, engines snarling—see how the urine slants to the left, Ethel thinks, a yellow horizon, the white lace the wings they ride beneath. Forney banks right—urine and lace coincide. Nose up, the liquid falls below the lace—she understands, a horizon in a jar. She finds it so clever, even sweet, turns to Forney with worshipful eyes. He can be wonderful too, worthy, even Forney. See how he steers there, firm-jawed, like some helmsman on a statue. Is this all narcotic judgment or not? she wonders. Perhaps—in that case, more of it, so this exaltation will never end. She puts the paper bag over her face, simply inhales and feels its bracing power. She laughs out loud—he looks across, laughs as well, for one sharp chortle. Lightning explodes somewhere close; there's a bind in the rudder cables all at once—he can barely move them. A brace wire busted, he thinks, fouling the hinges. There's another terrible lurch—something pours down the cockpit bulkhead onto Mrs. Booton. Gasoline, dyed-red eighty octane from those wing tanks—a seam has split, as he thought it might. Another line of rivets lets go somewhere, like a sheet tearing. "Whole damn airplane is coming apart!" he shouts.

"I know," she shouts back. "I know, I know!"

"You wanted to fly over the Andes in an airplane? Here they are—the Andes! I found them for you!"

"I know!" she shouts back. Gas is puddling in her seat—it's cold, like an alcohol rub. Forney's hand-pumping the remaining fuel into the other tanks. All at once, a deep bass boom resonates through the entire airplane; fear spills over and around her pleasure, smothers it. Another booming—Forney looks outside. A slab of rime ice an inch thick and four feet long is peeling off the underside of the wing, flashing aft. Boom—it smashes against the tail; the rudder pedals tingle, electric.

"Is that us?" she shouts. Forney's pointing out her window—ice curls off the airfoil like dead skin. "That's good," he shouts. "If the ice is thawing, it means ... "

Ethel's nodding, but he doesn't finish. Light blinds her—she blinks at the return of color, blue, black, brown. They're out of the gray all at once, the clouds sliced clean, floating in clear air, diamond-crisp. She looks slowly about—they're at the bottom of a vast bowl of mountains five miles across, surrounded by icy granite pyramids whose tops converge thousands of feet overhead. Neither of them speaks, stunned at the sight. More ice breaks off and bangs aft, loosened by the warmer air.

Those mountains before were just children, Ethel thinks, abruptly sober. This is where they come from—these are the parent mountains, oldest, grandest, without humor, without even voice. It's the center of the Cordillera, the very navel of the continent. Humbled, Forney banks slowly—the airplane begins a circuit of the bowl. Sheer walls pass in silence beyond the upturned wing.

Forney leans forward now, taps the altimeter. The needle unsticks, stops at 16,550. As high as he can climb—not bad for this old bird, he thinks, although it's a dry triumph; they're trapped here, no ridge in any direction lower than 18,000 feet. No retreat either—the storm they fought through still hovers on the western wall. And no place to land—granite facets below, spires, a plunging canyon with a frozen stream. You can't put an airplane down on a mountainside—it will fly at sixty, fall at fifty-nine. Forney sighs; he's come as far as he can. This lost bowl is where they will end, flying mindless circles until the gas runs out.

Ethel's staring over the side. The truth is, take away their personal problems and it's beautiful. Alpine scenery, blocks of granite, snow on the strata in white striations. A frozen river at the bottom, or a road. She'd like it to be a road, some last artifact of her own kind. Forney is standing beside her, cupping his hand. "Fly it again," he shouts. She's willing—can now, knows how. "Hold it in a bank like so," he shouts, showing her with his hand.

"Where are you going?"

He jerks his thumb back at the cargo. He has decided not to give up just yet, more as an experiment than out of any conviction. He squeezes her shoulder and leaves. She settles back to the job, but it's not easy—she'd been thinking about something. What? She looks down once more—the road slowly wheels below as she banks. Something about the road—she follows it north with her eyes, as far as a ridge crossing the valley floor. There's some sort of structure there, stone. Her point of view leaps to the road now, that muddy road, looking up past the ruins. She imagines what it would look like—her memory seems to add clues. A high mountain there, a peak like a stooped woman ... "Oh my God!" she says, out loud.

Forney's at the cabin's far end—he's pulled the emergency handle on the cabin door, and the wind's flung it away. The freezing slipstream curls around him—he's cut some tiedowns with his pocket knife, wrapped his arms around one sixty-pound crate, now staggers spread-legged to the open hatch. Bracing in the doorway lest the crate take him too, he lets it roll from his arms. The wind plays with it for a second before gravity snatches it away; it falls, clear against the white snow, deeper and deeper into the canyon. Now it's out of sight—there, a huge orange fireball rising from the canyon bottom, a plume of rocks and snow. Here's the explosion's boom, loud even over the din. As Forney heads for another, the plane suddenly banks hard, to the right. Half the load snaps its ropes, comes skidding down the cabin floor toward him, half a ton shoving and banging, butting in line like kids at a movie. Forney's foot gets wedged between a crate and the false wall—he yowls, grabs channels overhead, pulls himself free. "Level out, damn you!" he screams forward, without a chance of being heard.

Forgetting her instructions, Ethel's banked tighter, to better see the road. She knows these mountains, she does —on the horizon, a flattened mountain, much higher than any other. Illimani. The stooped woman is Santa Vela Cruz. That's the point: this is her valley—no, not exactly hers, but the next one south. There was a smelter, those ruins—she explored them with Gerald once, in the upside-down spring of November, a picnic with the super's wife from Cerro de Pasco. They buttered her up for more beds. Eucalyptus is that way—this is the Cordillera de Quimsacruz, her home mountains, where her mine is, the people that wait for her, the workers she tended, their children, wives. So if they could only land, she could lead Forney to safety, rescue him; she could save them both if they could land, but isn't that the point? she thinks. Isn't that it—they can't land. A thousand feet separates her and the road, food, friends, warmth, but there is no way to bring them together, might as well be a thousand miles. Forney could even turn north, fly over the mine, fifty feet over the stamping mill in the draw, the workers' barracks on the cliffs, even the infirmary, her tiny room in the super's house, the very room she started from a month ago when this prodigious loop began, except there's no way to span those mere fifty feet, not in an airplane. And suddenly Ethel understands something about Forney and flyers, about how they can take their machines anywhere on the earth's face, look down on any town, see its lights, its quiet and its calm, look into houses even, see husbands and wives close in their beds, children under their quilts, but all from a thousand feet above. See how they look up to the pilots, the kids at their bedroom windows, families on the beach, even her innocent miners if any by chance see them now, admiring their progress as they circle the bowl. They don't know that Forney's an exile, that he can't land, share their calm, join their peace, that flying is an overpassing, an act of solitude, that the aviator crosses a continent but comes down to earth where nobody lives, at some field on a city's outskirts, where they put the junk yards and the cemeteries. Oh George, she thinks, full of feeling for him, wanting to touch him, but his seat is empty. She looks aft—he's far at the back, sitting half out the doorway, hanging onto loose ropes, booting crates out with his feet. It looks precarious, the tilt of the floor; she shallows her bank a little. There they all go, she sighs, her crates, their reason for being here at all, dumped the way the cooks on the ship dumped trash over the taffrail.

Ten crates gone—ten more. Forney is doing all he can to save himself, a new role for him. Maybe a little climb—features below might be getting a little smaller, he thinks. He crawls back to the open doorway, squinting against the wind. A mile across the valley, another fireball, another upwelling cloud. It's not one of his—his mind speculates, slowly in the cold. Another explosion in line, nearer. He looks out, overhead, gets sunblinded for his efforts. He holds up his thumb, hides the sun behind it, searches. There's an airplane up there; a dark shape falls away, slab wings cross the sun. It's ABR—Slovak and Kinner, five hundred feet overhead, dropping their load, just like he's doing. He laughs out loud—the wind whips away the spittle. Slovak and Kinner, alive, dumping nitro.

Kinner's doing the donkey work, crouching in ABR's doorway with the wind yanking on him. Slovak, in the cockpit, waves him on. Shit, thinks Kinner, near collapse, half the load is gone—what more does he want, all? He wants all—Kinner waves back weakly, cuts more tiedowns. Ahead, Slovak pounds the altimeter—the needle unsticks a sixteenth of an inch, that much climb. Here's Kinner, tapped out in the cockpit doorway. Slovak unstraps, lifts him into the right-hand seat. "You fly for a while," he shouts.

"I can't," Kinner sobs. "I ain't supposed to." His frothy mind has slipped back to Coco Solo ethics. Too late —Slovak's gone aft. The nose slowly pitches down—Kinner blinks, hauls back on the yoke, nose over the horizon. Dried cakey stuff covers the instrument panel—his puke, he remembers, upchucked during the ice storm. Slovak had puked likewise, between his seat and the fuselage. The cockpit smells like rotten milk. Kinner groans at the memory: ass over elbow, so cold his nuts shriveled. It was like going crazy in a meat locker. Fuck flying, fuck it, he thinks, keep your aviating if this is all it is. He sees ACH climbing slowly to meet them, at last. They saw Forney a half hour back— it's taken this long to catch up. A crate of dynamite spills away from ACH, arcing down, lost to sight. Finally, it goes —kabloom, thinks Kinner.

Forney's mouth tastes blood—he touches his nose; his hand comes away red. Some blood vessel, he guesses. The wind swirls and doubles back in the doorway—his pants legs are tearing off, knees going, his vision screwed, eyes running away at high speed, no longer interconnected. He lifts one more crate, waddles to the doorway, lets it fall. That's all he can do.

When he slips back to his cockpit seat, blood is dripping from his nose and ears; his eyes are carmine red. "You're bleeding!" Ethel shouts. He nods, pointing. "So are you!" She touches her nose, feels dried blood, fresh on top of it. "Did it do any good?" she shouts.

Forney bends to the altimeter to read the numbers. Little hand between the seven and eight, big hand on the seven: 17,700. Forney looks out, pulling himself up to the windshield coaming. The ridges still rise above them, like castle walls. He snorts, a big bubble of blood expanding from his nostril. "Have to dump it all!" he shouts, coughing. Her face falls—she bites a knuckle. Bullshit, Ethel, Forney thinks, it won't be enough anyhow, won't get a thousand feet out of six more crates. He takes the coca bag, but the flakes stick to his bloody palms. He wipes his hands on his pants, snorts his nose dry. Why tell her? He'll do this first, he thinks, takes two more leaves, makes as fine a powder as he can, takes all the time he needs, snuffles it now. Things become clear, quickly positive. The blue overhead, streaked with cirrus, is the best blue, those massive ridges are the most noble, coated with the cleanest snow. Ethel Booton is the best co-pilot a man could ask for—her deft touch, her second sense for the air. Slovak and Kinner are the best of wingmen, comic, loyal, true to the end, tucking in beneath his wings and holding formation even into the side of a mountain. His hand rises from the wheel, begins to fly about.

He's dopey, Ethel thinks. Dopey, dopey. The water-skimmers have returned, skating across her pupils. She blinks, they change position—all except the biggest one, lower left corner. Her heart grows anxious—she senses danger in that bug, or is it power? Many emotions tumble and combine. Stop it, heart, she says, as it pounds harder. The more she tries, the more it pounds. Stop that now, she yells, calm down! Oh, it's getting worse—control just makes it angry. Is this how you die—by losing control, overspeeding? The image shifts—new visual distortion now, like the ones that machine in Ophthalmology gives you. The bug's not on her eye—it's out there. "What's that thing?" she yells.

Forney shakes his head, not listening. He's embracing the sky, the valley, those that are with him here, whatever forces brought him. Giving up hope he has found an emotion not unlike love, and he studies it, like a savage. Ethel pounds his shoulder. "George! What is it?" she points, a mile off, against a sheer rock face. A small dot rises, doubles back. "It looks like some kind of bird!" she shouts. He smiles, lets that drop slowly down the hopper. A bird's a feathered thing, many of them, large and small. It depends where you are. We're in Bolivia. Forney ponders all Bolivian birds. Mountain birds. Condor, comes the answer. It's doubling back once more, a little higher than the first time. Forney starts to move up and down in his seat. "Look at him! What is he flying with? He ain't got engines!"

"What? I don't know."

"He's soaring, that's what!" Forney's screaming louder. "He's found lift!" He banks toward the bird, hard as he dares.

Two hundred yards behind, Kinner sees ACH turn, banks sharply as well, dutifully following. Aft, Slovak loses his feet, slides helplessly toward the open doorway. He lets go of his crate, grabs for the doorway as he slips through it. Half-dangling out the airplane, he digs in his fingers, creases the duraluminum with his nails, hauls himself back inside. Furious, he scrambles forward to make Kinner pay. When he gets there, Kinner's pointing at the mountains. "He's heading toward that bird . . . "

Where the condor circles, Forney circles five hundred feet below, mimicking his every turn. The plane lurches, in turbulence again, but this is coherent lift air, rising from the mountain like spray where a wave hits a breakwater. Another surge of lift—the metal sighs, the rate-of-climb needle bangs against its peg, evens out at 1,000 feet per minute. The rock face falls away—they climb straight, silent, like an elevator. Forney tracks the bird in the sun; Ethel sucks in more coca. They're rising, delivered—she rises too, quitting her body, outside the airplane and faster, joining the condor, eyes bloody just like his, arms out and soaring, her fingers spread, 18,000 feet over the world. Below, an ugly metal airplane circles; there's one more below that, both chasing her up a spiral staircase. She calls down to Forney to join her—he does, puts the bag over his face, now ascends, pumping hard seventy-foot articulated wings, soaring up and past her like a bat out of hell. How they laugh, both of them, delighted. He starts his airshow now, smoke belching out his tail to trace his path: a vertical roll, stalling out, hard right rudder into a hammerhead, letting his head fall through up into a loop, so quiet on top, inverted, sudden stick and rudder, yank and bank, one snap roll, two, three snaps that suck his airspeed dry and he plummets, but as he plummets, gathers speed, the paradox of dive and lift, pulls out just in time, just spared above the sharp rocks. Hovering there, wing in wing, streaming blood, Ethel and Forney look down and see one Trimotor slipping over the ridge, diving away on the other side. Here comes the second, leveling out even with the rocks. One wingtip cleaves a slit in a snowy slope as it sneaks past; a snow flurry begins, barely a handful at the top, gathering mass as it rolls downslope.

THEY PARALLEL the mountains, picking their way south to Sucre. The warm smell of plowed land comes to them below the snow line. Now they fly over plateaus, fenced *fincas,* streams that swell into rivers, paths into roads. Forney wonders what they'll say at Sucre—he only has five crates remaining, doesn't know if Slovak has any at all. They might say the job was botched, but could they dare, after what they've gone through? He concludes he won't let them. Will he take Ethel out to dinner? Will he buy himself a tie?

The last checkmark's a river crossed by an iron bridge. Cars on the roads below, the outskirts of a city. Forney sees what looks like an airfield ahead, hangars, planes, SUCRE spelled out in whitewashed stones. "No, keep on going!" she shouts. "The field's five miles further, near the river." Forney nods, follows her lead. Ethel looks past the nose this way and that, sees the field she means ahead. What looks like some sort of military formation stands in ranks to one side. She squeezes shut her eyes. "Looks like a band!" Forney is shouting. "It should be a band—we deserve a band!" When he looks over, something's wrong—she's bawling, pulling at her hair. He takes it for an emotional release. "I got to hand it to you, Ethel!" he shouts. "You got me here! I don't think I could have done it on my own!" He reaches over and takes her hand. It's limp.

Forney's puzzled, but not too, throttles back to 1,500 rpm, looking for the wind. He sees smoke trailing from a mine smelter against the mountains, banks north, across the field. It looks like an army below; men salute, lower and raise flags. A long slow curve, slipping off altitude, the wind drumming against the fuselage. Straighten out ten feet above the hedge, wheels rumble on, cutting grass wakes, and they're down, all the way to Sucre.

ABR is just behind—in line, the two airplanes taxi up toward the soldiers. An officer marches over a squad of men—Forney shuts the mags; the engines clatter to a stop. He turns to Ethel, sees she's heading aft already. "I'm sorry," she murmurs, loud enough to hear but not facing him. "Sorry, why?" he wonders—following her, he sees she's taking out her nickel-plated automatic, opening the cabin door. "Hey," he says, hurrying after, but not fast enough—she fires twice, hitting the waiting officer in the groin. He screams; a soldier grabs her, slams her against the fuselage. Forney hears her teeth snap. "Hey," he yells at the soldier, leaping on his back from the doorway. Somebody rifle-butts him in the kidney—Forney howls, doubles up, falls gasping at Ethel's feet.

15

A GUARD'S BOOT fills his vision—the lace has been broken twice, knotted back together. Everything's dusty, pastel paints on the stucco house walls flashing past, pink, ochre. A muzzle pokes him away; Forney feels the front sight stabbing, looks up at the Indian who guards him. His uniform collar is held by a safety pin; his teeth look like odd stones glued there.

Forney's head is pounding—the truck hits a ditch, the flatbed rises, hits him in the jaw. He bites his tongue, sees tears. They rattle through a plaza—a machine-gun squad lounges at the base of a dried-out fountain. Narrow streets again, soldiers on every corner, waving rifles. Buildings pass by, homey store signs, a poster for a movie: "El Bandito de Amor." Kinner's beside him, head in his hands, blood seeping through his fingers—some kind of scalp wound, Forney figures. Slovak leans dazed against a stack of crates, a front tooth missing. Teeth, eye; Slovak is falling apart piece by piece, thinks Forney. The truck driver swerves playfully back and forth down the cobbled streets; he's probably never had the road to himself. Another intersection, another gutter—when the truck bounces, twelve crates rise, slam back again. Yellow stripes—the dynamite, all that's left of the load; don't they know what's in them? Another plaza, an armed car—a traffic cop waves them through with an exaggerated gesture. Forney looks back—trailing in their dust is a sedan, soldiers hanging from the running boards. Squeezed between the driver and an officer is Ethel.

They turn up a narrow street now; the driver downshifts for the grade. They grind past old houses, fronts draped with electric wires on insulators, women in the top windows leaning out. They turn a corner—over the cab, Forney sees a bullring rising, pitched on the hillside, a large oval supported on crossed-steel girders and concrete footings. There's a row of vehicles parked below it, military cars and trucks. The flatbed stops, the sedan alongside, and the dust settles. In the silence, Forney hears a volley of gunfire, far away, a third or fourth echo. The guards are prodding them to their feet—*"Andale,"* they say. Forney drops off the truck, Slovak and Kinner behind. He looks for a sight of Ethel—sees the car door open, she half-visible behind a circle of officers, hears laughter and her swearing before he's thrust forward, a hand in his back. A crowd of short men in hats and vested suits moves toward them, some carrying notepads. *"Qué hacen ustedes, qué falta?"* asks one. *"Y cómo se llama, de donde vengan?"* A red-faced photographer, a Yank by his look, raises a Speed Graphic —"Hey, pal, this way," he says, firing the flash when Forney turns to the sound of home. Slovak bumps against him; "More here than meets the eye," he mutters. They're herded past the reporters toward the huge double bullring doors. There's a smaller, man-sized door cut into one; a guard pounds on it, it opens, and they're thrust inside.

Forney's heart falters when he sees what he sees; oh shit, he thinks. The arena is full, up to the far top rows, two thousand people staring down at them without a sound; students in steel-rim glasses, old men in berets, Aymaras with woolen caps and their Oriental eyes, shriveled old women in limp black dresses, dandies with pencil moustaches and straw boaters, all totally silent. More rifle fire from far away. Soldiers stand at the bottom of every rising aisle, more in the sand ring itself, some chatting, some dozing against slat arena walls painted with beer ads and political slogans. Now a noise comes to him, vague at first, low and repeated. It's a chant, Forney realizes—it's coming from the stands. *"En-fer-mer-a."* It's getting louder; now the soldiers notice it, look around, as does Forney. *"En-fer-mer-a, en-fer-mer-a."* Oh oh, they're beginning to stand now, all two thousand, to this side and that. A kid in a cap vaults the wooden arena rail, runs toward him. *"En-fer-mer-a; en-fer-mer-a!"* they shout, approaching unison; Forney's frightened now. A girl drops over the rail, young men, two Indians, spilling into the arena from all sides. The guards don't know what to do—one laughs, nervous. *"En-fer-mer-a, en-fer-mer-a!"* The cry is louder, becoming a cheer: *"EN-FER-MER-A, EN-FER-MER-A!"* The guards cut off two men climbing the rail to one side—that leaves the other side open; three, four more sneak over there. They're being cheered, it occurs to Forney finally. The people are running toward them, cheering for some reason, the only one he can think of being that they made it here. Damn straight, he thinks—yes, we did. He waves back to the crowd—yes! *"EN-FER-MER-A, EN-FER-MER-A, EN-FER-MER-A,"* it replies, reverberating. The people are yards away—Forney spreads his arms wide to embrace them. Yes we made it—we're here, cheer us, raise the goddamn roof, tear the place goddamn down! We're alive and we made it.

They reach him, run past them, between Kinner and Slovak, ignoring them all. Forney turns—they're all around

Ethel, fighting through a cordon of officers that circles her, struggling for a glimpse, leaping over shoulders for just a touch. Guards are clubbing them now, from behind—the others pay no heed. *"EN-FER-MER-A, EN-FER-MER-A, EN-FER-MER-A!"* The whole arena trembles, two thousand on their feet, waving, shouting, blowing kisses. *"EN-FER-MER-A! EN-FER-MER-A!"* Ethel looks slowly up at the stands. Stomp, stomp—the girders sing, dust shimmers on the arena floor. Forney turns to Slovak; "What's *enfermera?*"

"Nurse" says Slovak, one eye narrow.

Forney doesn't get any of it, rubs his head. Gunshots ring in the archway the bulls enter through—out onto the sand rushes a platoon double-time, led by an officer with a whistle to his mouth who fires a pistol in the air every time his boots hit. The crowd scatters in all directions, clambering back into the stands. Those caught climbing are whacked hard on the head, the hands. The platoon surrounds the three of them, drives them back toward the bull gate; the cheering follows them out of sight into the tunnel beneath the stands. There, in the shadows, it's the stomping they hear; Forney can look up and see sunlight through cracks in the bleacher seats, see feet thumping up and down. They're dragged past horse stalls, all empty—soldiers look up, leaning on rifles, lighting smokes. They pass into a hallway built among the girders, stop before a line of doorways. It's quieter, cooler here, almost cold. On a bench nearby sit three prisoners, two Indians, one young man wearing his mineworker's union badge and high-topped shoes. They're shoved down on the bench to wait.

It smells musty, of horse piss. Forney stares hard at

Ethel, who knows he's there—it's a long time before she can speak. She clears her throat. "I haven't been entirely honest with you," she whispers at last.

"Shut up," says the officer with the whistle. "No talking."

Forney rubs his knuckles. He looks slowly around—where is this place, where is he? Still another goddamn world. He waits a moment, now speaks out of the side of his mouth. "Where's the mine on fire?"

Ethel shakes her head, fighting tears, squeezing her eyes tightly. "Shut up!" the officer repeats, turning.

"No mine?" whispers Slovak. Kinner groans, holds his bloody head, now begins to weep again. He's so afraid.

"What about Ramón, all them peasants?" Forney whispers.

Ethel won't meet his eyes, says nothing. She looks up finally at the young miner across the way, seems to know him by the way she hisses. *"Qué pasa—Qué fué mal?"* The miner makes sure the officer is turned away, places his hands together horizontally, hinged at the palm butts, fingers flapping and closing very fast, over and over. *"El médico,"* he whispers.

Ethel turns pale. "What's he mean?" asks Forney.

Before she can recover, a fat major with medals on a sash opens a door and motions to them. They stand and shuffle inside, followed by their guards. It's a matador's dressing room, small and white, the far wall solid wardrobe mirrors. A handsome middle-aged woman sits at a table beneath a graphic crucifix—she's wearing a full riding habit, high boots, tailored tweed jacket, high domed cap. With her riding crop, she shows them where to stand; on the desk, plates with food remaining, wineglasses showing dregs. A camera bulb flashes, blinding Forney—an aged general steps up to him, carefully laying a pistol under his chin. The fat major has done the same with Slovak, bookending the line with Kinner and Ethel between. An army photographer motions them all in closer—the officers squeeze from either end. Another flash, mirrors bouncing light around the room. Spanish wisecracks—there's an air of triumph, a good day's work. *"Cuantos arriven, en este vuelo?"* the woman asks the major. He holds up ten fingers, then two alone. She turns to Forney, smiling coyly. "Twelve crates? You could hardly expect to start a revolution with twelve crates of dynamite." The general nods. "Maybe you shouldn't have tried so hard to get here," he says; they all laugh at that, pleased as punch.

Forney looks around. "What about the mine on fire?"

"Qué dice el?" the major asks, the woman translates for him. He and the two guards titter. "Is that what she told you? A mine fire? Oh my," says the general. Slovak glares at Ethel—she's staring at the floor.

"Hardly an angel of mercy, are you, Ethel?" the woman smiles, coming around the table. "She's *La Enfermera*. She's in fact a terrorist, one of the most notorious, a ringleader of the dramatically titled December Twelfth Movement, a fugitive and a criminal." Forney and Slovak speak at once—the guards poke them quiet. "You're surprised?" The woman turns to Ethel. "Don't tell me you brought these men all this way and never told them why? How arrogant of you."

"Somebody tell me what's going on," Slovak mumbles.

"You were carrying dynamite for a coup d'etat. It was

intended for the army barracks." Slovak has a blank look. "A coup," she repeats. "They intended to take over the government by force. You do know what coups are?"

"Cooze is women," answers Slovak. They howl at that, almost in tears. Ethel looks up now, clears her throat. "Who talked?" she asks, quietly.

"You're sure someone did?" the señora smiles.

"We always knew which ones were your spies."

The woman's still smiling as she walks to a side door. "This will surprise you then," she says, pulling it wide. In the next room sits a man in a straight-backed chair, reading a newspaper. When he sees Ethel, he leaps up and hurries into the room. Ethel starts to faint, makes it as far as a chair nearby. "Oh my God, Ethel, Jesus, I'm glad to see you!" The man embraces her—flashbulbs pop. "I heard airplanes landing—I heard them chanting your name, but I had no idea whether it was actually you or not. You're fine, still in one piece?" He touches her hair. "No, you tell me—how are you?"

Forney raises his chin, studies the man. He's got a white shirt open at the collar, a pipe hanging out his back pants pocket, blonde hair, big hands and feet. Ethel's in his arms, but she's twisting awkwardly from his kiss. *"Mira la visage, hombres?"* whispers the woman to the other men. "Gerald, this is George Forney, also Mr. Slovak and Mr. Kinner," Ethel says, whispering mindless introductions. Gerald sticks his hand out—Forney won't take it, looks at her. "You told me you were down here taking care of miners."

"I was, for a year," she answers. "Until it became clear all the nursing in the world wouldn't give these people what they needed." Her strength is coming back—she turns to the woman, louder now. "That these people needed nothing less than a complete overthrow of the inhuman, bestial dictatorship that oppresses them, the same totalitarian ruling class that has oppressed this country since the arrival of imperial Spain five centuries ago!" She begins to cough, as though she's expended her breath and her politics at the same time.

The señora bats at a fly. "Rhetoric. Rhetoric and violence—this is what they offer the poor in place of food and security of employment. As if they could eat rhetoric, sleep under violence at night." Gerald is patting Ethel's back, but she flings off his hands. Forney shakes his head. "Jesus, how did people like you ever get involved with dynamite?"

"Clearly, known radicals couldn't obtain dynamite anywhere in South America," the señora explains. "Their solution was a foreign country—Miss Thorgaard was sent to New York with an amount of money to purchase a shipment and deliver it safely under the protection of her American passport." Ethel stares up at Gerald with bloodshot eyes. "Oh Gerald," she whispers. "How could you?"

"Obviously, by running out of options," he replies. She clutches herself, shaking her head. "Does it make any difference they were getting ready to torture me, Ethel? They had this telephone magneto—you know, the thing you crank. They were going to wire it to my testicles. One ring, Hello Central." Ethel drops her face into her hands, crying. "Nobody's going to come out of this with much honor, Ethel," he continues. "It's a case of *sauve qui peut.* I don't think there's any value in being strongly ethical about it." He bends down and takes her hand. "It upsets me you can't show a little more understanding, Ethel. I know your position; I wish you'd give a little more thought to mine."

"You sold us out," Ethel whispers.

Booton's getting rattled. "Yes, I suppose I did. What did I ever say that made you think I wouldn't?" He looks around the room for support—the woman and the soldiers nod understandingly, being the torturers.

Ethel is thinking, is that true, is that true? She recalls the time they drove forty miles in his old Dodge to try out a special tobacco blend. His dancing lessons—she thought it cute, kidded him about it. She knew he went to Newport for weekends now and then. She thought he might have another woman there, two, three, a whole other life—it was none of her affair, not until they were married. Good old Thorgaard, he used to call her, hospital last names. He was an awfully good kisser, enjoyed necking in dangerous places, restaurants, hospital supply rooms, his mother's house. Were there clues dropped all along—had she deluded herself that badly? No, no clues—she remembers none; she made no mistake. "Why did you come to Bolivia at all, if you felt that way?" she sobs.

Booton takes out his pipe, fills it from a leather pouch. His hand is shaking, Forney notes. "To help people, obviously. To cure illness. I *am* a doctor. To help my reputation as well, something compelling to write on my vita, I'll admit in total honesty." Ethel moans—Booton lights his pipe. "I'm being embarrassingly frank, Ethel—I wish you'd give me some credit for it."

"Oh Gerald. To help your reputation?"

"I'm not wealthy, Ethel—I don't have mom and dad

to buy me a private practice like my med school chums." Ethel moans, puts her hands over her ears. Shrill now, Booton shouts to be heard. "To hell with you, Ethel! I never did care much what you made of me. It was much too rigorous and never very accurate!" He looks up—only now does he realize he has an audience of glowing faces; provincial theater, he thinks, sitting on the table's edge, finding his composure again. "I don't expect you to approve of what I've done, Ethel, or even thank me. However, there may come a time when you will, and my guess is it will be some time after these men and all the rest outside are dead and gone and you're still thankfully alive." She looks up—Booton's nodding. "I didn't have much of a bargaining position, but I did manage to salvage that." He looks at the woman. "Tell her our arrangement."

The woman picks up her crop. "We decided the two of you could be simply deported as undesirables."

Ethel begins to shake her head. "C'mon," whispers Forney beside her.

"Ethel," says Booton, raising a finger.

"I'm not going to live my life at the price of others," she cries. "It's my life—I'll make my own arrangements."

There's a tapping, the riding crop on the table leg. "We did make the arrangement Doctor Booton speaks of," the woman continues. "However, we've discussed it among ourselves since, and we've changed our minds somewhat."

Booton starts for her—expecting him, she whacks his hand with the crop. Red-faced, screaming, he fights toward her—a guard falls; the major and the general lend a hand, pinning his arms. "You promised!" he shrieks. "We had an agreement! You gave me your word of honor!"

"Nobody's going to come out of this with much honor," the woman shrugs.

"That was our agreement, our agreement, goddamn it!" he hollers. Forney finds him embarrassing—the cameraman takes a fast series of him, burning his hands on the hot bulbs.

"You fucking swine!" Booton shouts. They drag him into the next room—the photographer follows, the door slams behind. "Stop—oh Jesus!" they all hear him shout, then a thud and no more.

The woman checks herself in the wall of mirrors, pulls back a curl of hair. "We concluded if we didn't execute you publicly, every revolution to come would insist on foreigners flying in dynamite. It's a bad precedent to establish." The general nods. "Understand our position. It's like manna from heaven—the dynamite appeals to both their romantic and their religious sensibilities."

The door to the other room opens now—the photographer enters, alone. Eyes screwed shut, Ethel shakes her head. The room is silent. Kinner hooks his thumbs in his belt loops, head low. "We didn't know nothing," he says finally, his voice trembling.

Slovak nods. "We thought it was some fire."

The woman bites a fingernail, tears off a sliver. "How can we let you go unpunished? The famous Panama Suicide Club . . ."

"Yeah, well I can explain that," says Forney, looking up. "It was a gag—there's no such thing." The woman glares, suddenly angry, snatches up the newspaper, translates the fat headline aloud: " 'Panama Suicide Club Off for Bolivia.' Do not patronize us, Mr. Forney," she hisses.

"Not only does the present government provide health facilities for miners but also newspapers." She leans back, glancing at the front page. "So romantic. The perilous pass at Chimbote. The deadly fog at Arequipa. Two comrades die in a terrible crash, but still they press over the Andes themselves ... "

"Yeah, well, this kid in Guayaquil needed a few bucks," Forney explains. "We made it all up ... "

The woman snorts out loud. The general joins in—they all chuckle now, even the guards, even the photographer, who smiles faintly. "Shut up, George!" screams Ethel, all of a sudden, loud enough to silence them all. "It's not all made up! You did fly through the pass—you did land at Arequipa in the fog and we did make it over the Andes! It's all true!"

Forney mulls that over, sensing a lapse, but unable to pin it down. The others do not wait for him—Slovak and Kinner glance at each other, silently communicating. Slovak straightens up now, clears his throat. "Well, I guess you got us, cuntface," he shrugs. The woman gasps. Ethel sucks mucous from her nose, now leans across the table and spits it in her face. "So do your worst!" The woman leaps up, groping—the general hurries over with a monogrammed handkerchief. Forney spins Ethel around. "Jesus Christ, why'd you do that?"

"It doesn't matter," Ethel shouts, giddy. "They're going to shoot us. We can do anything we want!" Inspired, Kinner tries to spit across the table at the woman but his gob lands short. The guards are clubbing them out of the room—Forney stumbles backward, protecting his head with his arms.

16

FORNEY TREMBLES; it's bitter cold, absolute zero, where even the molecules don't move. Low bass rumblings, random, incoherent—Forney floats an inch away from chaos. So much pain, stored like fossils in the set of his bones: a boot in the head some place in Ohio, a bar bet fudged, three on one behind a hangar, bleeding under a wing in the rain, plowed weeds and cowplop. A hooker's laugh, a six-foot queer with fists like bricks; drunk in the dark, running slam into barbed wire. Jack Welch dead, his instructor dead, Augie Pedlar belly-up, Brown, Queen, Frank Tomick with his chute on fire, unaware, jumping from his burning plane, pulling the D-ring, damn silk poof like toilet paper in a campfire. His stomach grinds, swallowed glass—ah, old Panama friend, gone on holiday two days, now returning. Stars overhead arc slowly across the sky, Southern Cross, Aquarius; Forney doesn't look, simply drifts below them. When Ethel stirs, he yields; when Slovak, sitting on his other side, bumps him, he offers no resistance. Voices he's never heard shout, strange accusations, forgotten crimes—his mind spins ungoverned in the thin air; he grabs his head to stop it. Wind over an airfoil, he shouts back, grabbing a ledge in the gale. Holder disappearing with the filing fee in Vancouver. This woman Ethel—oh Jesus. An airfoil, a cambered upper surface, flat lower. Broken bones, wet nose, grease in the folds, torn knuckles, kidneystones, veins twitching, the shits, old age. Cracked spars, zero compression, stripped threads and frayed cables, out of true, out of rig, props warped in the rain, rot, mildew, corrosion. Airfoil at an angle of attack, lift from a lower pressure forming on the upper surface—Forney concentrates on what he knows. Bullies, bullshitters, brownnoses, killers. The business of America. A butt is making the rounds—Forney takes it from an Indian behind who holds it with two hands when he puffs. Drag the resistance to the machine through the air, gravity the opposing force to life. Forney has fought gravity all his life, beat his head against drag. An engine for thrust, a tail to stabilize the four forces, a fuselage to hold them separate. In the freezing bullring, stars whirling overhead, Forney does what he can to save himself, constructs an airplane to carry him away. Bullets off stone, not far off, he thinks—they've moved closer, just up the mountain from the bullring, to make things go faster. Even now, two soldiers cross the ring, finger four at random. Rat-tat-tat, he hears. Nobody seems upset about it, neither guards nor victims. Somebody's always going off to Bolivia, Mossbach had told him. There's a scream now from the hillside, a woman's, first he's heard in a while. Rain, snow, ice, chop, mud, sand; if you've time to spare, go by air, they laugh. More gunfire, impersonal, like tool sounds at a building site.

Ethel coughs into her fist, whispers. "What if I'd told you I was a Socialist back in Panama? What if I'd told you the dynamite was for a workers' revolution? Would you have tried so hard?" What does she imagine he has against revolution, seeing how well he's done under the free-enterprise system? He thinks that but still keeps silent—she buries her head against his chest, frustrated. As she must have done with Booton, he thinks: damaged merchandise. The nerve—if she were a guy, he'd beat the shit out of her.

How he'd like to make her suffer, thinks of how he'd do it —they're both naked, sweating, sprawled on a bed. The vision jolts him. "Please, George, say something," she begs. Forney snorts—why should she be released and not him? What are grudges supposed to be, if not indelible? He turns back to his controls, trims for climb, elevator down, nose up, more wing into the wind. It's not love or affection he feels for her, should not be confused with it—more like obligation, necessary work to be undertaken. There's a scrape of heels behind him—a man in a thick leather tunic is working his way down the rows toward them, pausing at every move to see if the guards look up. "I didn't realize you could be so cruel," she whispers. "Is this the way we're going to die? Never saying another word to me?" She's crying; he never met anyone he thought worse off than him until he met her. He hears a voice whisper *"enfermera,"* turns; it's the man in the tunic, sliding between two Indians who shift sideways. Ethel wipes her tears, opens her arms —she and the man embrace but silently, so nobody notices. "Well, Ethel, too bad for us," he says quietly. "A setback." Ethel tries to smile back. "This is Wallo Empudia, secretary of the union at the Potosi mine," she says, turning to Forney. "George Forney, head of the pilots." The two men nod; Empudia sighs. "Just a setback—maybe next year." He's taking a bundle of rags from his pocket. "Tell me, would you know what to do with this?" Unwrapping the rags, there in his hand lies an old Webley revolver. Forney sighs—guns everywhere, he thinks, tired of their appearance. "Where did that come from?" Ethel whispers. Empudia wraps it up again. "It's been here all day, waiting. It's Ramón's, but he gave it to the Party." He points over to the side—three aisles away, a huge fat man in a llamaskin jacket gives them a fist salute. Ethel waves back, thrilled. That's Ramón? wonders Forney. "The delegation leaders have talked it over. We can't pay you the salary as promised; we were wondering if you'd consider this as payment instead?" The three pilots look at each other. "How come?" asks Kinner. "We didn't do you no good." Empudia shrugs his shoulders. "You delivered on schedule. We have no basis for complaint." Slovak grabs the gun, but Empudia won't let go. "Not so fast. If you're interested, then we all must vote. I'm only authorized to make the offer." "Shit yes, vote," says Slovak. "This place stinks—I want to go home." Kinner leans forward. "You told me you couldn't go home. You said they were after you." Slovak looks down, rubs his hands on his knees, hesitates. "That was bullshit. Nobody's after me." He turns to Ethel. "What about you, sister? What about your husband?" Ethel hesitates as well. "I'm not married," she murmurs, finally. Kinner grins, delighted. "No kidding." Slovak shrugs, relieved there's one less to worry about. The one left unheard from is Forney; Ethel fears his silence, touches him, feels the hardness in his shoulders. She could massage him, Forney thinks, smooth away the pain—it's what she does, isn't it? He feels white sheets, the smell of alcohol, roses, the squash of breasts. "Say something, George," she's pleading. Forney is thinking there's no sacrifice here; Brown is dead —nobody in this entire land knows shit about Hal Moxey. He can't even find his ghosts to bargain with, wonders if the cold has killed them all, like certain viruses. Could they in fact escape? He plots one now—kill a guard, steal a car, drive away before anyone stops them. Not very slick, he admits. Still, he already possesses the airplane, engines idling, safe in his mind, lift, thrust, what he needs to fly. He feels themes and resonance, harmonics cycling up and down his body. He spreads his fingers wide—now nods yes, committed. She clutches his arm—Empudia waves over to Ramón, quickly turns now to the Indians behind and begins to explain what's going on, that the vote will occur at three A.M., when the churchbells strike. Forney glances at his watch—only minutes away. The Indians nod, turn around themselves, each telling someone else; the word spreads on either side. The bowl reflects soft hissing; the guards are too sleepy to notice. Minutes pass—a bottle falls below the stands and shatters. Forney's watch hand snaps to three straight up—churchbells ring far away, three times, slowly. He looks around the bullring—not one light. Empudia leans forward, whispering. "Santa Teresa. Wrong church." Now another clock sounds the hour, loud enough to hear the mechanism whirring, just down the street. Empudia strikes a match on a box side, holds it up, flame steady with no wind. The Indians do the same—so do some students below them, an old man with a beret, his old wife. Matches flare on either side, twenty, forty. A second bell rings. A hundred matches flame across the ring. The third bell. Three hundred matches strike—a guard shouts, a whistle blows. Five hundred more matches twinkle, the entire bullring glowing stellar. Reinforcements for the guards clatter into the arena—too late: the matches blow out. There's the stench of sulphur, the murmur of voices. Forney must swallow saliva, cough, having not spoken in so long. "I'll tell you one thing," he says loudly. "I didn't come all the way down here to get shot by some Bolivian."

Does it take a long time, a little? Forney doesn't know. It simply happens, near dawn, when the two soldiers, tired by now dragging their heavy Mausers through the sand, cross the bullring and motion the four of them down. Somebody calls *adios* as they stand and leave—half the arena is empty seats now; those that remain sleep or freeze. The soldiers guide them toward the tunnel, too weary to notice the mayhem there, the clenched hands, the balled fists. Forney plans, choreographing his moves with dreamy contemplation; in a life of bad choices, he is experiencing the bliss of no choices at all. The soldier ahead is fat, broad-hipped, walks on the outside of his shoes. The one behind has glasses and a pointy nose. The tunnel mouth looms; they enter darkness. Boot shuffles, the slap of canteen on hip. Forney never gets in fights; he'd kill if he ever did, he's always assumed, rip, tear, and strangle, out of control, no modulation in him between cowardice and murder. All his life, Forney has sat on his anger, as a present to the world. This charity has never paid off, he now admits—the world has not been better for it. The fat soldier ahead has a leather shoulder strap, looped to his belt—Forney grabs it now, hauls hard as he can. Surprised, the man teeters backward, off balance on his heels—Forney finds it easy enough to spin him sideways, him flailing breathless at dark air, slam him head-first into the stucco tunnel wall. There's a crunching noise—a section of plaster where he strikes falls away, revealing adobe bricks. Scuffling behind him—Forney turns, sees Kinner tackling the small soldier by the ankles, football fashion, Slovak grabbing the rifle as he falls, lifting it axe-high, bringing it down on the soldier's face-down skull. There's a crunch—wood fibers give way; the riflestock splits. Slovak's hands are aching from the blow—he shakes his fingers, wincing. Forney has the Webley out of his waistband, barrel hard against the fat soldier's teeth. To Forney's surprise, he's not dead, in fact, more alive than before, wide-eyed, whispering no, no into the muzzle like a crooner into a microphone. A door opens to the side, dim light spills—Ethel's hissing from an unused room. Kinner and Slovak drag the smaller soldier inside—Forney leads the fat one after him, crouching low, shuffling backward. She shuts the door behind them all.

Forney paces, arms folded; hot air pumps from his nostrils. Easy, easy, he's thinking. The smaller soldier is out cold—Kinner strips off his uniform. Slovak has shoved the fat one into a corner, now ties his hands and feet behind him while Ethel gags him with his uniform tie. There's a basso blatz, a sudden wash of fecal smell—the fat soldier has filled his pants. He looks up, sheepish, under lidded eyes. Forney slowly shakes his head, disgusted, a conqueror's disdain. He paces, in no great hurry—all's unfolding as it should; they'd made no plans beyond agreeing the tunnel was do or die. He sniffs, makes a face—at his worst, at rock bottom in Panama, he did not befoul himself, he thinks. They are more afraid than he was, perhaps always were, all his life. Kinner is buttoning the uniform jacket; it's too small—he inhales deeply. Forney nods—the three of them raise their hands in sham surrender. Kinner plops the cap on, picks up the other Mauser and follows them out into the tunnel.

Ahead, an archway of false dawn, stars fading. They inch toward it, hands over their heads. A soldier shuffles past, slapping his arms in the cold—he grunts to Kinner, and Kinner grunts back, falsetto. They reach the outside portal—a guard dozes there on a crate. Forney would lead them past—Slovak stops, takes the Mauser from Kinner, brings it down on the guard's head. Once more the stock splits—green lumber, thinks Slovak. Kinner's hissing. "You're really pissed off, ain't you?"

Slovak nods. "I really am!" He raises his arms once more—Kinner marches them into the parking lot, tripping on rocks in the darkness. There are soldiers all around them, sipping *chicha* at garbage fires, snoring on truckbeds. Kinner follows them along the line of vehicles—while he stands sentinel, Forney and Slovak search quietly for an open door, ignition keys. There's a shout behind—Forney sighs, looks a little harder. A Chevy, keys in the steering column lock. The four pile in the car, Slovak at the wheel, Ethel and Kinner in back, Kinner stuck in the doorway with the long rifle. Out of the tunnel portal a hundred feet off hobbles the smaller soldier, barefoot and shirtless, clutching his head and screaming. Slovak fumbles around looking for the starter. "Shit, I ain't driven in ten years," he mutters. There's gunfire—tracer lofts in the wrong direction, toward town. The car engine starts—Slovak grinds gears in reverse, loud enough to wake everyone else not yet awake. Two soldiers run toward them—Forney finds the rifle in his arms, braces on the windowsill, blade and notch, feels the kick, watches one man fall as he jams bolt, ejects, slams closed, aims and fires again. A piece of something flies off the second man's shoulder; he twirls, screaming. The car wheels spin in the loose dirt, no traction, dust clouds in the faint light. Gay twinkles of gunfire from either side now; Forney fires back fast as he can. There is no great threat;

he will shoot or be shot—he resides in the middle of it now, can't really see a threat; what he can see is what's always there, always has been, sky, buildings, people. His head snaps back as Slovak skids around a corner, plummets down the steep street, too fast, hits a cross street; the car vaults, briefly aloft before it lands in the plaza at the hill's foot with a whang of springs bottoming. Shots from up the hill, off a wall beside him. Forney is interested in all this, wondering how this will turn out, decides this is bravery. Signs flash past—he struggles to remember landmarks from the drive into town. Soldiers stare at street corners—two stand in the street ahead to halt them, leap aside as they plunge past, Slovak banging on the horn.

At the bullring, soldiers are climbing on trucks and cars; the first pursuing vehicles rattle down the hill. The señora's there, shouting orders where she stands by the double gates—the major and the general twine through the confusion of backing and bumping. Vehicles jockey to either side, gears gnashing, drivers shouting old Aymara curses. More trucks pull out, soldiers hugging fenders, running boards, choking on their own dust. One truck backs full tilt for the señora—the major pounds its fender with his fist, reaches in the cab when the driver stops short, grabs him by his greased long hair and shoves his face against the outside rear-view mirror. With a look of shame, the driver beholds the señora reflected there, framed like a madonna. Horns bleat on every side; the driver's wedged himself crossway, blocking traffic, between the line of parked cars and the arena foundation. He cramps the wheel overhand, lets the truck roll forward, backs slowly now, staring in the mirror to give the woman a wide berth. The mirror does not reflect twelve crates, diagonally striped, stacked and forgotten in the corner by the bullring gates; he slowly but decisively backs into them.

The fiery explosion flips the truck end over end, thirty feet high, a sort of playful disintegration; flings ten cars in all directions, shreds every human being for thirty yards, hurls those beyond into walls, off cars, blows out half the windows in town, deafens half the inhabitants. When the great blossom of flame and the welling clouds of dust and smoke disperse, the main bullring gates have disappeared.

Inside, those that survive raise themselves up. The town spreads visible beyond the smoking opening. It's clear to Empudia what's happened; comrades, a committee he doesn't even know of, have managed to blow the dynamite and release them. He stands and shouts; the revolution begins. Rebels spill from the stands, overpowering the few soldiers; weapons are torn away. Men, women, and children squeeze through the opening, flood the parking area. The dead and dazed are overrun—Empudia is at the center, hollering; two assault teams gather around other union men, a woman comrade from the mine at Cerro Grande.

Two miles south, in the fleeing car Forney finds a switch on the dash, throws it—a siren on the roof screams authority. Soldiers at the next roadblocks wave them through, some even saluting. The buildings grow more modest, the streets widen—through gaps between the houses, he can see farmland beyond them in the half-light. Now the town falls away to countryside, dark shelters, cows hugging stone walls. Forney fears they're lost; Ethel glances about for the signs of the field. They cross an iron bridge —there's the river, a road alongside; she points Slovak down it and he turns sharply, back end drifting on the gravel. Kinner is pulling off his jacket, forgets he has the cap on. There, squat machines, a quarter-mile off, just visible in mist above the weed tops. Kinner looks out the back window—a line of faint headlights, flickering as they pass behind the bridge girders. Slovak skids onto a dirt road toward the field; they pass through a gate, grazing an army truck, two soldiers sleeping in the cab. They awaken, spill outside; one shouts, the other yawns. The sedan rattles across the field to ACH—Forney dives inside, scrambling up through the empty cabin to the cockpit. Below, Slovak and Kinner yank the chocks—mixture, throttle cracked, mags, starter cracked, all so fast, Forney praying the soldiers haven't fucked with anything. The nose engine coughs awake, wreathed in blue smoke—Forney turns sharply, taxiing downwind on one engine, starting the others on the fly. A slam aft—Slovak and Kinner are inside, Ethel just climbing into the other seat beside him. Lights turn off the road now, sparks to one side—the two awakened guards, firing. Forney hears a metal thump—not hard to hit something so large as them. Number three rouses, sluggish. There are headlights all over the field, some to one side, some to the other, hemming him in, denying him runway. He kicks rudder, fishtailing among the cars and trucks, looking for space. Tracer floats toward him, slow at first, fast as it rips overhead; Ethel screams and ducks. They correct their aim; the windshield shatters, panel ripping, slugs whining and rattling off the cockpit metal, dial glass flying everywhere. Forney hunches, peering barely over the coaming—dazzling headlights, shit-storm of tracer, everywhere but behind, back where he came from, six hundred feet toward the trees at the downwind end. No option once more, the liberation of necessity. Forney kicks hard right rudder, holds full brake, full left engine—the machine pivots hard, terrible torsion on the right strut. Now full power, three engines, right at the trees. A truck brakes there, a machine gun on its bed lazily throwing bullets down their throat. Again the panel shatters—Forney shoves the nose low, grabs Ethel by the hair, flings her down roughly between the seats, piles on top of her, covering her there while bullets lacerate the seats they just emptied. Face to face, almost touching, she looks up, wide-eyed; the airplane thunders toward the trees, no one at the controls. Forney has time to wink; copacetic. There on the cockpit floor, blind, hunched over, Forney still has what he needs to fly, can reach up, grab the control column, feel the lift building by how it stiffens, fingertips drumming, now slowly levers it back. Bullets whine off the nose engine, bend the prop, pierce the oil tank, gas line, throttle linkage, firewall, all no matter—they're gone; Forney takes off looking into Ethel's eyes. There's a jolt, an awful stagger—wheels tear through top tree branches, catch, then rip free. Tanks light, carefree, ACH lifts steadily into a sky pink with first light. Forney raises himself slowly up—the cockpit is mutilated, the panel a thing of shreds. She's holding on to him, uses him to climb, crawls up him and falls into the co-pilot's seat. Flames lick aft from the nose engine; Forney shuts it down, pulls mixture, doesn't need it now. Below, rosy fields in the morning, clear lakes, dots of cattle, ground mist. Slovak and Kinner appear in the bulkhead opening, pale, blinking. "You all right?" Slovak asks.

They both nod—Forney passes him the chart. "Give

me a heading," he says, his voice trembling. He feels his heart begin to pound, there now being occasion. "Are you?" Ethel shouts, not sure. He pats her hand. "Shit, I don't know!" shouts Slovak, too shaken to calculate. "Try zero-zero-zero!" Forney nods, slowly banks—the compass on the centerpost rotates with the turn.

THE SOLDIERS KNEEL in skirmish lines around the Presidential Plaza, firing volleys as their non-coms shout. They're trying to regroup toward the palace but rebels outrace them down side streets, flanking them through courtyards, backyard shortcuts. Snipers pick them off one by one from tiled rooftops—a student runs straight at a machine gun set up at the base of a marble statue, falls across it. Paving stones are torn up; women throw chairs from high windows, flatirons, dining-room tables. Children plunge bayonets into wounded soldiers, showing off for each other. Tripping, off balance, the soldiers attempt a last perimeter around the palace itself. The rebels, advancing into the square down every converging avenue, charge the line, throwing grenades, rocks. Steel whines, marble shatters, soldiers bellow pain. The perimeter is breached on this side, that; rebels pour inside, bayoneting soldiers where they cower. A handful race up the broad ornamental stairways, in through the high columns. Everywhere are shouts, explosions—Empudia is bellowing hoarsely. On the palace cupola, the flag comes fluttering down.

Overhead, above it all, the Trimotor climbs, rock-stable in calm cool air. Those in the cockpit look down onto the town as it passes beneath; the bullring still smokes, the streets are filled with running bodies. Now and then there's the swelling shockwave of an explosion, smoke, flame, but no sound. No one can explain what has happened; all assume responsibility of some sort. That will teach them to fuck with me, Forney thinks. He leans back, closing his eyes, letting the airplane do the work. Under the compass lubber line lies a white *N;* there's a full sunrise spreading to his east but Forney's not flying into it, rather magnetic north, up from the tropics, into the temperate zone, where most of the world lives.